TOO SOON FOR ADIÓS

ALSO BY ANNETTE CHAVEZ MACIAS

Big Chicas Don't Cry

TOO SOON FOR ADIÓS

ANNETTE CHAVEZ MACIAS

 Montlake

This is a work of fiction. Names, characters, organizations, places, events, and incidents are either products of the author's imagination or are used fictitiously. Otherwise, any resemblance to actual persons, living or dead, is purely coincidental.

Published by Montlake, Seattle

www.apub.com

Amazon, the Amazon logo, and Montlake are trademarks of Amazon.com, Inc., or its affiliates.

ISBN-13: 9781542039307 (paperback)
ISBN-13: 9781542039314 (digital)

Cover design by Caroline Teagle Johnson
Cover image: © anna42f / Getty; © Anna Kanishcheva / Getty; © mikroman6 / Getty; © Anatolii Poliashenko / Getty

Printed in the United States of America

This book is dedicated to my dad, Arturo.
Thank you for always being there for us.
I wish you could still be here now.

Chapter One

My mother was the type of woman who always made sure she looked her best. She felt naked without lipstick or a pair of earrings. And she never ever left the house in sweats or, God forbid, without a bra.

And although I'd done my best to make sure she would look perfect today, death did not become her.

I blinked back tears as I studied her face. The woman in the casket didn't look anything like my mom. But I couldn't really blame the mortician. The past three months had taken a toll on her appearance. Cancer hadn't just eaten away at her insides; it had destroyed everything my mom thought had made her beautiful on the outside. Her long, thick brown hair, her smooth olive skin, and her bright, infectious smile had disappeared long before anyone at the funeral home had touched her.

"Are you ready, Gabby?"

I knew Auntie Martha was asking if I was ready for the mortuary staff to open the doors so my mom's memorial service could begin. But she also could've been asking if I was ready to say goodbye.

Yes.

No.

"Sure," I finally said and reached out to straighten the collar of my mom's favorite turquoise-colored dress. The last time she'd worn it was eight months ago, when I'd taken her out to dinner to celebrate my new job at a very posh restaurant. She'd been in remission at that time. Then, six weeks later, she wasn't.

Martha hooked her arm around mine and walked me to the small chapel's front row, which had been reserved for immediate family. I took a seat closest to the aisle. Martha sat down next to me, and Lily sat next to her. No one else would be joining us in that row. We were it. We were my mom's immediate family.

I had no siblings, and my dad, Juan, had passed away when I was sixteen from a heart attack. Martha and Lily weren't related to my mom by blood, but they were basically her sisters. The three of them had been best friends since the first grade and had lived next door to each other in the Milagro Gardens housing projects in East LA for years. Lily was the oldest of the trio by about four months, and Martha was almost a year younger. While Lily and my mom bonded over shopping, makeup, reality TV, and their mutual love of fine wines, Martha and my mom loved going to concerts and musicals together, were the only two members of their murder-mystery book club, and for some reason had made it a mission of theirs to try every coffeehouse in the county. They were her ride or dies, walking with us—sometimes carrying us—through every horrible step of this horrible journey. When my mom's illness wouldn't let her continue working, Lily, who now lived in Las Vegas, hired someone to come to my mom's house to cook and clean. When my mom fell behind on her mortgage payments and lost her home, Martha insisted that my mom move back to Milagro Gardens and become her roommate. And when I made the decision to quit my job so I could spend every last moment with my mom, I had moved in too.

Lily and Martha were the only ones left in this world who knew how funny, sharp, charitable, opinionated, and bossy my mom could be. They definitely understood what I was going through.

Even still, there were moments when I couldn't shake the feeling that I was all alone in the world now.

For the next hour, I did my best to pay attention to the minister, who sermonized about life after death. I smiled at and then hugged the dozen or so mourners who had come to pay their respects. A few I recognized as some of my mom's former coworkers at the dental clinic where she'd worked as an office manager for almost twenty years. But most were friends from the neighborhood—the people who had wrapped us up in love and casseroles once we realized time was about to run out.

"How are you doing, Mija?" Señora Gonzalez asked as she hugged me tight.

"I'm okay," I answered, and she let me go.

The elderly woman dabbed the corners of her eyes with a tissue. She'd known my mom for ages and had been friends with my grandma Alicia. During Mom's last few days, it had been Señora Gonzalez who'd come by every morning to bring us pan dulce or croissants and do whatever needed to be done: wash dishes, fold clothes, or just sit and talk. She'd tell us stories about how she and my grandma would take turns watching each other's kids. My mom, she'd said, had given her many gray hairs. But she loved her like her own and owed it to my grandma to keep watching her until the end.

Señora Gonzalez took my hand and gave it a weak squeeze. "The service was beautiful."

"It was," I said and gave her a smile. "Mom was very specific with what she wanted."

The woman smiled back. "Well, she always knew how to throw a party."

Before she'd gotten sick, Mom had been known for her huge celebrations. New Year's Eve, Fourth of July, even Presidents' Day, were just excuses for her to hire a caterer and buy a new outfit. She had always been a spectacular hostess.

Why should her own memorial service be any different?

Señora Gonzalez and I walked out of the chapel together, arm in arm, and into the warm Saturday-afternoon sun. Lily and Martha were at the bottom of the steps talking with one of the neighbors. We were all headed to a nearby restaurant for a luncheon that Lily had arranged—with my mom's instructions, of course. There would be no burial or graveside ceremony. Instead, I'd return to the mortuary in the next week or so to pick up Mom and bring her back to the apartment. We still had to decide where to spread her ashes. Because for all her preplanning, my mom had never chosen her final resting place.

"I couldn't care less what you do with me," she had said. "Keep me on a shelf or toss me in the ocean. That's for you to decide."

It hit me then that, after today, I would never see my mom again unless it was in a picture. I would never be able to call her on the phone to tell her about something that had happened. I would never be able to just *be* with her.

During her last few days, when it was too hard for her to talk or even keep her eyes open, I would lie down next to her on the hospital bed that took up one corner of Martha's apartment. Sometimes I'd read her posts from Facebook, and sometimes I would even sing some of the same songs she used to sing to me. But most of the time, I would lie there and study her. I wanted to memorize every mole, every wrinkle. I wanted to etch everything about her into my memory. I regretted not taking more pictures together. I regretted not speaking to her for days at a time after one of our fights. Because as much as I loved my mom, our relationship had always been complicated, sometimes even messy.

Mostly because she hadn't approved of my life or the way I lived it.

She hated the fact that I wanted to be a chef instead of a doctor or lawyer. So much so that she had refused to help me pay tuition for culinary school. Then, after I'd graduated, she'd chided me for racking up thousands of dollars in student loans. I had never been a skinny girl, and my mom would always complain about how I was letting the beauty she gave me "go to waste." She was constantly trying to get me to go with her to her yoga and Pilates classes and emailing me articles on the latest fad diet. And the fact that I'd never had a serious boyfriend by the age of twenty-nine kept her up at night (something she made sure to tell me every couple of months).

Sometimes, when I was especially hurt or angry because of something she'd said or done, I'd let myself go to that dark corner of my heart and wonder if the real reason she was so critical of me was because she resented the fact that I'd made her a mom at only eighteen years old. I was the reason she couldn't go to college like she had planned. I was the reason she couldn't go to parties with Lily and Martha anymore. And even though my grandparents didn't kick her out, she always told me that they had refused to help her financially. So, for the first four years of my life, we lived off public assistance and whatever my mom earned working night shifts at a twenty-four-hour diner.

Then she met my dad. He had been a regular customer at the diner and had asked her out three times before she finally agreed. She told me she rejected him at first because he was twelve years older than her and she thought he would be boring. But Lily and Martha had convinced her to take a chance on him, and the rest, as they say, is history. They got married six months later, and he bought us a four-bedroom house in a nice middle-class suburb forty minutes east of Los Angeles. Mom quit her waitressing job and went to night school instead to get her AA degree in English. Eventually, she landed the receptionist job with Dr. Monroe and soon became his office manager.

Marrying Juan had finally given her the life she'd always wanted—the life I'd taken away by being born. At least, that's how it had always felt to me.

As I got older, I learned how to put distance between us before our relationship was ever permanently damaged. Because as much as she frustrated me, she was my mom and I loved her. And I knew that despite everything, she loved me too. That's why I had made myself focus on those last few days. I would curl up next to her, trying to make up for all the time we'd thrown away because both of us had been too stubborn to pick up the phone first.

But you couldn't cram a lifetime's worth of moments into hours.

I guess I had been naive thinking that all I would have to do was close my eyes and remember what it was like to just be with her. It had only been a few minutes since the memorial service ended, and I was already panicking that I wouldn't remember anything at all. Not one beautiful or good thing about the woman who had raised me on her own until Juan had come into our lives when I was only four years old. She once told me he was her second chance to make better first decisions. She had been devastated when he died because it had been so sudden and unexpected.

"I never got to say goodbye," she had cried to me over and over again. "Never hold in a goodbye. It will be the biggest regret you ever have."

Cancer, at least, gave you time to say goodbye. But no matter how many times you said it, it would still never be enough. Not when you knew the last goodbye would be for forever.

I had to go see my mom one more time. Even if, technically, it wasn't her at all.

"I think I left my phone on my seat," I told Señora Gonzalez as I unhooked my arm from hers and then went back inside the chapel. The mortuary employees were just about to close the casket when I yelled at them to stop.

"Can I please have one more minute alone with her?" I asked as I approached.

They nodded respectfully and disappeared into the back room, leaving me alone with my grief and my regrets.

As soon as they were gone, uncontrollable sobs racked my body. I don't know how long I stood there crying. Minutes? Maybe only seconds?

However long it was, I didn't think I'd ever stop.

Until I felt a hand on my shoulder.

The gentle touch helped to calm my shudders. The tears slowed, and I was able to finally catch my breath. When I was empty, I finally turned, expecting to see either Lily or Martha standing behind me.

It was neither.

"I'm very sorry for your loss," the man said softly. He looked familiar, yet I couldn't place him. He appeared to be the same age as my mom, even with his full head of silver-and-black hair. His eyes were hazel in color, a shade darker than my own. He wore a gray button-down long-sleeved dress shirt, black slacks, and dark shoes.

The man offered me his hand, and I took it.

"Thank you," I said as we shook.

"Sandra was a wonderful woman."

"She was. How did you know her?"

"I knew her from a long time ago. In fact, I—"

Before the man could finish his sentence, I heard Lily call out from the chapel's front door. "Gabriela, we're ready to go."

I waved at her to let her know I'd be right there and then turned my attention back to the stranger.

"You're welcome to join us for the luncheon. The restaurant's address is on the back of the memorial program."

The man nodded, but declined. "Oh. Uh. Thank you, but I'm not sure if I can make it."

I nodded. "Well, I appreciate you coming. It's nice to see so many of Mom's friends here today. I'm sorry, I didn't get your name."

"I'm—"

"What are you doing here?"

Both of us turned to see Lily standing in the aisle just a few feet away from us.

"Hello, Lily. It's nice to see you," the man said.

Judging by her squared shoulders and fierce expression, I could tell Auntie Lily was not happy to see him. "I asked what you were doing here," she said.

Her sharp tone startled me. The tension between her and the man was palpable. Obviously, they knew each other. And, obviously, they were not friends. So how did he know my mom?

I held up a hand. "Wait," I said and turned to him. "Who did you say you were?"

"My name is Raul," he said in that soft tone again. "I'm your father."

Chapter Two

Maybe someone else might have reacted differently to that sentence. I didn't believe him, so that's why the words fell flat.

"No, you're not," I told him matter-of-factly.

The man shrugged. "I am, Gabriela."

"My father is—was—Juan Olmos," I explained.

Lily grabbed my hand. "Don't listen to him. Come on. Let's go."

I went with her willingly because even though I didn't believe the man, I didn't want to talk to him any longer. But he called out after me.

"I really am sorry about Sandra. I wish . . ."

That made me stop and turn around again. I was angry now. How dare this man show up uninvited making such an outlandish claim. "You wish what? That you wouldn't have barged in on her memorial service spewing lies to her only daughter. I don't know who you are or why you're here, but I'm not wasting any more of my breath talking to you."

Lily pulled me out of the chapel and into the passenger side of her black Mercedes SUV. Martha was already in the back seat.

"Everything okay?" she asked from behind me.

"It's fine," Lily answered. "We just need to hurry. I want to make sure everything is set up before people start arriving."

I heard Martha blow her nose. "I still don't know why we didn't just have the reception at my place."

"Not this again," Lily said as she pulled the car out of the mortuary's driveway. "You barely have room in that apartment to shit. Besides, Sandra chose the restaurant. So, knock it off. We're going to go have a nice lunch and drink mimosas in honor of our girl. And that is all we are doing today, okay?"

Martha grumbled in agreement.

I looked over at Lily. Why wasn't she telling Martha about the man? Had it been any other day, I would've told her myself. But Lily's reaction made me hold back. I was too physically and mentally exhausted to care. It didn't matter what the man had said, because I wasn't ever going to see him again anyway.

We arrived at the restaurant less than ten minutes later. Most of the mourners from the memorial service had also shown up, along with a few others. None of my friends or former coworkers were there. Not that I'd expected them since I'd basically stopped talking to everyone once I'd moved in with Martha to help take care of my mom. After all, who would want to grab brunch or go shopping with the woman who was watching her mother die? And I was in no mood, either, for awkward conversations or forced attempts to make me forget my depressing reality. It was easier to decline phone calls and ignore texts. Eventually, I didn't have to do either since they stopped coming altogether.

And now that Mom was gone, I needed to figure out what to do next with my life. I had no job, and my savings probably wouldn't last me more than a few months. Martha told me I could stay with her for as long as I needed, and Lily invited me to go live with her in Vegas. They'd promised my mom that they would take care of me, but even on her deathbed, she had reminded me to never be a burden.

"We never take handouts," she'd said just as she had a million times before. "We are no one's charity, Gabriela."

"Do you want me to get you some dessert?" Martha asked, interrupting my thoughts. "They have delicious fruit tarts. Or what about a cheesecake shooter?"

I looked down at my barely touched salad and shook my head. "Not yet. I'll get something later."

Martha nodded and got up from our table to get something for herself. Lily, who sat on the other side of me, asked a passing waiter for coffee for the three of us.

"You should get something sweet to eat with your cafecito," she told me.

"I'm not even finished with my lunch," I said, pushing spinach leaves around my plate with a fork.

"Is something wrong with the food? Your mom made sure to select items she knew you would eat. That's why there's no fish. She didn't want a repeat of our San Francisco trip."

The memory of me retching all over the back seat of our rental car after our lunch at a seafood restaurant made me grimace. "That wasn't my fault. You guys didn't believe me that the shrimp tasted funny."

Even now I had to gulp down the rest of my mimosa to chase away the phantom taste of bad crustaceans and regret. I still refused to eat seafood after all these years because of that awful experience. Not exactly a great trait for a sous-chef to have. Instead, I just told everyone I was allergic. Which was kind of the truth.

Suddenly, the thought of Mom making sure there was no fish on her memorial service luncheon menu because of me was too much to take in. Only she would wait until she was dead to finally make sure I ate more than just a salad.

The room began to spin. My stomach churned. My palms began to sweat. My heart accelerated. And then I couldn't breathe.

I jumped out of my chair and mumbled to Auntie Lily that I was going to get some air.

A minute or so later, I'd found my way to the restaurant's patio, and luckily, it was empty.

I sat down on a nearby chair and covered my eyes with my hands as I tried to take deep breaths. It didn't matter that I was outside. It was as if someone were stealing my oxygen as fast as I could take it in.

My mom's voice whispered in my ear, "Slow. Slow. Slow."

Instead of gulping the air, I willed myself to take methodic sips.

"Gabby, Gabby, honey, Gabby."

This time it was Auntie Lily's words that cut through my anxious haze as I felt hands on my shoulders. My breathing slowed, and her concerned face came into focus.

"I'm okay now," I told her after a few minutes.

"Was it another panic attack?" she asked, tightening her grip on me.

I nodded. She had seen them before. So had Martha. The attacks had started when I was a teenager. As a chubby brown girl from a middle-class neighborhood, I was the literal round peg in a private Catholic school full of rich, skinny white squares. I missed so many days of high school because of my anxiety that I almost didn't graduate. But I'd managed to get the attacks under control in my twenties once I decided that I could tune out others' criticisms—including my mom's. Then the panic attacks had returned last month. We all knew the reason why.

"I'm going to get Martha," Auntie Lily said. But I grabbed her hand before she could walk away.

"No. I don't want to make her worry. I'm better, I promise."

"All right. But why don't we stay here for a few more minutes just to be sure. And if you want to leave, we will."

Despite feeling less than happy, I gave her a small smile anyway. "Thank you, Auntie Lily. You don't have to wait here with me, though. Go back inside. Finish your coffee."

She waved a hand at me. "I don't need any more caffeine. Besides, I don't mind hiding out here with you for a little bit. I'm a little tired of pretending to care about people I haven't talked to in a million years."

I remembered the man back at the mortuary.

"You definitely didn't want to talk to that man from earlier," I said. "What was his name again? Raul?"

Lily shrugged. "He's not worth talking to, that's all."

"Why?" I asked, studying her suspiciously blank expression. "It's obvious you don't care for him, but why?"

Lily straightened her shoulders and folded her arms across her chest. "Because Raul Esparza is a goddamn liar. I'm sorry he upset you. He shouldn't have shown his face today of all days. I honestly have no idea how he even knew about . . . Just forget about him, okay?"

But I couldn't forget. As much as I hated to give him another thought, I couldn't shake the feeling that she wasn't telling me something. Of the three, I could always count on Auntie Lily to be straight with me. She once told me that sugarcoating the truth didn't do anyone any favors, so she prided herself on being honest. Brutally if need be.

"A man I'd never seen before who shows up on the day of my mother's funeral claiming to be my father isn't something I can just erase from my memory, Auntie Lily. There has to be more to the story."

Lily's face pinched in frustration. "There's not. He's nobody. Why can't you just believe me and let it go?"

My chest tightened with dread. If the man really were a nobody, she wouldn't be so adamant. So defensive. Whatever it was she didn't want to tell me, it couldn't be good. Still, I had to know. "It's obvious you're not telling me something. I deserve to know who that man was and why he thought it would be okay to show up today."

"Gabriela, please just drop it!"

Lily's outburst stunned me into silence. She slapped her hand over her mouth and stared at me as if I were the one who had shouted at her.

"What's going on?" We both turned to see Martha walking onto the patio. "I can hear your raised voices from inside."

I walked over to her before Auntie Lily could say anything. "Auntie Martha, do you know a man named Raul?"

Martha's already ruddy cheeks burned even brighter. Her eyes flew to Lily, and I could see them ask permission. I stepped in between them and faced Martha. I wasn't going to move until she spilled their secret.

"Don't look at her," I said to Martha, trying to sound as stern as possible. "Look at me and tell me the truth."

Chapter Three

"Raul was at the service?"

I inhaled a sharp breath in shock. Auntie Martha's question answered a few of my own.

As I'd suspected, she also knew the man. And, although she seemed surprised about him showing up, it didn't look to be as much of a shock as it had been to Auntie Lily.

"Who is he?" I asked carefully. My heart was pounding now, almost as if I'd just run a mile. And if this conversation was going where I feared it was going, I might actually run away for real.

Martha cleared her throat. "He dated your mom when they were teenagers."

I swallowed my dread. "And?"

"Martha . . . ," Lily warned.

"Did you talk to him, Gabby?" Auntie Martha seemed more composed now as she stepped closer and met my eyes.

"Barely," I admitted, still trying to rein in my anxiety. "Can one of you please tell me who this man is and why on earth he would tell me that he was my father?"

"Because he is."

I almost laughed at Martha's words. But then I saw her eyes. They were sad. Regretful even. They weren't lying.

Even though I'd begun to suspect it, based on Auntie Lily's out-of-character behavior, the confirmation that this stranger was my biological father was literally too much to bear. My knees gave out and I dipped. Both of them reached out to steady me and then helped me to a nearby bench. Waves of panic resurfaced, threatening to pull me into a dark abyss of anxiety.

"Breathe, Gabby. Breathe," I heard Lily chant beside me. "Dammit, Martha. Why did you have to open your mouth?"

"I'm not going to lie to her anymore. Especially not today."

Someone, maybe Martha, left and came back with a bottle of water. After I was able to calm down for the second time, I took a few sips and tried to wrap my head around what I now knew to be the truth: Raul Esparza was my biological father.

I was eight when I'd finally asked my mom why we didn't have the same last name as my dad. After all, I knew they were married and I had always called him "Daddy." So I questioned why his last name was Olmos and why our last name was Medina.

"Because wives don't always have to have the same last name as their husbands," she had told me. "And because you came from my body, we have the same last name."

Even at that age I knew she hadn't really answered my question. So I pressed her for more information. "Auntie Lily's daughter has the same last name as her daddy, doesn't she?"

I remembered her pausing for a few seconds before finally saying, "That's because some kids have the same daddy when they're born and some kids, like you, get a different daddy later."

"What happened to my other daddy?" I asked, fearing that he had met some horrible and painful death.

Instead, all I got was the matter-of-fact reply, "He went away and he's not coming back. And that's okay because you already have the best daddy in the world, right?"

"But he's not my *real* daddy?" I remembered saying through my tears.

And I would never forget the look of hurt on her face. "Listen to me, Gabriela, and listen good. Juan Olmos is your real daddy. I never ever want you to call him anything else. Not stepdad, not your second dad. Nothing like that. As far as I'm concerned, he is the only dad you have ever had or will ever have. Got it?"

When I'd gotten older, I'd figured that my birth father hadn't wanted me or my mom. And even though I was curious, I told myself I didn't care. When a friend asked me if I would be sad if I ever found out that my birth father had died, I told her that I wouldn't because why would I care about the death of a stranger?

"Well, what if he just showed up on your doorstep one day?" she had asked.

"I'd slam the door in his face," I had replied.

Never could I have ever imagined that he'd show up at my mom's memorial service instead.

There would be no more wondering about what had happened to my birth father. Still, one question burned in my mind.

"Why was he there today?" I asked them.

Immediately, Lily shook her head furiously.

Martha, however, looked like I had after eating that spoiled shrimp.

"Auntie Martha, why was he there today?" I asked, making sure she met my eyes.

Auntie Lily seemed to finally realize that her friend knew something. "M-a-r-t-h-a," Lily said slowly. "What did you do?"

"He mentioned that he'd like to come and pay his respects, so I emailed him the information about the memorial service," Auntie Martha rushed.

I thought Lily was going to have a panic attack of her own. She held up her hand and began waving it in the air. "Hold up. *Raul mentioned?*

When on earth would he have mentioned this? Did you call him to tell him about Sandra?"

Auntie Martha slowly nodded. "He wanted to come see her . . . before. But I told him I didn't think it would be a good idea. So he said he would come for the funeral."

Her explanation shook me free from my stunned silence. "How did he even know she was sick?"

"He's known for a while," she admitted.

My heart dropped to the ground. Everything I had ever believed about my biological father was turning out to be wrong. He hadn't shown up out of the blue. The man had been lurking on the sidelines for some time. I immediately thought of my mom. Would she have wanted to see Raul? I couldn't imagine that she would have. After all, she'd never mentioned him to me by name—ever—when she was alive. I doubted he would've been someone she had felt the need to say goodbye to. At least she had been spared an awkward reunion.

Hearing that Raul had known about my mom's illness was the last straw for Lily. She exploded and began shouting at Martha in Spanish. I wasn't fluent, so I didn't understand everything she was saying, but I did recognize the barrage of curse words. For her part, Martha yelled right back.

After a few minutes of their heated back and forth, Lily finally pointed her finger at me. "Tell her, Martha. Tell Gabby how you betrayed Sandra."

"What is she talking about, Auntie Martha?" I asked. My stomach knotted even more in rising worry. *Betrayed* was a loaded and heavy word. I couldn't even imagine what Lily was accusing Martha of doing.

I didn't want to.

Auntie Martha heaved a long sigh and then pulled a chair from a nearby table and set it next to me. She sat down and took my hand in hers.

"Before your mom and Raul started dating, he was her friend. In fact, he was our friend too. We all went to junior high together and then high school. I've known—we've known him—for a long, long time."

I nodded but didn't say a word. I was worried that if I did, she would stop talking and Auntie Lily would start yelling again. Morbid curiosity made me want to know what happened next in a story I already knew the ending to.

"So," Auntie Martha continued, "a few years after you were born, I ran into Raul in the neighborhood. He was visiting his cousin who used to live down the street from me. Anyway, he wanted to know all about you, and Sandra too. He wasn't the same guy I had remembered. He seemed more mature and had his life together. So, when he asked for me to set up a meeting with Sandra, I did."

"Did she meet with him?" I asked calmly, as if Auntie Martha were telling me the plot of one of her favorite books instead of a true story that would have significant ramifications in my real life.

"She did. And that's when she let him know that she was going to marry Juan. Sandra told Raul that Juan loved you like you were his own daughter, and she asked him to sign some papers so Juan could adopt you after they got married. He refused."

My heart sank. Juan had wanted to adopt me. I had asked my mom once about why he hadn't, and she'd gotten angry. "For what?" she'd said. "You're already his daughter. A piece of paper isn't going to change that."

Anger kicked whatever sadness I'd been feeling out the door. "Why would he do that?" I asked Auntie Martha.

She shrugged. "He told Sandra he had his reasons. Anyway, they got into a huge fight, and Raul told your mom that he was going to take her to court and try to get visitation rights. A few months went by, and then one day Sandra told me that she had had a long talk with him and he had agreed to not fight for custody because he was going to be moving out of state. But he asked if she could send him pictures of you and just let him know that you were okay. And that's when Sandra asked me if I would be the one to keep in contact with Raul because she didn't want Juan to know anything about it."

Auntie Lily gasped. "She asked you to?"

"Yes, she did. I would never go behind Sandra's back like that." Auntie Martha's voice was steady, but defensive. It was obvious that Lily must have had some pretty harsh words for her before.

"Oh, but you were okay going behind mine?" Auntie Lily scoffed. "I never knew about this, Gabby. Sandra never said a word to me about it. I swear."

I believed her. And I believed Auntie Martha.

But that didn't mean I accepted it. Or that I still didn't have questions.

"How can this be happening?" I asked.

Lily and Martha may have been the only ones within earshot, but I was really saying it to my mom. Why had she kept something like this from me? She could've said something when I was older. She had the chance after my dad had died. She could've had a real-life dramatic deathbed confession, for God's sake.

"Gabby, I'm sure you want answers. And you can ask me whatever you want, and I'll tell you whatever I know. But there is someone else who can tell you even more than I can."

"Absolutely not!" Auntie Lily said. "She should stay away from that man."

Auntie Martha seemed to ignore her. "If you want, I can give you his number so you two can talk."

Talk to the man who didn't want to have anything to do with me for nearly thirty years? Up until that moment, I hadn't even considered the possibility of seeing him again, let alone having a conversation with him. Of course, I had questions. But did I want answers?

Auntie Lily, however, was very clear about what she thought about the situation.

"Unbelievable!" Lily yelled. "Why are you doing this, Martha?"

"Because Gabriela deserves to know the truth," she said. "I'm not forcing her to talk to the man, but she should have the choice. Finally."

Auntie Lily took another step closer and met my eyes. "This is ridiculous, Gabby. That man is nothing to you—he never was. You don't need to ever talk to him again."

The thought of seeing Raul made me queasy. Only because I wasn't sure if I was ready to hear if there were more secrets my mom had kept from me.

But Auntie Martha had a point. Raul was the only one who could tell me his side of the story. That is, if I ever decided that I even cared to know about it.

"Gabby, you don't have to decide right this minute," Auntie Martha said, grabbing my hand again. "Everything that happens next will be up to you and only you."

Why did that sound so ominous?

Chapter Four

When I was fifteen, I'd made the very bad decision to take my mom's car to a friend's house a few blocks away.

It was a late-July afternoon, and my friend had invited me over to go swimming. My mom and dad had gone to her coworker's wedding, leaving me alone in the house and very, very bored. So, when my friend had called and asked me to come over, I was more than ready. The only problem was that it was way too hot for me to walk to her house. I had my learner's permit, and my dad had already taken me driving a couple of times around the neighborhood. He had told me that I was a pretty good driver. And I had believed him.

So, I convinced myself it would be a good idea to drive myself to my friend's house.

It wasn't.

Needless to say, I was way more confident in my head about my driving skills. Because once I got in the car and turned on the ignition, it was as if I had forgotten everything my dad had ever taught me. And that was the day I had my first car accident. Luckily, the only victim was our garage door.

It wasn't the first time I'd made a bad decision. And it was far from the last. I had a long list of ex-boyfriends to prove it. The point was, sometimes my gut was my guardian angel.

And, sometimes, she was a fucking liar.

Sitting on the small couch in Raul's motel room, I hadn't yet decided whether she had led me astray once again.

It had been two days since my mom's memorial service. By the time I'd collapsed onto Auntie Martha's sofa bed that night, I knew I'd be calling the man who was my biological father. I had felt that, despite Auntie Lily's conviction that I was better off not talking to Raul again, I wasn't so sure. Maybe he didn't deserve my time. Actually, I was sure he didn't. But I had decided that I deserved answers. I told myself I would listen to what he had to say and then I would never have to see him again. He wasn't, nor would he ever be, my father. Raul Esparza was a sperm donor. Period.

By luck or fate, I'd caught him just before he was going to head for the airport for a flight back to New Mexico, where he now lived. He had said he'd reschedule and we could meet whenever I was ready.

I knew myself, though. And if I had let myself wait even one more day, I'd chicken out. So I'd shown up five minutes earlier and braced myself to have what I knew would be a very uncomfortable conversation.

"Are you sure I can't get you a bottle of water?" Raul asked as he took a seat on the chair in front of me.

"No. I'm fine," I said, forcing myself to meet his eyes.

He gave me a big smile. "I'm really glad you called. After our meeting at the memorial service, I wasn't quite sure how to reach out to you again."

I shifted in my seat, trying to steady not just my balance but also my nerves. "Well, it was kind of a shock."

He nodded and cleared his throat. "Yeah, of course. My timing isn't always the best. I realize now I could've handled it differently. I could've handled a lot of things differently."

"Auntie Lily said you were a liar," I blurted. I wanted Raul to know that just because I was here, it didn't mean that I was going to make this easy for him.

He crossed his arms against his chest. "I see Lily is still as blunt as ever."

I shrugged. "Actually, I think she's worse. Whatever filter she used to have is pretty much gone now."

That made him laugh. I didn't join him. When he stopped chuckling, an awkward silence filled the small space between us. Part of me wanted to bombard him with all the questions that had kept me awake for the last two nights. The other part wished he wouldn't speak to me ever again.

It turned out that when it came to absent parents, there was a delicate line between curiosity and indifference.

"So . . . ," Raul began.

"Why did you show up at the memorial service?" I rushed, interrupting him.

"I wanted to pay my respects to Sandra."

"Then why say anything to me? You could've said your goodbye and then been on your way, and I wouldn't have known a thing. So, why come up to me at all?"

Raul sat back farther into his chair. "I guess I wanted to talk to you. See how you were doing. I know you and your mom were close. I can't imagine how hard it's been for you these past few months."

Irritation pricked my nerves like the annoying sticker balls that fell from the tree in front of Martha's building. "Well, since you don't know a lot about me in the first place, that's understandable."

"I know some things," Raul insisted.

I raised my eyebrows at his statement. "Such as?"

"I know you lost Juan when you were a teenager," he said. Then, before I could ask, he answered my immediate question: "Martha told me."

Why did it surprise me that Martha had told him that too? It made me wonder what other news she'd shared about my family over the years. Was I a regular topic of their conversations? For some reason, I had always believed that my biological father wasn't interested in me or my life.

When I didn't say anything else, he continued, "I know that you landed your dream job earlier this year working as a sous-chef at a popular restaurant, and then you quit so you could help take care of Sandra. And I know you're staying with Martha in her tiny one-bedroom apartment."

It was jarring to hear how he'd kept tabs on me all this time, yet I knew nothing about him. I squared my shoulders defensively. "So what?"

"So, the reason I came, the reason I'm here, is to help you."

"What do you mean?" I scoffed.

"I mean I have a house in New Mexico. It's yours if you want it."

His words hit me like a splash of cold water. They startled me, and he had my full attention now. "I don't understand. You want me to move in with you?"

Raul waved his hands. "No. No. Of course not."

"Then what?"

"My abuela's house—your bisabuela's home—has been vacant since she passed away last year. She left it to me, but I already have a house of my own. I keep saying I'm going to sell it. It needs some improvements, though, and I just don't have the time to deal with all of that. So, you can move in there, fix what needs to be fixed and sell it. And you can keep the money."

"You want to give me a house?" I asked the question, not even believing the words myself. How could I? The man had been a ghost for almost thirty years. It was hard to trust someone who had basically appeared out of thin air. And he was offering me a gift? No. Something wasn't right.

Despite my apparent doubts, Raul continued to explain himself. "In simple terms, yes. Yes, I want to give you a house."

"Why?"

"Isn't it obvious?"

"It's not. That's why I asked the question."

Raul let out a long sigh. "All this time I've told myself you were better off without me—that I couldn't offer you anything. Now I have something."

Although I thought I heard sincerity in his tone, I still couldn't trust it.

I sat back and crossed my arms against my chest. "And what do you want in return? What's the catch?"

"No catch," Raul said.

I studied the man before me and tried to figure out if he was lying. I had an ex-boyfriend who used to answer my question with a question when he was being less than truthful. Mom would look everywhere but at me, as if I needed eye contact to see right through her dishonesty. But Raul was a stranger, and if he was lying through his teeth, then I couldn't tell. At least not yet.

Even my stubborn brain couldn't deny that his proposal, if for real, was tempting only because I had no income at the moment. I had some money in my savings, but even without having to worry about rent, it would only last me a few more months because of my regular bills. Not to mention the fact that just before she died, Mom had confessed that she had opened several credit cards in my name to help her pay her mortgage after she was forced to stop working. But all that had done was delay the inevitable.

I had been shocked when she'd told me. Stunned. Because I already owed thousands in student loans, I never wanted to add to that debt. I didn't even have a gas card, for God's sake. And the only reason why she finally owned up to it was because I'd found a stack of bills hidden at the bottom of her hamper. Barely able to speak, she weakly explained how she had maxed out her credit cards first to pay for doctor visits, prescriptions, and utilities. But when a preapproved application arrived at her house in my name, my mom said she only filled it out once she got behind on her mortgage payments. Then, before she knew it, one card had turned into three. She'd begged for forgiveness. Of course, I couldn't tell her how angry I was or how betrayed I felt. At that point, we knew she only had days left and I wasn't about to spend them being mad at her. We'd already lost so much that way.

The day after she passed, Auntie Lily, Auntie Martha, and I called each bank to find out exactly what she had owed—well, what I legally owed now. All in all, it was nearly $40,000. Plus, that didn't include the $76,345 balance left on my student loans. Needless to say, I'd had no idea how in the world I was going to pay off any of it. Having a house to sell would be the answer to my money problems. Again, *if* it was all true.

Did that mean I was considering getting to know this man? Was I actually leaning toward accepting his offer?

Mom would be appalled. It didn't matter that I was mostly in my current financial crisis because of her either. She had never gotten over the shame of having to use vouchers at the grocery store to buy staples like milk and cereal or shop at thrift stores and yard sales for baby clothes. She would be furious at me for accepting what she considered "charity" from someone. And the fact that it was being offered by the man who had abandoned us? I wouldn't have put it past her to disown me. If I accepted Raul's offer, it would be a huge betrayal.

No, there had to be another option.

Suddenly, the small room seemed even smaller. My heart was racing toward a full-on panic attack. I felt trapped. Anxious. I needed to get away from Raul and his promises.

I shot to my feet and grabbed my purse from the table. "I appreciate your offer, but I don't want it. I don't want your house."

Or you in my life.

"Gabby, wait, at least think about it for a few days. I know this has all been very hard on you, to say the least. Don't make any rash decisions you might regret later."

"I can't move to New Mexico!" I didn't realize I was yelling until the last syllable.

"It's not going to be forever," he said softly.

My head shook back and forth. "Even if it were for only a day, I wouldn't move. My home is here. My mom is . . . ," I began and then stopped. I was about to tell Raul that my mom was here.

But she wasn't.

Familiar grief gagged me as I began to choke on the escaping sobs. I slapped my hand over my mouth in an attempt to trap them until I could get as far away from this man as possible. As I took a step toward the door, Raul took a step toward me with his arms open.

That's when I ran.

Chapter Five

I felt like fighting.

It had been a week since I'd run out of Raul's motel room. Although seeing and talking to him had been more painful than I'd expected, at least it had given me the kick I'd needed to call Chef Dean and try to get my job back. Sure, it was embarrassing having to basically beg for a second chance. I'd started as a hostess at Sky Grill when it opened three years ago as the signature restaurant of the new Sunset Towers luxury hotel. Despite my culinary training and years of experience working in kitchens all over LA, Chef Dean required new hires to begin at the front of the house. I'd finally worked my way up to sous-chef, and then my mom had gotten sick again. When I'd given my notice, he told me I'd basically spit in his face and then listed all the reasons why he always knew he'd wasted the opportunity on someone like me.

Crawling back wasn't going to be easy. But Sky Grill was the hottest restaurant in the city at the moment. So, I was ready to get on my knees and put up with whatever verbal insults came my way if it meant getting another chance to work with him. It was better than accepting a house from a stranger.

Wasn't it?

I left messages on his cell and at the restaurant for five days without a return call back. I had expected that. Chef Dean was an arrogant, stubborn bastard who was known for his fiery temper and sexist attitudes.

He'd only ever had two female sous-chefs before me in his restaurants. Others had either been fired on the spot or walked out because of his tongue lashings. I'd prided myself on building up a shield to his insults over the years, so when I finally was in the kitchen, anything he verbally hurled at me just slid off the back of my white chef's jacket. Eventually, I began to get a few grunts of appreciation.

I knew I had proven that I deserved to be in Chef Dean's kitchen. Now I just needed to prove to him that I deserved to come back.

I wasn't ready to give up. Not yet.

Armed with a container of potato salad from his favorite German deli and a six-pack of his favorite Belgian beer, I showed up on a Friday morning at the hotel that housed Sky Grill on its roof and waited for him outside the employee parking lot. He drove up in his black Tesla just after ten in the morning. Of course, he ignored me. Only stopping long enough to grab the potato salad and beer from my hands. My heart sank when he disappeared into the hotel. I waited for another ten minutes before deciding I'd come back tomorrow and try all over again. Then, just as I was about to get back into my car, he texted me to get inside.

Chef Dean was sitting behind a desk in his small office off the kitchen's pantry when I arrived. He had already opened up one of the beer bottles and had just stuck a spoonful of the potato salad into his mouth. I took a seat on the opposite side of the desk and waited for him to swallow.

It was a good five minutes before he even acknowledged my presence.

"So, you want to be a hostess again?" he said as he typed away on his laptop.

Panic fluttered in my chest. "No, Chef Dean. I want to be your sous-chef."

"I already have enough sous-chefs," he said, still refusing to look at me.

"I bet none of them are as good as me," I said, trying not to sound like I was whining. Chef Dean hated whiners. However, he tolerated arrogance as long as it was deserved. "I did a good job for you when I was here, didn't I?"

"I wouldn't say good," he said, scrunching his nose. "You were sufficient."

The ding didn't deter me. "I already know your kitchen. You wouldn't even have to train me."

Finally, he closed his laptop and finished off his beer. "Why should I take you back? You clearly didn't appreciate everything I gave to you."

It couldn't have been further from the truth. I wanted to tell him just how much it had meant to me to finally be able to wear one of his sous-chef jackets. But I couldn't trust myself that I wouldn't be overcome with emotion—the one thing Chef Dean hated to see. So, I paused and swallowed my feelings. "I did appreciate it," I told him in an even voice. "But I knew I couldn't give you my full attention because of what I was dealing with in my personal life. I know you deserve only the best, so I made the difficult choice to leave."

I almost choked on the last sentence, but I knew Chef Dean's narcissistic personality would appreciate me taking full responsibility for leaving. He didn't care that my mom had been dying. All he cared about was how it had affected him and his restaurant.

When he nodded back, I knew my instinct had been right. Hope bloomed in my chest.

"If I take you back, you have to do whatever I say without complaint," he said, pointing his finger at me.

His crystal-blue eyes darkened with a look that made a chill run down my back. But I dismissed the uneasy feeling in the pit of my stomach. Chef Dean was going to make me pay for quitting. I told myself that it didn't matter. I was no stranger to hard work, and I could keep my mouth shut as long as I focused on the reward at the end.

"I will. I swear I will do anything to show you that I deserve to be here."

"Fine. You start tonight . . . as a hostess."

My heart and my stomach sank all the way back down to the parking lot of the hotel. "But, I thought . . ."

"You will be a hostess, or you will be nothing," he said before opening his laptop again.

It wasn't what I wanted. And although every fiber in my being wanted to argue with him, I knew I couldn't. This was the second chance he was offering, and I had to take it. I had no choice. So I swallowed my anger and my pride.

"Okay. Thank you," I said.

Without giving me a second glance, he pointed at the office's door, and I knew I was being dismissed. The conversation was over.

As I walked back to my car, I tried to be more excited. I had a job again. It was going to be a huge pay cut from before, but it was still better than the zero dollars I'd been making the past few months. It was something. And something was an improvement over nothing.

And it meant that I could forget all about Raul and his offer.

◆ ◆ ◆

I returned to Sky Grill a few hours later dressed in the black long-sleeved shirt and black pants I used to wear during my hostess days. Part of me was a little nervous about seeing the rest of the staff again. I was also curious about the other hostesses and whether any of the ones I'd once worked with were still around.

"Hey, Gabby!"

I turned around. Immediately, my nerves slightly eased at the sight of Andrew—Sky Grill's assistant executive chef. He jogged across the parking lot and met up with me at the hotel's employee entrance. Andrew had taken me under his wing right from the beginning. He and I would stay after everyone else had gone home so he could teach me how to prep for one of the menu items. I knew Andrew was the one who'd vouched for me when the sous-chef opening had come up. So it had been especially hard to tell him that I had needed to resign. But he'd been supportive and understanding. The complete opposite of Chef Dean.

"Hey there," I said and gave him a tight hug. "It's so good to see you."

Andrew gave me one of his bright smiles after letting me go. "Hey, what happened to the purple?"

I instinctively touched my hair where the vibrant streaks of color used to be. My mom had been horrified when I'd done it. "You'll never get a professional job now," she'd warned. "You're not a teenager, Gabby. When are you going to grow up and start acting like an adult?"

Despite her hysterics, I'd kept the streaks. Sometimes I'd change it up with pink or green. But I always went back to purple. Now they had turned into straw-colored strips of blahness. Lily had wanted to take me to a salon before the memorial service, but I had refused. It had seemed wrong to try to look perfect when my life was anything but.

"Oh, yeah," I said, trying to laugh. "Just haven't had the time, you know?"

He nodded. "I was sorry to hear about your mom. I would've gone to her service, but I had no idea she'd passed until this morning."

Guilt unsettled my stomach. "I'm sorry. I know I should've texted you. I guess I just didn't think about telling anyone here, especially after going radio silent when I left."

He reached out and squeezed my shoulder. "No need to apologize. You were going through a lot. You didn't owe us—or me—anything. I'm just glad you're back. Which, by the way, I have no idea how you even managed it. Do I even want to know?"

I grimaced. "Probably not. Let's just say I'll probably owe Chef Dean my firstborn if I ever have a kid."

"No, he hates children. You're probably going to have to give him a kidney or something."

That made me laugh, and a familiar lightness brightened my mood. Andrew had always been a good friend. Just being around him again was going to make whatever pain Chef Dean inflicted worth it.

"I'm glad you're still here," I told him honestly.

He seemed to consider my admission for a moment. "Me too. Well, now I am."

We both smiled at each other for a moment before Andrew swiped his employee badge and held open the door for me. "Let's get cooking," he said.

Andrew must have seen the disappointment in my face because he quickly asked, "What's wrong?"

I shrugged. "I'm back to being a hostess again."

"Are you fucking kidding me? That bastard. I'm going to say something to him."

"No. Please don't," I begged and then tugged on the hem of his jacket to keep him from barreling through the door straight to Chef Dean.

"You worked your ass off to become sous-chef, Gabby. That son of a bitch is just being petty by making you be a hostess again."

"I know he is," I said after a long, deep sigh. "But if this is what it takes, then so be it. Beggars can't be choosers, right?"

Andrew didn't look convinced, but he also didn't argue. He'd worked with Chef Dean for years, and he knew better than anyone that it wasn't a good idea to get on our boss's bad side. One night, after a particularly rough service, Andrew had confessed that he'd begun looking for investors so he could open his own restaurant. Although I had never told a soul, Chef Dean had somehow gotten wind of it. The people who had once promised Andrew they were interested in his venture suddenly stopped returning Andrew's calls, and we both knew why. Chef Dean was probably the most influential restaurateur in town at the moment. No one dared cross him. Andrew had fully expected to get fired. Instead, Chef Dean had only threatened to let him go—torturing him with the threat for weeks. Andrew said that had been worse.

We walked together to the employee elevator and took it up to the hotel's rooftop, where Sky Grill was located.

"Let's grab a drink after, okay?" Andrew said before he headed for the kitchen.

I nodded and gave him a smile. "Definitely. Have a great service," I told him.

He saluted me before walking away, leaving me alone at the empty bar. I debated following Andrew and checking in with Chef Dean. But before I could, a woman and a man I didn't recognize entered the restaurant.

"Are you Gabby?" the man asked.

"I am," I said with a quick nod.

"I'm Sal and this is Jessica. She's going to be your trainer tonight."

"Oh, I don't need to be trained. I've worked here before."

They both exchanged looks. "We know," Jessica said. "Chef Dean texted and told us all about you. He still wants me to train you. The menu has changed a little and so has our reservation system."

"Okay," I said, not missing the woman's irritated tone. I wondered what Chef Dean had told them about me. "I'm just going to put my stuff in a locker, and then we can get started. Is the staff break room still by the restrooms?"

Jessica didn't even look at me and disappeared into the dining room. Sal laughed nervously and then confirmed that at least hadn't changed.

A few minutes later, after securing my belongings for the night, I walked into the ladies' room and into the last stall to tuck my shirt into my pants. I was just about to unlock the door when I heard a woman's voice. Although I'd just met her, I instantly recognized it as Jessica's.

"I wish you were on shift tonight. I already know I'm going to hate working with her." I didn't hear a second voice, so I guessed that Jessica must have been on her phone.

"Who cares if she has the experience? We all know she's here because Chef Dean is probably fucking her. Why else would he give her a job again? You told me he was so furious when she quit. Do you really think he let her come back because of her cooking?"

Rage exploded inside me, and it took everything I had not to run out of the stall and start screaming in Jessica's face. I'd bet good money that the person on the other end of the phone was Belinda. We'd worked together as hostesses for a few months but never became friendly. I could tell she didn't like me, and frankly, I didn't care for her. We'd both applied for the sous-chef position, and when I got it, she basically accused me of sleeping with Andrew since it was pretty obvious that he had wanted me to get the promotion. The fact that Belinda still wasn't a sous-chef was a little satisfying—even if I was still seething about Jessica's assumption.

When Jessica finally left, I counted to twenty before walking out of the stall. I needed a calm head and heart before facing her so she could train me. I needed to prove to Chef Dean that I was a kick-ass hostess who deserved to be his next sous-chef. Jessica and Belinda and their stupid opinions meant nothing to me. And they weren't going to stand in the way of getting what I wanted.

It turned out I didn't need to wait that long.

Before Jessica could even start explaining the new reservation system, Chef Dean barked my name from the kitchen entrance.

"Get in here, Gabby," he yelled.

Jessica gave me a look that told me she wanted to say something, but she kept her mouth shut. I couldn't help but smirk and jogged over to where Chef Dean was standing.

"Joseph got into a car accident on the way over here. Get a jacket and start prepping."

I felt bad for whoever Joseph was, and I honestly hoped he was going to be all right. But I couldn't hide my excitement. "Yes, Chef. Thank you, Chef."

Chef Dean raised his eyebrows at me and then leaned down until his face was only inches away from mine. "Don't fuck this up."

I nodded and then followed him into the kitchen.

As soon as I saw Andrew, we exchanged sly smiles. Somehow, I knew he'd had a hand in bringing me back to where I belonged.

I thanked my earlier self for wearing a black tank top under the dress shirt. I took off the shirt and grabbed a clean, neatly pressed white sous-chef jacket from the rack in the hallway outside Chef Dean's office. It felt so good to put it on.

And for the first time in months, I felt like my old self again. Who knew that the thought of chopping up carrots and celery again would bring me such a sense of peace?

It took me an hour or so to keep up with the chaotic pace that Chef Dean conducted in the kitchen. But once I got into the groove, it felt like I'd never left. It also didn't take me that long to figure out that Jessica wasn't the only one at Sky Grill who wasn't too happy about me being back. Ian, the sous-chef who had been hired to replace me, seemed hell bent on reminding me that things had changed since I'd worked in the kitchen. He made a big show of letting everyone know that Joseph was faster at plating. And when we fell behind clearing tickets, Ian let Chef Dean know that I was the one holding up everything even though he was the one who insisted on redoing everything I touched.

But if Ian thought he could intimidate me, he was wrong.

After Chef Dean unleashed his usual profanity-laced insults on me, I apologized for my slowness and told him I'd speed things up. That seemed to satisfy him, and he turned his attention back to the meat he was grilling.

By closing time, I was both exhausted and exhilarated. It had been a high to be cooking again and just to be doing something I knew I could control. Despite having been slow in the beginning, I knew I had done a good job. I only hoped it had been enough to show Chef Dean that I was ready to be back for real.

"So, where do you want to go?" Andrew asked as we grabbed our stuff from the lockers.

"It doesn't matter," I said. "As long as it has chairs so I can sit down and get off my feet, then I'm good."

Andrew laughed. "I can do that. How about we just hit the hotel bar?"

"Perfect," I said. "Just let me go put this jacket in the laundry hamper."

The sous-chefs' jackets were the property of Sky Grill, and we weren't allowed to take them home. I couldn't wait for the day when I could wear my own personal coat like Andrew did as Sky Grill's assistant executive chef.

I took off the jacket and threw it in the hamper in the hallway outside Chef Dean's office. As I walked back to the kitchen, he called for me.

"Come in here, Gabby."

Why had I thought I'd be able to escape without seeing him? I had wanted to keep the high going at least until tomorrow. I wasn't ready for him to tell me that I was going back to being a hostess.

Or, maybe he wants to tell you what a good job you did.

I rolled my eyes at my own naivete. Quickly, I texted Andrew, who had gone to wait for me at the elevator, and told him I'd meet him downstairs after I talked to Chef Dean.

Taking a deep breath, I walked into the office and found my boss at his desk again. He wasn't on his laptop this time. Instead, he was leaning back in his chair holding one of the beer bottles I'd given him earlier that day as a peace offering. I was surprised when he offered it to me.

"Let's have a drink," he said. Part of me wanted to tell him I was too tired. The other part knew I had to take the bottle.

"Sure," I said and sat down. "Thanks."

He opened up another bottle for himself. But while I took a small sip from my bottle, he gulped his down until it was finished.

"You did okay," Chef Dean said, grabbing another bottle from the case. "You're definitely out of practice, though."

"I know. It's been a while since I've done that kind of prep work," I admitted.

"I'll put you on the schedule two nights a week as a hostess and two nights as a sous-chef. After three months, we can look at making you full time again."

My heart soared, and I couldn't hold back a large grin. "Really? Oh, wow. Thank you, Chef."

He downed his second beer and then stood up. Thinking it was my cue to leave, I set my bottle on his desk and stood up as well. Chef Dean walked around the desk and came up to me.

"Don't make me regret giving you this second chance, Gabby."

I shook my head furiously. "I won't. I promise I'll do whatever it takes."

"I'm glad to hear you say that. How about you start now?"

Before I realized what was happening, Chef Dean slammed his mouth against mine. It took a few seconds for my body to catch up with my brain. When it finally did, I managed to pull away and take a step backward.

"What are you doing, Chef?" It was as if shock had numbed my brain. It wasn't working. It couldn't decipher what had just happened, so all I could do was ask the question.

He smiled and shrugged. "Well, I thought I was kissing you, Gabby. It's more fun, though, when you kiss back. I hear you Latinas can get pretty passionate."

My adrenaline began to spike from the rising fear of where this was headed. My internal danger alarms were blaring, and I knew this was going to be bad. Very, very bad.

Chef Dean reached for me again, and I moved just out of his grasp. "I don't think this is a good idea. You're my boss."

"That's right," he snarled. "And you promised to do whatever I said, didn't you?"

My gut wrenched with dread. This couldn't be happening. "I meant I'd do whatever you wanted in the kitchen," I explained desperately, even though deep down I knew it didn't matter anymore.

If Chef Dean seemed amused before, he definitely wasn't now. His face contorted into red fury. "Are you really going to pretend that this isn't exactly what you meant when you begged for me to give you your job back?"

I shook my head furiously. "If I gave you that impression, I'm sorry."

Chef Dean waved his finger at me. "Nobody makes a fool out of me. Especially not twice."

Before I could try to talk some sense into him, Chef Dean grabbed both of my upper arms and threw me onto his office's small couch. In an instant, he was on top of me and holding my arms down while he tried to shove his tongue into my mouth. I shut my eyes so I couldn't see his face as he continued to kiss and lick my lips. He tasted bitter and salty. It disgusted me. Bile burned the back of my throat as the nausea began to build. He moved his mouth to my throat and then cleavage. The scruff of his beard raked against my skin, and it began to burn there. I went rigid, hoping the less I moved, the less he would move.

"Nobody rejects me, Gabby," he growled. "Especially not some Mexican bitch."

My eyes flew open. Rage replaced the shock, and I summoned all my strength to wriggle free.

He moved his mouth back to my neck. "That's it," he breathed into my ear. "Put up a fight."

I tried to do just that, but his weight continued to pin me into the cushions, and my shifting and kicking didn't seem to make much difference. Then, just as I'd opened my mouth to scream for help, he let go of one arm so he could stick his hand down the front of my pants.

That was all I needed. With my free hand, I reached up and scratched Chef Dean's right cheek. He swore and instinctively moved his hand to touch his wound. That gave me the opening I needed to knee him between his legs and push him off me. Chef Dean grunted, lost his balance, and rolled onto the floor.

I jumped off the couch before he could get up, grabbed my purse, and ran out of the office and right into Jessica.

"Whoa, slow down," she yelled.

"Sorry," I mumbled and headed for the elevator.

As soon as I got inside my car a few minutes later, I tried to stick the key into the ignition. But I was shaking so much that I couldn't get it into the hole. Frustration and anger finally spilled over, and I couldn't hold back the tears anymore. I let out a wail and sobbed into my hands. I felt so stupid. So clueless.

Then the second-guessing started. Had I actually implied to Chef Dean that I was willing to trade sex for a job? Had I unknowingly given him some sort of signal that I was willing to sleep with him if he made me a sous-chef again?

My phone pinged with a new text. It was Andrew asking if I was on my way yet to the bar. I wiped my tears away and texted back.

"Sorry. Rain check? I'll call you tomorrow."

Even as I typed the words, I dreaded telling Andrew what had just happened. But there was no way I was ever going back to Sky Grill, and he was going to want an explanation.

But, it turned out, the decision wasn't up to me after all.

When a second text came in, I assumed it was Andrew asking questions. But it was Chef Dean.

"You're fired. And if you start spreading lies about me, I'll make sure the only chef job you ever get is inside a fucking taco truck."

Even though I had always known that Chef Dean had a reputation for harassing women, he'd never said or done anything sexually to me before this. Or maybe the signs had been there the whole time and I had just been oblivious because it'd never occurred to me that Chef Dean would ever see me that way. I knew now that was bullshit. Sexual harassment and assault had nothing to do with desire. They were all about control and power.

Chef Dean had both, and he could use them to destroy my career. It would be his word against mine. There was no way I could get a sous-chef job in this town or any other place without his recommendation. And there was no way he was going to give me one after tonight, even if I kept my mouth shut about what he had done.

What on earth was I going to do now?

Chapter Six

If I had been living in my own apartment, I probably would've stayed in bed for days.

But I was sleeping on a couch in Auntie Martha's living room. That meant I had to get up and go on with life. Even if it was only eight in the morning.

Auntie Martha busied herself while I folded up my blankets and put them in her bedroom. I grabbed my things and headed into the bathroom. I could barely stand to see my reflection in the tiny oval mirror above the sink. My hair was a mess of tangled clumps, and yesterday's smudged eyeliner and mascara only enhanced the dark circles that already lived under my eyes. Gingerly, I touched the streaks of pink across my cleavage and the marks on my upper arms. Even hours later my skin screamed with irritation where Chef Dean's coarse beard had rubbed against it. And I prayed I wouldn't have to see any bruised reminders of my awful night.

By the time I'd taken a shower and gotten dressed, breakfast was waiting for me on the kitchen's small round table.

I didn't have much of an appetite, but I forced myself to eat some of the scrambled eggs on my plate.

"So, how did it go?" Auntie Martha finally asked from across the table.

Images of Chef Dean on top of me flashed before my eyes, and I willed them to go away. It still didn't seem real. The marks I'd seen on my body had been ugly reminders that it had indeed happened. But I wasn't going to say anything about it—especially not to Auntie Martha or Auntie Lily.

I took a sip of my coffee before answering. "Um, it was okay. But I really don't want to be a hostess again, so I'm not going to go back."

Auntie Martha set down her mug and seemed to study me. "You quit?"

"It was more like me and Chef Dean agreed that it wasn't going to work out."

If that wasn't the biggest understatement of the world, then I didn't know what was. At least it wasn't a real lie. Auntie Martha could always read me like a book when I was trying to hide something from her.

"I'm sorry, honey," she said, obviously believing my reason. "I know how much you were excited about being a sous-chef again."

"I was, but I didn't really fit in there anymore."

She reached out and patted my hand. "I know you'll find something better."

"Yeah, well, about that. Um, I decided something."

"What's that?"

"I'm going to go to New Mexico."

I said the words still not quite convinced of the decision I'd reached at about three in the morning. As I had lain awake, trying to stifle my sobs so Auntie Martha wouldn't wake up, option *never* had become my only option.

I had considered staying in Milagro Gardens for a few more months, but almost immediately dismissed the idea when I readjusted my position on the sofa bed mattress, only to have to move again so the springs underneath wouldn't dig into my back. Besides the less-than-perfect sleeping accommodations, staying with Auntie Martha would mean staying in Los Angeles, and I'd already established that the job opportunities would be zero to none because of Chef Dean.

Las Vegas could have worked for a little while. I liked the city enough and had even lived there with Auntie Lily during the summer after high school. Mom, who still hadn't wanted me to go to culinary school, thought Lily could change my mind by giving me a part-time job working in her real estate office. Of course, she had no idea that Lily had no such plan. All she had wanted was some extra help for the summer and someone to go to the spa with. But as much as I loved spending time with her, Auntie Lily had been just as opinionated and nosy as Mom. I valued my privacy and, frankly, I missed living on my own.

Moving to New Mexico would have more benefits than I had allowed myself to consider at first. And selling Raul's abuela's house wouldn't just pay off my debt; it would give me the cushion I needed to get back my independence and get back to what I really wanted—to become a chef. Not to mention the fact that putting hundreds of miles between me and Chef Dean's threats sounded like the best thing I could do for myself and my mental health.

When Auntie Martha didn't say anything right away, I began to panic, though. "Do you not think I should?"

Of the two, she had been more open to the idea when I'd told her and Auntie Lily about Raul's offer after our meeting at his motel. Auntie Lily, on the other hand, not so much.

She shook her head. "It's not my place to say either way. You're an adult, Gabby. You need to do what's best for you and not what others think is best. I guess I'll just miss having you as a roommate, that's all."

I nearly choked on the sudden emotion tightening my throat. "I don't even know how to thank you, Auntie Martha. For what you did for my mom and for me, I'm always going to be grateful."

She wiped away tears and nodded. "This will always be your home, Gabby. No matter what. My door is always open, okay?"

I got up from the chair and walked over to her. As soon as she wrapped her arms around my waist, I began to cry. We cried together for a few minutes. Me standing, her still sitting. We had been through so much together, especially in the last few months. Moving away, even though it was only going to be temporary, was going to be hard. I estimated it would take about three months to clean out the house and get it on the market. And it wasn't like I had any interest in getting to know Raul, so there would be no need to stay longer than necessary. I knew it was going to be a huge change, and I also knew it wasn't going to be an easy one. But it comforted me to know that Auntie Martha would still be here waiting for me to come back.

When our tears finally subsided, Auntie Martha looked up at me with concern in her eyes.

"When are you going to tell Lily?"

I stopped by a liquor store to pick up a bottle of wine and then showed up at the hotel where Auntie Lily was staying. She had stuck around to help me close Mom's accounts and wanted to come with me to pick up her ashes the next morning.

She opened the door right away, clapped when she saw the wine, and promptly took it from me.

She raised the bottle and examined the label. "Very nice. I taught you well."

"Yes, you did."

I dropped my purse on the side table next to the suite's couch and then plopped down.

Auntie Lily joined me a minute later with the open bottle and poured us each a glass. "This is why I never leave home without a corkscrew," she said, taking the seat next to me.

"You taught me that as well."

Auntie Lily reached over and patted my hand. Although she smiled at me, I could tell it was forced. She looked tired and still very sad.

I took a long gulp of my wine before beginning what I knew was going to be a difficult conversation.

"Martha says you're not talking to her right now," I said.

"I am not."

"Auntie Lily . . ."

"What? It's not right what she did. She went behind your mother's back all these years, feeding Raul information about you. Sin vergüenza."

"She says Mom knew," I reminded her.

"*She* says. Doesn't mean it's true," Auntie Lily said. "And even if Sandra knew, you didn't. So she betrayed you too."

I let out a heavy sigh. "I'm not happy about it, either, but I understand, I guess."

Lily waved her hand in the air. "Well, I don't. If Sandra had wanted Raul in your life, then she should've been the one to tell you. Martha should've kept her big nose out of it."

"Probably. Maybe. Either way, I can't change what she did."

"No, but you could ignore it. You can just forget you ever met him."

I raised an eyebrow at her naive suggestion. "You know that's not going to be possible."

"Fine. But it doesn't mean you have to keep talking to him, or go live with him."

"I'm not going to live *with* him. I'm going to live in his grandmother's house and then sell it."

Lily stopped midgulp. Her eyes morphed into solid brown pools filled with surprise. Why did I feel like I was already drowning in her look of betrayal?

She moved the glass away from her mouth and said, "You're going?"

I nodded my head, and I struggled to keep my emotions in check. "I am. I have to. I've practically blown through my savings."

"I thought you got your old job back?"

"It didn't work out," I said, trying very hard not to show any emotion about it.

"I don't understand. If you need money, I'll give you money." Lily yanked her purse off the glass coffee table in front of us and pulled out a checkbook. "Let's see, you'll need first and last month's rent, a security deposit, and some money for furniture and groceries. I'll give you ten thousand, and if you need more, then I'll give you more."

I waved my hand. "We already talked about this. I'm not taking your money, Auntie Lily."

"But you'll take a house from a man you just met a few days ago?"

The hurt in her voice was loud and clear.

"Well, he does kinda owe me. There's no time limit on back payment of child support, is there?" It was a crass characterization, but I wanted her to know I had no other emotions tied to this agreement. Well, not the kind she might be assuming. At first, I'd balked at Raul's offer because of my mom. But the more I thought about it, the more I began to realize that the house wasn't a handout. It was repayment for the years my mom had struggled to make ends meet as a single parent.

"Fine," Lily conceded. "I get that this is only about getting the money you deserve. But why do you have to move there? We can go spend a weekend to check it out, take some pictures and then post them online. Raul can handle any showings. All you need to do is sit back and wait for the check."

"Okay, even I know selling a house is a little more complicated than that," I told her. "Besides, I think it might be good for me to just get out of LA for a little while. I need to figure out what to do next."

"You can figure things out in Vegas," she said.

"Auntie Lily, you know I appreciate you. But I don't want to be a burden."

"Qué burden? You're family."

"And I'm also an adult. I need to take care of myself. I can't always come running to you or Auntie Martha when life gets hard."

"Of course. I understand that. All I'm saying is that you can take all the time you need without having to worry about getting a job or finding a place. You just lost your mom, Gabby. There's no rush to move on."

"I can't stay on Martha's couch forever."

"God, no. Of course not. But I got a guest bedroom in Vegas for you instead. Hell, I've got two."

Auntie Lily lived by herself in a big, beautiful home in North Las Vegas. Her older daughter lived in Colorado with her husband and new baby. And her younger daughter had just moved to Boston for work. A divorcée three times over, Auntie Lily had told me she would never marry again and was perfectly happy being single. Auntie Lily's successful career allowed her to travel all over the world, and she had the money to buy what she wanted when she wanted without having to explain her spending habits to anyone else.

Why on earth would I ruin my good life by getting another husband? she would always tell me.

Still, I couldn't help but wonder if she ever got lonely. Maybe that was another reason why she wanted me to come stay with her? I knew both Auntie Martha and Auntie Lily had promised my mom that they would always be there for me. Did they know that I had promised her that I would always be there for them too?

That didn't mean I had to live with them, though.

"I need to do this, Auntie Lily."

"You don't, Gabby. That man doesn't deserve to know you."

"I know. But I'm not going to New Mexico for him. As far as I'm concerned, I don't need to see him again until it's time to sell the house. Just because we're going to be living in the same town for a few months doesn't mean I'll ever consider him to be my dad."

Auntie Lily poured herself more wine and took a long sip. "I don't like it. Nothing good ever comes from dwelling on the past."

"I couldn't care less about the past. I'm doing this for my future," I explained.

"Something tells me that Raul doesn't see it that way."

"Well, it's not up to him, is it? You were right, Auntie Lily. I don't need to know anything about him other than the fact he can help me get out of this mess. I honestly don't care what he wants. And I'll make sure I'm very clear about that."

Her expression softened. "I still don't trust him or his offer. If you ask me, that man is only going to cause you more grief. I really don't think you should go."

I loved Lily, but she was as stubborn as they came. She was never going to give me her blessing to move to New Mexico. So, I would just have to go without it.

Chapter Seven

Sonrisa, New Mexico, surprised me.

When I arrived three days after that awful night at *Sky Grill*, the small town was nothing like I'd pictured it. I wasn't sure why I had expected to see more tumbleweeds than people making their way down a lone main street spotted with decrepit-looking shops. I guess I'd pictured something similar to the set of one of those old westerns my grandpa used to watch on Saturday afternoons.

But as I pulled my Honda Civic into one of the spots in a small public parking lot, the scene before me looked more like it was straight out of a Hallmark movie than a John Wayne classic. The street was bustling with all sorts of traffic, while colorful storefronts sat along the cobblestone sidewalks.

Of course, Raul had painted it as a charming small town that I would immediately fall in love with as soon as I saw it. After all, the town slogan was "Where Smiles Grow." He'd been so happy when I'd called to tell him that I was going to take him up on his offer. And even though I stressed that I had no interest in building any sort of relationship with him while I worked on the house, Raul hadn't tried to hide his excitement. So I'd packed up two large suitcases and a backpack and headed for New Mexico.

I double-checked the address I'd used on Google Maps as the final destination on my two-day drive from Los Angeles.

I only had to walk past one building before finding it—Carlita's Cocina. Raul had told me to meet him here, and he'd leave work to take me to the house.

A bell rang as I entered the restaurant, and a man behind the counter told me to sit wherever I wanted. Instead, I walked up to him.

"I'm looking for Raul," I said.

He set down the tray of dirty dishes he'd been carrying. "Are you Gabriela?" he asked.

I hadn't been expecting him to know my name, and I felt a twinge of uneasiness at the knowledge that Raul had mentioned me to his coworker. Who else had he told that I was coming?

"Yes, I'm Gabby." It felt important for the man to know that, even though I doubted I'd ever see him again.

"Que bueno. I'm Antonio. Mucho gusto," he said and held out his hand.

Antonio looked to be around the same age as Raul, but was bald and heavyset.

"Nice to meet you. Is Raul here?" I said after we shook.

"No, sorry. He had to deliver a catering order out of town, and he ran out of gas. He says for me to give you these, and he will meet you there when he gets back."

Antonio handed me a piece of paper with an address on it and a key.

"Oh and he says to make you lunch because there is no food at the house because he was going to get you some groceries, but then he had to go deliver the order."

I shook my head and tried not to let my irritation show, now that plans were already changing and I'd only been in town five minutes. "That's okay. I don't want you to go to any trouble. Is there a McDonald's close by or something?"

"McDonald's?" another man's voice asked.

I turned my head to the left and saw that it belonged to the guy sitting at the counter. He wore a faded blue baseball cap, a gray Henley shirt, and dark-blue jeans. My simmering annoyance bubbled up at the stranger sticking his nose in our private conversation. Hunger, exhaustion from driving, and the fact that Raul wasn't here combined for a very bad attitude.

"Yes," I answered, not caring anymore if I sounded bothered. "You know the place with the golden arches?"

"Why on earth would you want McDonald's when you're standing in a place that already has food? Are you craving a Big Mac that bad?"

"Actually, I'm more of a Quarter Pounder girl. I don't really like that special sauce. And who are you and why do you care?"

"He's the mayor," Antonio declared.

The man with the baseball cap shrugged. "I am."

Mayor or not, my irritation level was quickly rising. "How nice for you," I told him.

"How about tacos?" he said, obviously undeterred by my sarcasm. "They have the best tacos in town."

"Who says they have the best tacos?" I asked.

"Everyone in Sonrisa. Carlita's Cocina has a four-star rating on Yelp. And if you don't want tacos, they also have a killer carnitas torta and carne asada burrito."

My stomach grumbled its approval. "Fine," I said after a long sigh. "Tacos it is."

Antonio clapped his hands. "Muy bueno. Just give me a few minutes."

I took a seat at the corner of the counter—a few feet away from the mayor of Sonrisa, who didn't seem very mayor-like at all. First of all, why did he care so much that I tried the tacos here? Also, what mayor hung out in the middle of the day wearing a baseball cap and jeans?

I told myself to stop giving any more thought to the man. I stole a glance at him, and my original irritation stayed put. Even now, as he loudly talked on the phone, I could tell he was obviously arrogant and a busybody. I was mad at myself for letting him convince me to eat there instead of getting a burger. What had I been thinking?

I was thinking of tacos, that's what.

That's what I got for not stopping for breakfast back in Albuquerque after checking out of the motel room I'd rented for the night. But I'd wanted to get an early start on the long drive I had in front of me that morning. The beginnings of a migraine and a queasy stomach probably had made me more prone to irritation. Because if the guy had been anyone other than the mayor of Sonrisa, there was no way I would've let his comments slide. Although, if I was being completely honest with myself, I probably would have still kept my mouth shut. I wasn't here to make enemies, but I wasn't here to make friends either. I was here to fix up Raul's grandmother's house, sell it, pay off my debts, and get on with the rest of my life. And that life was going to happen as far away as possible from Sonrisa.

My gut squirmed thinking about the stack of credit card bills sitting in one of my suitcases in the car—right next to Mom. I'd brought her with me, of course. Auntie Martha had offered to keep the mahogany burial urn on her mantle until I came back to LA, but I'd decided at the last minute to bring her along for the ride. I knew it seemed a little strange to want my mom with me for this very big step.

"So, I hear you're from LA?"

I looked over my phone to find that Mayor Baseball Cap had moved and was now sitting two spots away from me.

"Yep," I answered, making sure I sounded uninterested in having a conversation with him.

"I like LA," he quipped. Then added, "To visit. Not to live there, though. Too much traffic and too many people."

That made me put my phone down. "You're a mayor. Aren't you supposed to like people?"

"Well, I like the people in my town, of course. Doesn't mean I have to like people in general."

For someone who supposedly didn't like people, the guy was sure chatty. I picked my phone up again, hoping he'd get the hint that I was not in the mood to talk.

Luckily, another man entered the restaurant and made a beeline for Mayor Baseball Cap.

"Mayor Paz!" the new customer said and slapped the mayor's back as a greeting. "Cómo estás?"

I watched to see if Mayor Paz, a.k.a. Mayor Baseball Cap, would pull away or say something rude about having his lunch interrupted. Instead, his face beamed with a charming smile and bright eyes.

"Alfredo!" he said and shook the man's hand. "I'm doing great. Y usted? Cómo son los nietos?"

"They're little traviesos. They give me all this white hair," the man said, pointing to his head.

Mayor Paz laughed. "But they're your traviesos, right? Hey, did everything go okay with your inspection?"

"Sí, sí. I'm going to be able to start construction next month. Thank you again for doing that walk-through with me. I made the changes you recommended and passed the inspection no problem."

"That's good. Have a seat. I was just finishing up lunch, but I can talk for a little bit."

"I wish I could stay. But I'm just picking up a torta to take with me. I need to drive over to Santa Fe for some supplies."

Antonio appeared then carrying a white bag and handed it to the man named Alfredo. "I put two extra containers of jalapeños in there for you."

"Gracias, amigo. You know me so well."

Antonio and Mayor Paz said goodbye to Alfredo, and then Antonio turned to me.

"Your food is almost ready. Can I get you anything to drink? We have Coke, Sprite, iced tea, and horchata."

"I'll take an iced tea. Thank you."

"Antonio, can I get a refill on my horchata?" Mayor Paz said.

The bald man nodded and gave us both our drinks before disappearing back into the kitchen.

"So are Antonio and Raul the restaurant's only employees?" I asked Mayor Baseball Cap after realizing I hadn't seen a waiter or waitress around.

"No. There are a few others, but your dad doesn't just work here—he owns the place too."

"He's not my dad," I rushed. "I mean, I guess, technically he is. But I don't consider him my dad."

"Right. Well, Raul is the owner and main chef. Antonio is his backup."

I couldn't help but be impressed to find out that Raul owned the restaurant. But the fact that he was also a chef threw me for a loop. It was a strange and uncomfortable coincidence.

I leaned over. "I'm not going to get food poisoning, right?" I whispered.

Mayor Baseball Cap raised his eyebrows. "Why would you say that?"

"Antonio seems like a nice guy, but all of the empty booths don't really scream great food."

"You missed the lunch rush. It will pick up again around three," he explained. "How about you try the food, though, before making any judgments?"

My tacos arrived a few minutes later, and I let out a breath I hadn't realized I'd been holding. Everything *looked* and *smelled* appetizing, at least. My mouth watered as I surveyed the spread of lightly charred corn tortillas topped with sizzling strips of grilled steak dressed with a mix of diced white onions and sprigs of dark-green cilantro. Hints of tomato and garlic wafted from the perfect mound of orange-tinted grains of rice, while melted white cheese crisscrossed a generous serving of refried beans.

Both Antonio and the mayor watched with rapt attention as I picked up one of the tacos and took a bite.

I made sure to keep my expression neutral when I then spooned some rice and beans into my mouth. The beans were creamy and smooth and coated my mouth in a warm blanket of slightly sweet and smoky flavors. The rice was soft, but not mushy, and had a hint of salt and tanginess that enhanced the beans.

After what seemed to be an eternity of chewing, I finally released a smile.

"Very good."

Antonio nodded proudly. Then Mayor Paz said something in Spanish, and both of them looked at me and started laughing.

"What?" I asked.

"You don't speak Spanish?" Mayor Paz asked with his eyebrows raised in judgment.

"Not fluently," I said defensively. It was the answer I'd given numerous times in my adult life.

"So, that's a no."

"I can understand most conversations if I'm paying close attention," I explained. "I wasn't right now so, no, I didn't understand."

"I told Antonio that his tacos must taste like a Quarter Pounder," he said.

That made Antonio laugh all over again. I ignored the joke and continued eating my meal.

The mayor shook his head and said something again to Antonio in Spanish. Although I wasn't fluent, I definitely heard the word *tough*.

Antonio shrugged and asked, "Mayor, can I get you anything else? How about some flan?"

Mayor Paz patted his very flat stomach. "No, thank you. I think I've had enough. I'm stuffed. But why don't you bring Gabby here some instead."

"Let me guess. They also have the best flan in town as well?" I said to the mayor.

Antonio, obviously oblivious to my sarcasm, nodded. "Sí, we do!"

"Hmm," Mayor Baseball Cap began, "based on your expression, I'm guessing you don't like flan."

I don't know why, but it sounded like the mayor was challenging me. It was true, though. I had never liked the custard dessert. Something about the texture always turned me off. But I had no intention of telling him that.

"Actually, I do like it. Antonio, I'd love to try your flan."

"You got it."

Annoyed beyond measure, I excused myself and went in search of a restroom. It took me a good ten minutes to wash my hands and cool down.

I couldn't blame the food for the waves now rolling through my stomach. Everything had tasted excellent. And I would know. Antonio's carne asada was on par with that of some of the best steak houses in the country. But Mayor Paz was getting under my skin. I made a note to steer clear of city hall while I was in town.

Satisfied with my renewed determination to ignore the man I planned on never seeing again, I left the bathroom and headed down the small hallway that led back to the counter area. But I stopped in my tracks when I heard Antonio say my name.

"Ella? No way," Mayor Paz responded after a short pause.

"Por qué no?" Antonio asked.

"She's not my type."

"Why?"

"Because she's not. I prefer to date women who aren't so opinionated and judgy."

58

Judgy? Judgy!

How dare that man call me opinionated and judgy? Not that I would ever consider dating him anyway. He didn't deserve any more of my time.

I walked back to the counter and told Antonio that I'd changed my mind about the flan.

"I'll just go wait for Raul at the house. How much do I owe you for my lunch?"

Antonio waved his hand. "Your money is no good here. You're Raul's daughter."

I bristled at the word *daughter*. But I wasn't going to argue. I just wanted to get out of there. I pulled a five-dollar bill out of my wallet. "Then this is for you." I set the money on the counter. "Have a good day."

I walked briskly past Mayor Paz and headed for the front of the restaurant.

"Welcome to Sonrisa," I heard him call out.

It took everything I had not to flip him off.

◆ ◆ ◆

About three minutes later I arrived at the house I would be living in for the next few months.

A white van was already in the small driveway, so I parked on the street right in front of the house. I decided to leave my suitcases in my car. If the inside was a decrepit disaster, then I'd drive back to LA tonight.

It was a one-story house built in the same southwestern architecture style I'd seen back in Albuquerque and on the short drive here. The outside was more rocklike than stucco, and the edges were rounded instead of sharp. The small front lawn was mainly dirt, rocks, and overgrown weeds.

"You're here."

I looked up to see Raul walking out of the blue front door.

"Here I am," I said with a shrug.

We stayed staring at each other for a few awkward seconds before he finally invited me to come inside.

Right away, I noticed all the . . . stuff.

All kinds of figurines, knickknacks, and other things seemed to line every shelf and table in the house. The living room still held a couch, a recliner, and a coffee table. From what I could see, the kitchen and dining room seemed just as full.

"It's an authentic adobe home," Raul told me. "My great-grandfather helped build it in 1920, along with other homes on this street."

I walked to the middle of the room and pointed. "I've never seen a fireplace like this."

The beehive-shaped structure had a narrow top, a broad base, and seemed to protrude from the corner of the living room's wall, as it appeared to be made from the same beige-colored plaster.

"It's called a kiva," he explained. "They're pretty common around here. I'll show you how to use it if you want, although I don't expect you'll need it much. We got our last snow of the season a few months ago. The weather is already starting to warm up."

"You get snow here?" I knew we were close to the mountains, but I hadn't realized just how close. I was glad that I was only going to be around for the early part of the summer season. Either way, I had no desire to buy snow gear anytime soon.

"Sure do. But just enough to dust the ground. The sun melts it pretty quick."

I nodded and walked into the dining room off to the left. "You said your abuela passed away a year ago?"

"Yeah, that's right."

"Well, it's almost like she never left," I said, looking at the woven place mats set out on the dining room table as if dinner were about to be served.

Raul coughed. "There's a lady from church who comes once a week to dust and vacuum for me. I just didn't want cobwebs or other critters living here when no one else was, so she just leaves things as they are. You're welcome to keep or sell whatever is here."

I studied him. "Don't you want anything? Or anyone else in the family?" The possibility that I could have other relatives in Sonrisa, or anywhere else for that matter, seemed unbelievable. And honestly I didn't have the bandwidth to even entertain the thought. The people who knew and loved Raul's abuela should at least be given the choice to take something to remember her by.

"Nah. Let's just say my abuela and I didn't have the same tastes. Besides, she didn't really have anything of much value. I'll rent a dumpster, and you can toss it all if you want."

I thought it was strange that Raul was fine with throwing away everything in his abuela's house. In a way, he was also throwing out the house itself by giving it to me. But it wasn't for me to judge or analyze.

"A dumpster would be great. What else do you suggest I focus on fixing? I'm only going to be able to do some minor repairs, though. I just don't have the money . . ."

Raul waved his hand to interrupt me. "Don't worry about cost. I'll take care of it."

I couldn't help but be suspicious. "Why? That doesn't seem fair, if I'm already going to get the money from selling the place."

"Well, I'm not saying I can pay for a large-scale remodel. But my abuela did set aside some money in her will for some improvements. She probably thought I was going to live here."

"Oh."

More suspicions and questions erupted in my mind. But I kept them to myself. I was getting more uncomfortable being in this house with him. I didn't belong here. I would never belong here.

But I'd made my choice, and my stubborn pride wouldn't let me get back in the car and return to LA. I was determined to make the best of the situation—at least for the next few months anyway.

"Okay then," Raul continued after more awkward silence. "I'll come by tomorrow with Diego, and we can figure out together what needs to get done."

"Diego?"

"Yeah, he's kinda the go-to construction slash handyman in town. He's also—"

Raul's phone interrupted him, and he excused himself to answer it. I took the opportunity to walk around the kitchen. It was a pretty good size, but it seemed to be stuck in the 1970s, with its dirty yellow cabinets and stained Formica countertops. I opened the basic white refrigerator and was surprised to see it full of food and drinks.

"I wasn't sure what you liked, so I kinda bought one of everything."

I glanced up to see Raul back in the kitchen. I shut the refrigerator door as if I'd been caught snooping. It was ridiculous, I know. This was where I was going to be living for a while anyway. And apparently I was also going to be going through cupboards and closets and deciding what pieces of Raul's abuela's life were going to be sold or thrown away.

A chill ran through me.

For the millionth time I wondered if I had made the right decision coming to Sonrisa.

Raul pointed behind me. "There's a small walk-in pantry right there next to the back door, and it has a few more things like cans of soup and oatmeal. But, if you want something that's not there, the grocery store is just at the end of the block. And for everything else, you'll have to drive about half an hour over to Santa Fe. There's lots of stores, a mall, and a Target and Walmart."

"Okay." It was all I could muster at the moment. My uneasiness and unreasonable anger were threatening to provoke an anxiety attack. If Raul had thought this was going to turn into a teary family reunion, he would be wrong.

All I wanted was to be alone.

Actually, all I wanted was to be back in LA. I couldn't even say *home*. Auntie Martha's apartment wasn't mine either. So, did I even belong there?

Raul finally seemed to get the hint. "Well, I'll get out of your hair now and let you get settled. Do you need help with your suitcases or bringing in stuff from the car?"

"No," I replied. "I don't have a lot. I can manage on my own."

"All right then. If you need anything, you have my cell and my house is only a few blocks away. When I'm not there, I'm at the restaurant, and that's even closer."

"Okay. Well, I guess I'll see you tomorrow then."

As soon as the front door closed behind Raul, I let out a long, relieved sigh. And then I sat down in the middle of the faded linoleum kitchen floor, covered my face with my hands, and cried.

◆ ◆ ◆

I'm not sure how long I sat on the kitchen floor. After sobbing like a little girl for a good several minutes, I just stayed where I was, trying to comprehend how I had gotten here. How had my life veered so far in the wrong direction? And what if it was too late to change course?

Eventually, I noticed that the bright beam of sun that had once warmed the back of my head had disappeared and I was now sitting in the shadows.

I told myself to get up. It was time to do what I'd come here to do. I needed to see the rest of the house.

First, I discovered a small guest bathroom just past the living room and a bedroom right across from it. Except for a twin-size mattress on a simple black metal frame and a dresser, it was empty. No knickknacks in sight at all.

The next room was a little smaller. A desk with a roll-up top and a plain wooden chair sat in one corner, while a sewing table, complete with sewing machine, sat in another. One wall was covered in faded and torn pink-and-white-striped wallpaper. It was as if someone had tried to take it off once and then just gave up. The tall brown bookcase next to the desk was stuffed with small plastic containers, magazine holders, and of course, books. Lots and lots of books.

The bedroom at the end of the hall must have been the master. A large four-poster bed, matching armoire and dresser filled the large, dark room. I was surprised to see jewelry and other items on top of the dresser—again like Raul's abuela was still using it. I walked over to the closet and slid open the door. Clothes hung from the rack, and shoeboxes lined the shelf above it and the carpet below. A light flowery scent emanated from the space, and I recognized it immediately.

Chantilly Lace was the powder my grandma—my mom's mother—used to wear every day. Although she had passed away when I was still little, I never forgot that smell.

I shook off the old memories and headed out to the backyard. If the inside of the house was a bastion for clutter, the outside was probably ten times worse.

It was a graveyard for the broken and the forgotten.

Chairs with missing arms or cushions, empty cracked plant pots, and a rusted shovel were just some of the items I could see that seemed to be rising from their dirt graves. The patio I was standing on had oil stains and cracks throughout the concrete. Chunks were even missing from some spots.

Carefully I made my way around to the side of the house. But I couldn't even walk through it. More junk was piled on top of itself, as if the band of idealists from *Les Misérables* had built another makeshift barricade in an attempt to overthrow the French government.

"Who are you?"

The voice came out of nowhere, and I jumped. I looked behind myself, but there was no one there. I tried to peek into the makeshift junkyard in front of me and couldn't see anything in there either.

If I had believed in ghosts, I might have scared myself into thinking the voice belonged to Raul's late abuela.

But I didn't believe in them. So when my heart rate finally slowed down, I yelled out, "Who are *you*?"

I waited for a few seconds, but there was no response. Maybe I had imagined it?

"You don't belong here," the female voice finally said. "She doesn't want you here."

Another chill ran down my back.

That's when my phone rang, scaring me for real this time. I pulled it out from the back pocket of my jeans, glanced at the caller ID, and shook my head.

In the corner of my eye, I thought I saw some movement just beyond the thick bushes that lined the other side of the backyard's rusty chain-link fence. Relief swelled in my gut. The voice must belong to the owner of the property next door. And even though my new neighbor didn't seem very neighborly, I was just happy that there had been a perfectly reasonable explanation for what had just happened.

I took a deep breath and finally answered my phone. "Hi, Auntie Lily," I said quickly, before she said anything.

"It's about time. Are you there or are you still driving?"

"I'm here at the house. I was just about to unpack my car."

"Is he there?" she whispered, as if she could be heard by others.

I laughed. "He was. He left a while ago."

"And?"

"And nothing."

"You guys didn't talk about stuff?"

"No. We just talked about the house. He's going to pay for all of the repairs and improvements."

"He is? Well, isn't that nice of him," she said, the sarcasm coming through as clear as day. "I guess that's one way to try to get you to think he's a good guy. Don't fall for it, Gabby."

"I told you I didn't come here to get a dad. I'm only here for one thing."

"The house," she said.

"The house," I confirmed.

"You know, though, that he's going to make every excuse to see you, right?"

"I know. But I'm going to make sure it's only when necessary." I still hadn't changed my mind about not wanting a relationship with Raul. He was a means to an end; that was it. I wasn't going to pry, dig, or research. In fact, the less I knew about him or his abuela, the better. "He's going to come back tomorrow with some handyman, and we'll talk about what work needs to be done in order to get ready to put it on the market."

Auntie Lily smacked her lips. "Well, I could tell you that. I know what sellers are looking for."

"I know you do, and I'm definitely going to get your opinions once I have a chance to really look around. I'm going to take pictures and email them to you and then let you know what the handyman thinks too."

"What's your gut telling you?"

I walked back inside the house, making sure to lock the back door behind me, and sat down on the plastic-covered sofa in the living room. "For the area, it looks like a decent-size house. The front yard is tiny, though, and the backyard is a mess. But the kitchen is probably going to need the most work. Everything in there will need to be updated."

"Of course. But don't go wild. Just do what's cosmetically necessary and functional. It's not like you're going to be cooking in there, so you don't need to blow your budget on state-of-the-art appliances or gadgets."

"I know. I know. But, Auntie Lily, the counters are Formica."

I heard her gasp through the phone. "Dios mío. Counters are definitely going on the list then."

We talked for at least another hour. I got updates about her new clients she'd already secured back in Vegas and what was going on with her daughters. And I found out that she and Auntie Martha were talking again.

After we hung up, I brought in my suitcases and rolled them down the hall to the master bedroom. But I stopped in the doorway.

I couldn't explain why, but I couldn't shake the feeling that I shouldn't sleep in that particular room. I almost felt like I didn't deserve to. After all, Raul's abuela didn't know me, and now I was going to sell her house—the house she had given to her only grandson.

I might not have believed in vengeful ghosts, but I did believe in karma and bad vibes.

So that's why I turned my suitcases around and took them to the room with the only other bed in the house.

Its empty walls, empty dresser drawers, and simple bed made it the perfect room for someone like me.

Temporary.

Chapter Eight

The numbers on the back of the envelope refused to change.

No matter how many times I rearranged them. No matter how many times I scratched them out and then wrote them down again. They still added up to the same conclusion.

Not enough.

"Are you still there? Did you hear what I said?"

I tossed the envelope onto the dining room table, picked up my cell phone, and took Auntie Martha off speaker.

"Sorry," I said quickly. "No, I didn't hear. What did you say?"

"I said that I found another credit card bill stuffed inside her knitting bag."

I covered my eyes with one hand, as if that would stop what I knew Auntie Martha was going to say next. But it didn't work that way. "And?"

"And it's for five thousand. It went to collections last week."

The frustrated sigh escaped before I even realized. The low sniffles on the other end of the line tightened my own throat with emotion. I gulped it down and blinked away the wetness from my eyes.

"It's okay, Auntie Martha."

"I'm just missing her a lot today," she whispered.

I understood. Mom's credit card bills were tied to some of the worst shared memories we had. They were reminders of how she had suffered. And it didn't seem fair that they were still here and she was not.

"I know. Me too," I admitted, grabbing a tissue from the box on the table.

"I'm sorry for being such a chillona. I told myself I wasn't going to cry, but honestly I don't know what we are going to do about all the bills."

"I already told you. *We* aren't going to do anything. They're in my name, so they are my responsibility. I'll figure something out." I glanced at the envelope again. My dwindling savings might take care of my regular bills for the next couple of months. But there was no way I could afford to make a dent in what Mom owed—what I now owed—to the credit card companies. The repercussions of Mom's illness and eventual death continued to take their toll in more ways than one.

"I could apply for a loan," she said quietly.

I shook my head. "And I already told you that wasn't an option. You're on a fixed income, Martha. I can't take your money."

"Well, you won't take Lily's money either. So what are you going to do?"

"I'm doing it. I'm going to sell this house, pay off the bills, find a new job, and then get an apartment."

"And who knows?" she said after blowing her nose. "Maybe you'll even like Sonrisa and stay there."

I didn't tell Auntie Martha that I already knew the town wasn't for me. My face grew hot just thinking of its especially rude mayor.

Instead, I said, "Or maybe I could just move to Vegas?"

"No. Don't you dare. I couldn't stand it knowing that you and Lily were over there together having fun without me. Do you know Sandra never visited without me?"

"I didn't know that. How sweet."

I heard a long sigh on the other end of the phone. "Not really. She just hated driving all the way over there."

That made me laugh until tears welled up again, thinking about how there would be no more trips or vacations with the four of us. I hated that they came so easily now. Is that what happened when you were in mourning? I was so tired of everything being so fucking tragic.

After I trusted myself to speak, I said, "Well, I don't mind driving. So when I'm back in LA, we'll take a road trip to go visit Lily. I heard you guys are talking again."

"Kind of. She texted me a picture of her new haircut and asked me if it made her look like her mother."

I laughed remembering the photo I'd also been texted the other day. I had told her that it didn't but only because her mom's hair was white.

"How much do you think you can get for the house? What if it's not enough?"

"It will be enough. Don't get me wrong. I'm not getting rich off this place, but it will get me out of debt and let me start over. That's enough."

I'd stayed up until almost one in the morning on Zillow and other Realtor sites researching comp sales from the area. As I'd suspected, most averaged around three hundred thousand or below. The size of the lot might get me a little more than the neighbors had. But, I wasn't going to haggle. All I cared about was selling as soon as possible.

I sighed into the phone. "Please try not to worry, Auntie Martha. Everything is going to work out. Okay?"

"Okay, I promise I won't worry about this anymore," she said, and I almost believed that she meant it.

"Mail me the bill you just found, and I'll call to see if I can set up some kind of payment plan."

There was a knock on the door. For a second, I wondered who on earth it could be. Then I remembered that Raul had said he was going to come by with the handyman. Still, it seemed weird that he was knocking since this was still technically his house.

"I gotta go, Auntie Martha. I'll call tomorrow," I said as I walked over to the door.

"Okay. Have a good day. Love you," she replied.

"Thanks. I will. Love you too."

My promise, though, to have a good day went out the window when I opened the door and found Raul and Mayor Baseball Cap standing on the front porch.

"What is he doing here?" I spat out before either of them could speak.

Raul looked confused and seemed like he didn't know what to say. Mayor Paz, however, gave me a big smile and said, "Hello, Gabby."

I purposefully refused to look at him or address him directly as both men walked inside. "The mayor of Sonrisa is your handyman?" I asked Raul.

Raul cleared his throat. "Well, yes. How did you know . . ."

"We met yesterday at the restaurant," Mayor Paz explained. "I suggested that she try the tacos."

I couldn't help but roll my eyes at his limited explanation. The aggravated tick of his jaw gave me more pleasure than I'd anticipated. He must have been one of those guys who expected people to fall down on their knees and thank him for his help. If he had expected that from me, then he was definitely in the wrong house.

"Oh, okay," Raul said, obviously still confused by my attitude. "Well, like I told you, Gabby, Diego is our resident expert when it comes to home-improvement projects and construction. He also helps a lot of the townsfolk get their houses ready to put on the market, so he's pretty familiar with what buyers are looking for these days."

Out of the corner of my eye, I could see Diego, and he definitely looked completely unbothered. That annoyed me. He was obviously amused that he'd caught me off guard. Why didn't he see that this arrangement might be a mistake or tell Raul that he couldn't do the job after all?

I tried to remain composed and collected. "Well, that's all nice and good for Mayor Paz. But I'm also going to be consulting with my aunt Lily. She's actually a real estate agent and might know a little more about how to sell houses."

Mayor Paz shrugged like he couldn't care less about who I talked to about the repairs.

Raul, on the other hand, looked pleased. "That's a great idea. I'm so glad she's going to help you. I wasn't sure . . . you know?"

"Oh, she still thinks this is a bad idea, but she's going to support me no matter what. Just like she always has."

I hadn't meant for it to sound like a dig, but I could tell by Raul's tight expression that it had.

"I've got to fix Mrs. Lindell's washer in an hour, so how about we get started?" Mayor Paz announced. Judging by the stiffness of his shoulders and the way his lips pressed into one thin line, he was definitely bored with the small talk and wanted to get down to business.

Which was fine with me.

We went through the house as Mayor Paz—Diego—did his inspection. He scribbled things down with a short pencil on a little notebook. He directed all his questions and comments to Raul—who would then turn to me and ask for my opinion. It was obvious that Raul was trying to let me know that he'd been serious about putting me in control of the project. I was pleasantly surprised.

As for Diego, I was becoming more and more annoyed with him for basically ignoring me. But I was taking my own notes and had already decided I'd only do the repairs that Auntie Lily agreed with. Diego could suggest and recommend all he wanted. But Raul had made it clear that he was going to let me run the show because he just didn't have the time.

And in my show, Diego didn't even have a speaking role. He was just there to make sure the stage looked pretty.

When we were done, Raul said he had to make a quick call and left me and the mayor by ourselves at the dining room table.

"All right," I began. "What's the verdict? How much are we talking?"

"About fifty grand," the mayor said.

I burst into laughter. And then I stopped when I recognized the seriousness in his eyes.

"Wait. You're serious?"

"Of course I am," Diego said. "I never joke about estimates."

I didn't appreciate the exasperation behind his words. What was it with this man? I didn't know him. Why should I trust him?

And as if the doubts in my mind were written all over my face, Diego seemed to only grow more agitated. "I realize we may have gotten off on the wrong foot yesterday, but you don't seem like the kind of woman who'd let her personal feelings about me get in the way of a professional relationship. You are welcome to get a second or third opinion and even hire someone else for the job. But I can promise you that my prices are fair and I only want to help Raul. He told me you want to get this place ready pretty quickly. And some ridiculous sense of pride isn't going to help you sell this house or pay your bills any faster," he said as he scanned the table.

Embarrassment burned my cheeks as I spotted the envelope on the top of my laptop—the one with the words *PAST DUE* stamped in big red letters on the front of it. It might as well have said *DESPERATE*.

Pros and cons of saying yes ran through my head. There was no denying that paying off all that debt needed to be done sooner rather than later.

I'd prayed for a miracle, and here it was. What was the big deal? All I cared about was the money. Nothing else. Because once it was done, then I would be free.

"What kind of timeline are you talking?" I asked.

"Depends on the budget and scope. I can do everything on the list, or I can do half. It's going to be up to you, and Raul since he's footing my bill."

Begrudgingly, I admitted Diego was my best option at the moment. I studied his face for a few seconds and then laid out my expectations. "I want your word that your estimates are one hundred percent on the up-and-up and you're going to do whatever it takes to keep the delays to a minimum."

He stared right back at me. "You have my word."

I couldn't read him. But my gut was telling me that he was being sincere. He was the mayor, and obviously, Raul trusted him. I had to take a leap of faith that both men wouldn't let me down.

"Fine. I'll consider your suggestions."

"Lucky me," he deadpanned.

I'd had enough of the mayor and his seeming insistence on pushing my buttons. "Look, I agreed to let you work on the house, but that doesn't mean we're friends. I don't like you. Or trust you. I'm just doing it because I don't have a lot of choices. Understood?"

He looked up with a smirk. "Understood. But can I ask why you're such a cynic?"

Raul came back inside before I had the chance to tell the mayor what I thought about his assumption about me. But I thought better of it and kept quiet as Diego began to go over his extensive list. As he spoke, all I could focus on was how much I disliked the smugness behind his words and on his face. If only I could take it back, tell him I'd changed my mind and slam the front door on his arrogant ass. But the satisfaction of doing such a thing wouldn't fix the house or get me out of Sonrisa as quickly as possible. No, I was going to hire the mayor and turn this place into an interior designer's dream home—on a budget. And when it was all said and done, I'd leave this town and never have to speak to Mayor Baseball Cap or Raul ever again. That was enough to help me sleep like a baby at night.

After Diego finished talking, Raul looked over at me. "Well, what do you think, Gabby?"

I shrugged. "I think it sounds like a lot."

"Like I said, you can do as little or as much as you want," Diego offered. "There are a few things on here that I think are musts—like replacing the water heater and fixing the leaks in both bathrooms. But there are others that can be Band-Aids just to make sure it passes an official inspection. If you have a budget in mind, then we'll make our decisions based on that."

"Gabby," Raul began, "why don't you go over Diego's list with Lily first? Then let's work on a list of priority projects and go from there?"

Both of them stared at me and waited for an answer.

"Sounds like a plan," I said, surprised again—this time by Raul's mention of Lily. He knew she didn't like him and that she was against this entire plan. Yet, he seemed to be perfectly fine with her having a say in it.

I nodded at him in appreciation, and he smiled.

"Bueno," Raul said. "Now that that's settled, I gotta run back to the restaurant. Apparently, Antonio is having some sort of issue with our meat supplier. Diego, can you give Gabby some rough cost estimates on each item? That way she has all that info when she talks to her aunt."

"Sure," Diego said and stood up from the table. "I just need to retake some measurements in the master bedroom."

Raul headed to the front door, while Diego walked toward the back of the house.

I grabbed the credit card bills I'd been going through earlier and stuffed them back into the manila envelope I'd been collecting them in. I didn't want to risk Diego making any more comments about them. I also took a few seconds to digest everything that had just happened. So far, Raul had made good on his promise. I let out a small breath of relief. Things were moving forward. I told myself I could put up with

Mayor Baseball Cap as long as he came through with the promises he'd just made.

Diego returned to the dining room a few minutes later. As he collected his things, I studied him again from across the table. I still couldn't believe he was the town's mayor. Based on the conversation I'd overheard at the restaurant, I'd assumed he wasn't married. That meant he was a bachelor mayor who also happened to be very good looking. And he was a handyman too? I couldn't help but wonder how many of the town's females were trying to become the first lady of Sonrisa.

Remembering what he'd said about me yesterday made my blood boil all over again. Raul and others in the town might believe he only had the best of intentions. But I recognized something else behind his good guy facade. The man was hiding something behind the jokes and needling.

Well, Diego might have gotten the best of me at the restaurant and today, but not anymore. I wanted to let him know that he shouldn't be talking about others behind their backs because those others might just be listening around the corner.

"Here's my business card," he said, handing me a card that read *Paz Handyman Services*. "You can text me your email address later, and I'll send you an updated list with cost estimates."

I nodded and waited for him to step outside. Waited for my chance to defend myself.

"You were right about one thing, Mayor Paz," I said, making him turn around to face me. "My pride won't pay my bills. But don't think for one second that you know me or my life. I'm not a cynic—I'm a realist. Which means I'll do whatever's necessary to get what I want or need. I also only believe what I can see. So if you and Raul are willing to do the work to get this house ready so I can sell it as fast as possible, then I'm all in."

He nodded in agreement. "Good. Because we have a lot of work to do. I'm glad we're on the same page. See? That wasn't so hard, was it?" he said, offering me a smug smile.

I was so ready to make it disappear. "Oh, and one more thing. You know, so we're both on the same page? You're not my type either."

Then I slammed the door in his shocked face.

Chapter Nine

It took three days for Auntie Lily, Raul, Diego, and me to come to an agreement on the final list of repair and maintenance projects for the house. Some of the bigger ones couldn't get done until supplies were ordered and delivered. So the priority projects were the ones that Diego could start with what he already had or could get in town.

The goal was for everything to be done in eight weeks.

I was anxious to get started, but Diego had told Raul he would need another few days to finish his other contracts and tackle some city business.

In the meantime, I'd bought about a dozen plastic tubs from the local hardware store and begun working on what I could inside the house. I hadn't stepped in the backyard since that first night, so I hadn't heard or seen my faceless neighbor again. It wasn't that I was afraid. It was more like I just didn't want a confrontation. It was obvious she wasn't happy about someone moving in. Maybe she was worried I'd start throwing weekend parties or playing loud music late at night. I'd done neither of course. But I had no interest in finding out what other grievances she could have.

I wasn't even going to ask Diego if he knew her. As far as I was concerned, there was no need to learn anything extra about the town of Sonrisa or the people who lived here.

Although I was a little apprehensive about having to face him again, I was more excited for him to start working. So, when he showed up that morning with tools in hand, I decided to play nice.

I even offered him a cup of coffee before he got started.

"I'm good, thanks," he said after following me into the kitchen.

I, on the other hand, definitely needed a second cup just in case Diego was going to bring up what I'd said to him before slamming the door in his face. Luckily, he didn't.

"What's all this?" he asked instead.

I turned around and saw him pointing at the two large plastic containers sitting on the dining room table.

"Oh. I started cleaning out closets. Those are books and some board games I found in one of the bedrooms. I was going to donate them to a thrift store if Raul didn't want them."

Diego picked up one of the boxes. "Somehow I don't think Raul plays Candy Land."

I didn't think so, either, but I was struggling with what to do with most of the things I had found. "Probably not. But you never know?"

"He told me that he told you to just throw everything away."

I shrugged. "He did. But what if he decides in a few days or a few weeks from now that he should've kept stuff? It just feels wrong to get rid of somebody else's possessions without them being here."

My voice nearly broke at that admission, and emotions I hadn't expected choked me so hard that I had to cough them out. But it had nothing to do with a board game from the 1970s and everything to do with the boxes piled up in Auntie Martha's garage back in LA. Everything my mom had brought with her after selling the house was in those boxes. And now they were waiting for me to go through them and decide what to keep and what to toss in a dumpster.

I still couldn't wrap my head around discarding her life's possessions as easily as a piece of trash.

Maybe I'd imagined it, but I could've sworn that Diego's face had softened. Embarrassment at nearly crying in front of him made me turn my attention back to my mug.

I heard him clear his throat. "Well, if he decides he doesn't want them, you could try to sell them at the Sábado Mercado."

"What's that?" I asked as I focused on stirring my favorite oat-milk creamer into my coffee. I'd finally finished the half-and-half that Raul had bought, and it had been the perfect excuse to make the drive into Santa Fe and pick up a few of my go-to essentials.

I turned back to face Diego and noticed he was still holding the game.

"It's a monthly flea market the city holds over at the Plaza de la Revolución park in the center of town. You pay twenty dollars to reserve a spot, and then you can sell whatever you want. We don't do garage or yard sales in Sonrisa, so Sábado Mercado is pretty popular. There's one happening in two weeks."

My cleaning efforts *had* been pretty extensive. It would be nice to get some money out of it.

"I'll look into it," I told him. "So, what's first on the list?"

"I'm going to start clearing out the side yard. Raul said the large trash bin is going to be delivered tomorrow, so I'll just make some piles for now. I also have a few things to do in the front yard."

I thought it was a little unusual that Raul hadn't told me that himself. In fact, now that I thought about it, it had been a few days since I'd heard from him. Our texts were always initiated by him and always revolved around house updates. I'd had no reason to reach out to him in the past few days, so I guess he'd had no good reason to do the same. He seemed to be keeping his distance as I had asked.

And that was fine with me.

"Okay. Well, I'll be in here still cleaning out closets."

Diego nodded and headed out to the backyard. I finished off my coffee with a delicious chocolate-filled croissant I'd picked up at a bakery in Santa Fe. And then went back to work. Today, I was going to tackle the closet in the master bedroom.

Magdalena, the cleaning lady, had stopped by a few days ago to do her usual routine. Raul had said he would tell her to stop coming if it made me uncomfortable to have her in the house while I was there. I saw no need. All I asked was that she didn't come into the bedroom I was using. I hadn't wanted to risk Magdalena knocking over the box with Mom's ashes and then trying to vacuum her up.

And based on the fresh tracks deeply pressed into the brown shag carpet in the master bedroom, I could see how meticulous Magdalena was with a vacuum.

I decided to start with the clothes. I grabbed as many hangers as I could and carried them over to the bed. On my second trip, one of the hangers got caught on the strap of a hatbox on the top shelf, and before I realized it, I gave it a tug and the box came crashing down on my head.

"Ouch," I yelled.

After picking up the clothes and hangers and placing them on the bed with the others, I knelt down on the rug and began to shove everything back into the hatbox. It was mainly old receipts, magazine clippings, and other random items. But when I picked up the box's lid, I noticed a photo wedged into the inside rim. It was a photo of a family—well, I assumed it was a family. There was a man and a woman who looked like they were about my age, and they were standing with a young boy and young girl in front of a waterfall. Based on everyone's clothes, it looked like the photo had been taken in the fifties or sixties. I brought the picture closer to inspect it. Although the image was covered in spiderweb-like creases and somewhat faded, I could make out the faces of the kids. The boy bore a striking resemblance to Raul. But the ages didn't add up. Raul wouldn't have been born yet. He couldn't have been the boy in the photo. So maybe it was just someone related to him, like a cousin perhaps?

I closed the box and put it back on the shelf. But I placed the photo on top of the dresser. Raul had said he'd already taken what he'd wanted, but maybe he hadn't seen it since it had been in the hatbox?

The more important question, though, was why did I even care? If I saved everything for Raul to take a second look at, I'd never get anything accomplished.

I went back to what I was doing. One by one, I sorted. Outfits I thought I could donate or sell went into another large plastic tub. Everything else went into a trash bag.

Teresa—Raul's abuela—basically had the wardrobe of a nun. I'd learned her name in the past few days during my cleaning/exploring activities. She had owned mainly plain brown or black dresses, with a few white blouses and beige skirts sprinkled in between. It jibed with the numerous crosses and other religious figurines that still decorated the house. But as I pulled things out from the back of the closet, it became obvious that the woman had probably kept everything she had ever worn as an adult. And before her Sister Teresa phase, the woman had had some style. Outfits that had been in fashion during the 1950s through the 1970s had been preserved immaculately in plastic covers from the dry cleaners. My first thought was to throw it all away. Then I remembered some of the vintage stores I used to drive by on Melrose, back in LA. The mannequins in their window displays were dressed in clothes like Teresa's.

Perhaps the retro outfits might even sell at Sábado Mercado. If not, then there was always eBay.

I had just filled up one tub when Diego walked into the bedroom.

"Can I pull you away from that for a few minutes? I need some help outside," he said.

"What are you doing?" I asked as I continued to sort.

"I'm cleaning the scuppers in the front of the house."

I stopped and looked at him. "What the hell are scuppers?"

"They're gutters," he explained.

"Then why not call them gutters?"

"Because they're different," he said after a long sigh. "The adobe houses around here use scuppers because the roofs are flat."

"And?"

"One of the scuppers is really impacted with debris, so I need your help to get it loosened."

I balked. "Me? Don't you have an assistant or something?"

"Nope. I like working on my own. But there are some projects that take two people. Usually, the homeowners don't mind helping."

"So they pay you, but you also make them do the work?"

"I guess," he said. "At least you're not the one paying me, though, right?"

I rolled my eyes. "Oh believe me, I'm paying for this in more ways than one."

"Are you going to help me or what?" he said after shaking his head. "The faster we get this done, the faster I can move on to the next thing on the list, and the faster I'll be out of your hair."

"Well, you should've just said that in the first place," I said, making a face to let him know I still wasn't pleased with the situation.

I followed him to the front of the house, where a ladder was resting against the house's front wall. Diego handed me a long, thick branch.

"I'm going to use a high-pressure hose to force the debris through the scupper. I need you to use this branch to kind of poke it from this end to help loosen it up a little. Got it?"

"Got it," I said.

Diego climbed up to the roof and turned on the hose. But nothing happened.

"Are you sure this is going to work?" I questioned as I continued to shove and twist the branch into the scupper. It was barely going in. Whatever was stuck in there was really jammed tight.

"It will work. Just keep poking it."

I stepped off the walkway and onto the dirt bed below the row of scuppers and used both hands to hold on to the branch. Finally, I felt a little give.

"I think it's loosening up," I yelled.

"Don't stand too close," Diego warned. "Once it breaks through, it will come down fast."

"Well, I've got short arms. I can't reach unless I stand here."

Then a loud whoosh filled the air, and before I realized what was happening, a long, thick brick of mud, twigs, leaves, and other debris came sliding out of the scupper and plopped onto the ground right in front of me.

"Dammit," I yelled as mud splashed all over my shoes, jeans, and even all the way up to my denim shirt.

But what pissed me off even more was the sound of Diego chuckling right above me.

"I told you," he yelled.

I looked up and gave him a hard stare. "Thanks for the reminder."

As I moved back onto the walkway, I pulled off my denim shirt before the mud soaked through to my tank top underneath.

He came down the ladder, obviously entertained by the situation.

"Now I know why you went on the roof and made me stay down here," I accused. Using my already dirty shirt, I attempted to wipe the mud from my jeans and shoes before going back in the house to change. I didn't want Magdalena to have to scrub mud out from the carpet when she came back next week.

"What happened to your arms?" Diego asked, the amusement gone from his voice.

"What?" I was so focused on cleaning myself off that I didn't think I'd heard him right.

Diego walked over to where I was standing. Then he pointed to the purplish marbled patches just below both of my shoulders. "What happened?"

My chest tightened as I realized what he was looking at. "Nothing. They're just some old bruises."

"They don't look that old. How did they get there?"

Why on earth was Diego so concerned with my bruises? "I don't know," I lied. "I must have hit something."

"On both arms? In almost the exact same spot on each?"

"I guess," I said, trying to sound nonchalant.

"They're handprints," Diego announced. "I can still see the imprint of the fingers. Who hurt you? Raul?"

His accusation made me flinch. "What?" I said. "Of course not."

Diego stepped even closer and met my eyes. "Then who?"

I was shocked by the anger I saw reflected in his hard stare. His taut jawline and flared nostrils made me believe that if I gave him a name, he'd go track that person down right then and there. But there was no way I was going to be sending him after Chef Dean. I didn't need Diego or anyone else defending my honor.

"Nobody did," I lied. "I told you I must have hit something."

"I don't believe you. I know what it looks like when someone has been grabbed hard like that."

That made me raise my eyebrows at him. "How on earth do you know that?"

"I just do."

"Well, you're wrong," I said. "I'm going to go inside now to change."

"Gabby, wait."

I stopped walking and turned around, bracing myself for more questions that I didn't want to answer.

"There's an aloe vera plant in a yellow pot in the backyard." Although his voice had been hard and loud just a few seconds earlier, his tone now was softer. Even gentle. "Cut off one of the leaves and squeeze the liquid onto the bruises to help them heal," he said. "You can also soak a washcloth in hot water and press it against the area for as long as you can stand. The heat and compression will boost the circulation and clear away any trapped blood under the skin. And if you still have any pain, take some Motrin. That will help alleviate any inflammation as well."

"What are you? A doctor?" I joked.

Diego shrugged. "I used to be."

Chapter Ten

Friday nights in Sonrisa were almost just as busy as the afternoons.

I'd learned that the downtown shops stayed open until ten and most residents took advantage of the extended hours, usually after enjoying dinner out at one of the town's three eat-in restaurants.

After two days of being stuck in the house having to listen to Diego hammering or sawing away, I decided I needed a night out. And since I planned on sipping some adult beverages, that meant not driving all the way to Santa Fe. So, I decided to walk the two blocks from the house to downtown.

As I strolled past the neighboring houses, I couldn't help but notice all the scuppers and wonder if they ever got clogged like mine had.

Wait. Why was I thinking like the scuppers belonged to me? Which then led me to other questions—questions like, Why wasn't Diego a doctor anymore?

I'd never pressed him for an explanation after his admission. And he hadn't offered one. Instead, we'd spent the past two days only talking when we had to and never ever working in the same place or on the same project again. It was clear Diego didn't want to broach the subject, just like I hadn't wanted to discuss my bruises. We both kept our mouths shut as much as possible.

Raul, on the other hand, must have found my phone number again. He was texting me several times throughout the day, asking for random updates on what Diego was doing and how my cleaning was going. Then he invited me to come have dinner at his restaurant.

Part of me had wanted to decline. It was one thing to accept the house. It was quite another to let him be a part of my life. I wasn't about to pretend that he hadn't hurt my mom or abandoned her when she'd needed him the most. No amount of money would ever buy my forgiveness for that. Besides, I'd only known Raul had existed for less than a month. He was still a stranger to me. And I didn't want to make him think that I'd changed my mind about having a relationship with him. I hadn't. I was still determined to sell the house as fast as possible and leave Sonrisa in my rearview mirror.

But another part of me—the part that was starving—craved those tacos.

Carlita's Cocina was jam packed with customers this time. In fact, there were even people waiting outside. I was surprised, but then I remembered the town only had three real sit-down restaurants.

Although I couldn't discount the fact that the food was also delicious. It was why I was here, wasn't it? It had nothing to do with Raul.

He saw me as soon as I walked through the door, as if he'd been waiting for me since I'd texted him half an hour ago to take him up on his offer of dinner.

I went to the counter, and he pointed to the empty seat at the end. "I saved this one for you. We're pretty busy tonight," he said, the pride in his voice unmistakable.

"I can see. Thanks for not making me wait. I'm starving."

"Of course. You're welcome here anytime. But your money's not, okay?"

I gave him a quick smile and then looked at the menu. I hadn't seen it that first day since my meal choice had been practically decided for me by Diego.

The number of selections impressed me. Besides the typical Mexican-restaurant staples, Raul also offered classic diner options like sandwiches, T-bone steaks, and burgers. He also had a couple of vegetarian entrées that sounded interesting.

But my mind was already set on what I wanted, and I put down the menu.

"Hey, Gabby. Nice to see you again," Antonio said from the other side of the counter.

"You too," I replied. "I had to come back for the tacos."

He beamed. "I knew it! I'll put your order in right now. Anything to drink?"

I told him I'd take a beer and then pulled out my phone to check Instagram. I was curious if there were any posts about the restaurant. Sonrisa wasn't a big town, but I knew from my research that it was a natural stopping point in between Santa Fe and Albuquerque. Tourists also flocked here to visit popular hiking trails, caves, and waterfalls. And given the barely existent local competition, I assumed Carlita's Cocina must get even busier during the summer, which was just a few weeks away.

It took several seconds, but I was able to find a couple of posts. The photos of the food were pretty good, and the posters seemed to have enjoyed what they'd eaten. It did make me wonder, though, why there weren't more posts.

"Okay if I take the seat next to you?" I looked up and saw Raul standing by the counter again. "It's been a long day, and I try to sit for a few minutes when I can."

"It's your restaurant. I think you can sit pretty much anywhere you want."

He didn't reply and instead plopped down next to me. "So what did you end up ordering?"

"Tacos," I said with a shrug. "They're really good. Your meat is perfectly cooked. And that marinade is amazing."

Raul nodded. "It's my great-grandfather Miguel's secret recipe. This was his restaurant, you know. Carlita was my great-grandmother. She ran the front and he ran the kitchen."

He pointed over to the wall lined with old black-and-white photos. "That's them in the center. They're standing in what's now the parking lot behind the restaurant."

I squinted until the image of a young Mexican couple standing side by side on a dirt clearing came into view. They weren't smiling or even really posing for that matter. It was as if the photographer had simply captured a moment in time, and they just happened to be there.

"Did Teresa work here too?"

"Yeah, and so did my grandfather. They took over the place in the sixties. Then Ernesto, one of their cooks, ran it for a while. When I moved here, I worked for him in the kitchen. Basically taught me everything I know."

"Yeah, I had this teacher in cooking school who sort of became a mentor to me like that. She showed me the basics, but also taught me that one ingredient in every dish I made was me and my experiences. She would say that's why no two chefs can ever cook the same exact meal. They're different, so their food should be different."

"That's a great lesson," he said, nodding in agreement. "I never expected I would end up owning a restaurant—and I certainly didn't get anything like the training you did in school. But I like to think that's what makes this place different."

"Definitely," I replied.

My grandma used to say that the universe worked in mysterious ways. It was the only explanation I could come up with for how I'd ended up becoming a chef just like the biological father I never knew. Or how I ended up eating tacos in his restaurant almost thirty years after I was born.

Okay, maybe not that mysterious. But definitely unexpected.

"Here you go, Gabby," Antonio said as he placed my food and then my beer in front of me.

"All right, I guess I better get back to it. I hope you enjoy your dinner," Raul said.

"And I'll make sure you get some flan this time," Antonio said.

I was about to protest when Raul grimaced. "Sorry. I sold the last piece just before you came. We have cheesecake?"

"No, that's okay. I would take a caffe latte to go, though, if you have it."

"Sorry again," Raul said. "I'm not exactly a coffee master. But there's a bakery two shops down that has a pretty good selection. And they're open late tonight too."

I smiled. Tacos and gourmet coffee? It was turning out to be a fantastic Friday night.

◆ ◆ ◆

Half an hour later, I walked out of Carlita's Cocina feeling full and content.

I walked over to the bakery Raul had mentioned but began having second thoughts about whether I really needed a coffee at eight o'clock at night.

Then I saw Diego. And he wasn't alone.

He and a very pretty woman were sitting at a small table next to the bakery's main window. They were talking, and she was laughing. I also noticed that she couldn't keep her hands off him. Not that he was doing anything of the same back to her. In fact, it looked to me like he was a little uncomfortable.

So naturally I wanted to make him more of that.

I walked into the bakery and straight up to the counter. A nice young man took my order right away and told me it would be ready in just a few minutes.

Perfect.

"Oh, hey, Diego," I said, feigning surprise as I walked by their table.

"Gabby!" he said, with actual surprise. "What are you doing here?"

"I just had dinner at Raul's, and he told me about this place, so I stopped to get a latte." I smiled sweetly at him and then turned to the brunette, who was very obviously giving me the once-over. I silently thanked earlier me for putting on actual makeup and clean clothes.

"Hello," I said, meeting her eyes. "I don't think we've met yet. I'm Gabby Medina."

"Hello. I'm Carolina Valdez." Then the woman reached over and placed her hand on Diego's arm. It didn't escape me how quickly Diego pulled away from her.

"Carolina is a friend from high school. She's also Sonrisa's top Realtor," he explained. "And, um, Gabby here is from LA. She's the one living in Teresa's house until it gets sold."

The woman's demeanor seemed to change once she realized I wasn't planning on becoming Sonrisa's next resident. Or her competition.

"That's great! Let me give you my card for when you're ready to put it on the market again," Carolina said and reached into her purse.

I held up my hand. "That's not necessary. I used to work for a Realtor back in a different life; plus my auntie runs a very successful office in Las Vegas and can help me out if needed. So, I'm going to do everything on my own. No offense, but I need every penny I can get from this sale."

The woman offered me a small smile and put her hand back on the table. "How nice," she said.

Then it hit me. *Again.*

"Wait. Did you say the house has been on the market before?"

"Yes, multiple times, in fact," Carolina said with a nod. "Raul took it off about three months ago."

Three months ago. When my mom's cancer came back.

In other words, when he found out I'd be desperate enough to actually consider moving here.

"Hey, Gabby. Are you all right?"

Diego's voice sounded muffled, as if he were a thousand yards away from me instead of just a foot or two. I didn't answer him. But I wasn't all right. I was far from it.

I booked it out of the café, not caring that the latte I'd paid for was going to go to waste.

It took me less than a minute to walk back into Carlita's Cocina. I ignored Antonio's wave and just asked, "Where is he?"

Antonio pointed toward a small hallway off the kitchen. I nodded and headed for the single door labeled *Office*. Raul smiled when he saw me, but then a look of concern crossed his face.

"What's wrong?" he asked.

I shut the door and confronted him with what I'd just learned. "Why didn't you tell me the house was on the market before?"

"Because technically it wasn't," he said with a shrug.

"I don't understand."

"Every time I was going to have Carolina list it, I changed my mind because I didn't have the time to make the improvements I knew it needed. I told you this already."

"So you haven't had any other offers?"

Raul shook his head. "I haven't. Who told you that I did?"

Although I was angry at Carolina for misrepresenting the facts, I didn't know her well enough to say for certain that she'd done it out of malice. So, I decided I would give her the benefit of the doubt. But she had definitely triggered my defensive radar, which meant I was going to be careful around her.

"I just overheard some people talking at the bakery. I'm sorry for accusing you of lying to me."

Raul stood up and came around his desk. "Look, I know you don't know me very well and I know how hard it's going to be to get you to trust me. But I swear I'm not hiding anything from you. Hopefully, one day, you'll believe that."

I wasn't sure what else to say. So, I just nodded and turned to leave his office.

That's when Diego walked in. He seemed to search my eyes for an explanation, but then looked over at Raul. "Everything okay?" Diego asked him.

"Everything is fine," I answered.

"Yep," Raul agreed.

Judging by the confused expression on his face, Diego didn't seem to believe us. But I was too tired to care. "Okay then," I said. "I'm going back to the house. Good night."

I had only taken a few steps outside the restaurant when someone grabbed my hand.

It was Diego.

"What happened back there?" he said. Then, realizing he was still holding my hand, he abruptly let it go.

"Nothing," I said with a shrug.

"It sure didn't seem like nothing when you practically sprinted out of the bakery."

"Well, it's nothing now." I couldn't help but wonder why Diego was so concerned.

"Did you and Raul get into an argument?"

"No," I told him. "But maybe you should tell your friend to get her facts straight before sharing them with other people."

He looked at me quizzically. "What are you talking about?"

Was he really going to play dumb? "Carolina said Raul had put the house on the market before, and he says he didn't."

Diego shrugged. "She was mistaken then. But what difference would it have made?"

I sighed and crossed my arms against my chest. "Because if the house had already been on sale and there were no takers, then that could mean it could take longer to sell now. And I thought Raul had lied about that in order to trick me into moving here."

Diego took a step closer and met my eyes. "Raul wouldn't do that."

"Maybe. But I just met the man a few weeks ago. Some people lie to get what they want. I have no idea if Raul is some people."

"That's because . . ." Diego didn't finish his sentence. I could tell he wanted to, but something was holding him back.

"What? What were you going to say?"

"It's not my place," he said.

"That's never stopped you before," I said sarcastically.

"Fine. I think you automatically assumed the worst about Raul because of who he was and what he did in the past. If you took the time to get to know the man he is today, you'll see that all he wants is to get to know you, Gabby. It's what he's always wanted. But you seem determined to punish him for a decision he made a long time ago."

Anger and hurt welled up inside me. How dare Diego defend Raul?

I pointed my finger at him. "It wasn't just one single decision. It was thousands. He had twenty-nine years to make things right with my mom, yet he doesn't show up until after she's dead? Uh-uh. Neither of you will ever understand what she went through when he left her. So neither of you get to tell me that I should just forget all of that and give him a chance to play daddy. Do you really think that I should automatically believe he's a good guy just because he's giving me a house?"

"Of course not," Diego said. "But how can he prove it to you if you don't let him?"

"What do you mean?" It was hard not to feel so defensive, and I didn't like how this conversation had taken a turn.

Diego continued. "You keep Raul at a distance. I see it. He sees it. Every once in a while, you seem to crack open the door a little by laughing at something he says or, like tonight, letting him give you dinner. But then you slam it shut again as soon as you find yourself getting close to him. And I'm not saying you should forget what he did either. But maybe you can forgive and give him a chance and finally let him in?"

I was crying now. But I didn't care that Diego could see my tears. I also didn't care about the concern—or was it pity—that I saw in his eyes. Old frustrations and buried hurt feelings had been reawakened and were on the rampage.

It was Lana Moran all over again.

Lana had been my high school nemesis. She was the leader of my own personal mean-girl hate club. It didn't matter that we had been best friends in elementary school. Once we got to junior high, Lana decided she didn't want to be my friend anymore. Not only that, she didn't want anyone else to be friends with me either. Any girl who hung out with me during lunch or walked home with me was automatically ostracized by her and her groupies. And because Lana was more popular than I was, the other girls usually chose the side that wouldn't make them teenage social pariahs.

A few years ago, my mom ran into Lana and her mom at the mall. For some reason, my name came up, and Mom shared that I was working as a chef at Sky Grill. I was still a hostess at that time, but Mom had decided to stretch the truth. Of course, Lana was impressed and gave my mom her number under the pretense of wanting us to catch up. I knew it was bullshit. I knew that Lana only wanted to use me to get a reservation at the restaurant. Mom told me to still call her, but I refused.

"She made high school hell for me, Mom. Why on earth would I want to talk to her, let alone have her come eat at the restaurant where I work?" I said.

"Well, she seemed very sincere about wanting to see you again. Maybe she's changed? Why can't you be the bigger person and give her a second chance?" Mom replied.

That's when I decided that I was tired of being polite and being the one who always made concessions for people who didn't care about my feelings—then or now. I never called Lana and even blocked her on social media. She had hurt me and made my life miserable. I couldn't care less if she was the sweetest person now—although I doubted it. Either way, Lana Moran hadn't deserved to have that kind of access to me or my life.

As far as I was concerned, the jury was still out on Raul, and no one—especially not Diego—was going to make me feel guilty for protecting myself.

"It was Raul's choice to stay out of my life all these years," I told him. "So, now I get to choose whether I let him back in it. And right now, I don't."

Diego reached out to touch my shoulder, but I moved away from him. I didn't want to have this conversation anymore.

"I'm tired. I'll see you Monday," I said and then turned to walk away.

Later, when I was back at the house, I sat on the edge of the bed and stared at the box that held my mom's ashes. My suitcase sat in the corner of the room, and I was tempted to pack it.

It had been such an emotionally exhausting night. I wasn't sure if I could handle another one.

"I know you think I should leave," I said to the box. "I know you probably hate that I even came here in the first place."

I waited, half expecting a response. But the only thing that answered me was silence.

I thought about what Diego had said about me punishing Raul, and he had been right. It was as if I had wanted to believe that he had lied to me. Part of me had been waiting for him to disappoint me—to prove that I couldn't trust him. That way I'd have the excuse I needed to leave and take the easy way out of what had become a very complicated new chapter of my life. Because I would've given anything to go back to my normal, boring existence where the only real decision I had to make was whether to go home after a shift or go out drinking with my coworkers. And I would've done anything to call my mom on the phone and hear her tell me what I should do instead of sitting alone in a strange house talking to a wooden box.

But this was my life now. And I was the only one who could tell myself how to live it.

I wiped the tears from my face, got up from the bed, grabbed my suitcase, and stuck it back in the closet.

Chapter Eleven

The Sábado Mercado was the place to be on this particularly warm May morning.

I had arrived at seven in the morning at the Plaza de la Revolución park as instructed in my reservation-confirmation email. I was told to bring my own table, chair, and canopy. I didn't have a canopy, but I'd found two folding card tables in the garage, a metal lawn chair, and a drying rack. It was far smaller and more basic than the other setups I'd seen on my way in.

While there were a few people like me who were selling used items, most of the vendors looked to be artisans and small business owners. I saw tables filled with beautiful leather bags, candles, jars of honey, and handmade jewelry. Teresa's bell-bottoms and platform shoes suddenly didn't seem like the hot sellers I thought they'd be.

Determined to make the best of the day, I began unpacking the tubs and tried to make my displays as enticing as possible. Well, as enticing as a ceramic donkey or macramé plant holders could be. As I worked, I couldn't help but notice the woman setting up next to me. She had long jet-black hair, dangling silver earrings, and she wore a floor-length flowy caftan with exaggerated bell sleeves topped with a black sheer shawl embroidered with colorful flowers. It was obvious this wasn't her first time at the mercado, because she didn't just have a canopy; she had a very large square tent with panels on three sides. I couldn't exactly see what was under the tent, but the two tables outside it held jars of incense sticks, assorted burners, baskets filled with sage bouquets, and a display rack of dream catchers.

If I'd had someone else to watch my table, I would've gone over to shop myself. But I couldn't leave it unattended and risk losing out on even five dollars. I had checked my account last night, and it was now only three figures instead of four. I had to figure out how to make some money another way while I was waiting for the house to be ready.

But two hours into the Sábado Mercado, those five dollars might as well have been five hundred based on how difficult it was to get customers over to my tables. Even though I'd had a few lookie-loos, the only things I'd sold so far were one dollar's worth of yarn and miscellaneous threads.

It was clear that if I was going to sell any of the outfits I'd brought, I'd have to go outside Sonrisa and straight to the internet.

I began scrolling through Instagram and checking out popular hashtags for vintage and retro collectors in the hopes of luring customers with creative aesthetics featuring my inventory. An older woman wearing a floppy straw hat walked up to my booth, and for a second I was amazed by the magic of social media.

But based on her constipated expression as she looked through the items I'd hung on the rack, I knew she wasn't really interested in what I had to sell. After only a minute or so, she moved on and began inspecting the rings and other costume jewelry I'd laid out on top of a towel.

"You're the woman living in Teresa's house, aren't you," the woman said as she tried on a silver and turquoise cuff bracelet.

"Yes I am," I said, offering her a big smile even though she seemed far from friendly.

"And this is all of her stuff, isn't it?"

I forced another smile. "It is. I'm getting the house ready to sell, so I've been cleaning it out."

The woman shook her head. "Sin vergüenza."

"Excuse me?" I said, no longer caring about trying to be nice.

She took the bracelet off and stared at me. "No hablas español?"

It was supposed to be a question, but I took it like an accusation. Because I'd heard the judgment behind those exact three words all my life.

"No," I responded, bracing for the reaction. Because there was always a reaction and it usually came in three stages:

First, there was disbelief. As if being bilingual was something I felt the need to lie about.

Second came anger. For some reason, my not speaking a language some stranger assumed I spoke was somehow offensive to them.

And third was pity. They felt sorry for my parents because obviously I must be a disappointment.

Sometimes, there was a fourth response. And it was the one I hated the most—discrimination. They now saw me as less than. I wasn't worthy of cooking Mexican food, enjoying Latin music, or taking part in any kind of cultural tradition. Like there was some rule that because I didn't speak Spanish, I couldn't call myself a Latina. Instead, I was labeled a coconut, a pocha, or—the newest insult—a "no sabo."

The woman with the hat went with response number three.

"Your poor mama. I'm sure it hurts her heart that you can't speak her language."

Fury heated my core, and I felt myself trembling with emotion. I told myself not to cry. "Well, my mama purposefully didn't teach me Spanish because she wanted to make sure I didn't get teased by the gringos at my very white private Catholic school. And her heart can't hurt anymore, because she's dead." Then I grabbed the bracelet from her. "And this is no longer for sale."

The lady gasped. She made a very dramatic turn and walked away calling me all sorts of names in Spanish.

I was feeling pretty good about myself for standing up to her, until I heard a voice.

"She doesn't want you in that house either."

It was the voice from the side yard.

I whipped my head around and found the lady from the tent standing behind me.

"You," I said. "You're my neighbor, right?"

The woman shrugged. "Technically, it's not your house, so, no, I'm not your neighbor. But I used to be Teresa's neighbor."

I put my hands on my hips. "Whatever," I scoffed. "What are you doing here?"

She shrugged again. "Same as you," she said, pointing to the table with the incense and dream catchers. "Selling. Well, I'm selling. I'm not quite sure what you're doing."

My cheeks burned with irritation. "Don't worry about what I'm doing. Here or at the house, okay?"

The woman smiled, but it wasn't genuine. So when she took a step closer and stared at me as if she were trying to solve a puzzle, my hands curled into fists at my sides just in case.

"Careful," she whispered. "That ball of anger inside you is going to ignite a fire you can't control."

I was about to go off on her when a customer asked if she could help him find something in her tent.

Part of me wanted to follow her and find out why she didn't want me staying at Teresa's house. Maybe they had been friends. Although I couldn't imagine eighty-nine-year-old Teresa in her conservative nun clothes hanging out with the incense-burning Latina Stevie Nicks wannabe. It didn't add up.

Luckily, the arrival of two women—a.k.a. potential customers—distracted me. I recognized one of them as Carolina, Diego's friend and town Realtor. I hadn't seen her since the night she basically lied about the house having been on the market before. I thought better of confronting her about it, though. I needed all the sales I could get.

"Ooh, these are fun," the other woman said, spotting some neon-green vinyl slip-on shoes. "Can I try them on?"

I nodded with a smile. "Yes, go ahead. I think they're a size seven. Most of the shoes are."

"Perfect," she said and proceeded to kick off her sandals.

"Hi, Carolina. How are you?" I asked politely.

"So I see you're still in town," she responded. Not politely.

"Yep. I am."

Carolina gave me an exasperated look. "Diego says you gave him a long list of things to do. I barely see him anymore because you're keeping him so busy."

"Oh. I didn't realize you and Diego were a thing," I said sweetly just as the other woman came over holding the pair of shoes she'd just tried on.

"They're not. Although Carolina wants them to be," the other woman said. "I'm Lupe, by the way."

If looks could kill, poor Lupe would be dead twice over.

"Diego and I are friends," Carolina explained after regaining her composure. "Well, he did move to Sonrisa to be close to me. But neither of us are ready for a relationship, so we agreed to just be friends . . . for now."

I didn't know how to respond to that overexplanation, so I just turned to Lupe instead. "Did they fit?" I asked.

She nodded enthusiastically. "I'll take them. How much?"

I froze. I had no idea what to charge for them. But she'd kinda put Carolina in her place, so that deserved a discount in my book. "Two bucks."

"Really? Are you sure?"

I wasn't. But I'd already said it, and I'd look like an idiot if I changed it. "Yeah. You're doing me a favor by taking them. Just one less thing I have to lug back to the house."

"Diego says Teresa left behind a lot of junk. You couldn't pay me enough to clean out that woman's house," Carolina droned.

Lupe opened up her wallet and handed me a five-dollar bill. "Here you go. I don't need any change."

"Thank you," I said and stuffed the money into my back jeans pocket.

"Carolina, look," Lupe said, pointing to one of my tables. "She has that old-style CorningWare stuff you like to collect."

And just like that, Carolina was interested in my junk.

Lupe and I watched as she looked over several pieces of the white ceramic casserole dishes and other kitchen items with the blue cornflower design.

"Whatever you think you should sell them for, charge her three times more," Lupe insisted. "She told me she once paid sixty bucks for the stove teapot from that collection."

I laughed. "Good to know. But since you're her friend, I would've thought you'd try to get me to lower my prices, not raise them for her."

Lupe made a face. "Oh, I'm not her friend," she whispered behind her hand. "I mean I know her, obviously. She actually helped me and my husband buy our house when we first moved here a year ago. But we don't hang out or anything. I ran into her at the candle booth, and now she's just following me around."

Suddenly, I really, really liked Lupe. Then she told me she was the town librarian, and I knew she was good people.

"In fact, while she's preoccupied I'm going to sneak away and go get me some incense."

She put her finger over her mouth, waved goodbye, and disappeared into my neighbor's tent.

I took a deep breath and went up to Carolina.

"Well, see anything you like?"

"Maybe," she said as she fingered an appetizer tray. Then she turned around and noticed Lupe was gone. "Where did she go?"

"I'm not sure," I lied. "Maybe she had to go home."

Carolina scanned the area for a few seconds, and then her eyebrows furrowed. "There she is. Ugh. I told her not to go over there."

"Where?"

"To go see the Bruja."

"Who? The lady selling the incense?"

"Have you seen the inside of her tent? It's filled with all of these weird concoctions that are supposed to be healing remedies. But we all know the truth. Lola Allende is a witch."

I laughed. "I highly doubt that woman is a witch. She's my neighbor."

"Exactly!" Carolina exclaimed. "She and Teresa were friends, which made sense. Toxic people tend to attract toxic people. Anyway, I wouldn't be surprised if she cursed Teresa's house and that's why Raul could never sell it. Lola doesn't want anyone else living there. I once made the mistake of asking if she wanted to sell her house, and she immediately started telling me all kinds of horrible things about my future."

I also wanted to laugh at that, but I didn't for a couple of reasons. One, I knew how it felt for the neighbor—Lola—to tell you things you didn't want to hear. And two, part of me wondered if it could be true. Not the witch part. The part about Carolina ending up with a horrible future.

Although I barely knew the woman, I knew her type: entitled, self-absorbed, and jealous. It was obvious she was threatened by the fact that Diego was spending all his time at my house, even though he wasn't spending that time with me personally. I couldn't help but be surprised—and a little disappointed—that he would be friends with her.

If Diego had a type and Carolina was it, then I had been offended for nothing.

"Well, witch or not, it's not like I'll be here long enough to be her friend. So I'll be surprised if I ever talk to the lady again."

Carolina raised one eyebrow. "You're still planning on leaving Sonrisa after the house is sold?"

I nodded furiously. "Oh, definitely. I have a life back in LA that I need to get back to."

She didn't need to know that life included sleeping on my aunt's couch.

This time, the smile that crossed Carolina's face was big and bright. "Good for you," she said. "Let me help by taking more stuff off your hands. I'll give you fifty dollars for all of the CorningWare."

The quick calculations in my head confirmed that despite her new friendly demeanor, Carolina was still trying to be a sneaky bitch. There were at least fifty pieces sitting there if you counted the individual glasses. I would've sold them to her for three dollars each. But one dollar? That whole being grateful even if I only made five dollars went out the window.

"I'll take fifty dollars for the eight-piece casserole set only. The other sets are twenty each, and the serving trays are ten dollars or thirty for all four."

The smile disappeared.

I expected her to haggle a little more or walk away. But instead, she agreed. That's when I knew I should've done what Lupe had said and charged her triple.

Ah well, at least I wouldn't have to pack all that back up. It was worth it to have two fewer heavy tubs to carry to the car.

Despite the slow start, I ended up making about another hundred bucks in addition to Carolina's $120 sale. And thanks to my creative social media posts, I had even connected with a reseller in Santa Fe who was interested in stopping by the house next week to look through the rest of the tubs I hadn't been able to fit in my car.

By one in the afternoon, the crowd had dwindled, and I noticed other booths starting to pack it up, so I decided to start doing the same. But even though I had less stuff than I'd arrived with, I barely had the strength to pick up the containers and take them to my car on the other side of the park. It probably didn't help that my head was now throbbing and my stomach was threatening to eat itself.

Feeling weak, I dropped back onto the chair. My stubbornness surrendered, and I admitted there was no way I was going to be able to load the car on my own. I was about to call Raul to come help me when I remembered him mentioning he was going out of town this weekend.

"How did you do?"

Using my hand to shield my eyes, I looked up from my phone and saw Diego standing on the other side of the table. He looked different out of his usual uniform of work shirts and paint-spattered pants. He was newly shaved, his hair was wet and nicely combed, and he wore a Hawaiian-print shirt, khaki shorts, and loafers.

"What are you doing here?" I asked, annoyed that he looked so fresh and cool while I felt like an overheated blob.

"I was on my way to a barbecue at Councilman Larson's house and decided to stop by to see how everyone fared. Usually the Memorial Day weekend mercado is pretty busy."

Maybe for some people.

Diego stepped closer to the table and looked at me as if I had three heads. "You're red," he stated.

I nodded slowly. "I forgot to put on sunblock. And next time I'll definitely need a canopy or a big hat."

"I bet you didn't eat either."

Even though my stomach turned at the thought of food, I nodded. "I had a yogurt before I came. But I'll stop by Raul's and pick up some tacos."

"Didn't you bring some water?"

I pointed to the plastic bottle sitting on the corner of the now-empty table.

Diego picked it up and frowned. "It's almost still full."

"I didn't want to drink it all, because I didn't want to have to go to the restroom and leave all my stuff. And now it's too warm to drink."

"Dammit, Gabby," Diego muttered and walked away.

Well, okay then.

"Have a nice barbecue," I croaked in a hoarse whisper. If he heard me, he didn't turn around or even wave goodbye.

But I couldn't waste any more brain cells wondering why Mayor Baseball Cap always seemed so grumpy around me. I needed to get out of the sun and into my bed. Even though I felt exhausted, I forced myself to stand up.

And then I fell back down.

I was still sitting there trying for a third attempt to get my legs to lift me up when I noticed Diego stomping back in my direction.

He shoved a new water bottle in my face. "Drink it all. Now."

He didn't have to tell me twice. The water was ice cold and felt so good going down my throat. Suddenly, I couldn't quench my thirst no matter how much I gulped down. I began to feel dizzy again, and my temples throbbed with pain.

"You don't look so good," Diego said.

"Gee, and people wonder why you're still single." Even though I felt like crap, the sarcasm still flowed freely.

Diego walked around the table and squatted next to my chair. He leaned forward and touched the back of his hand to my forehead. "Jesus, Gabby, you're burning up."

"Duh. I told you I felt like I got sunburned," I said, feeling the heat emanating off my face.

"I think you might be suffering from heat exhaustion. Let's get you home."

I wanted to argue that Raul's abuela's house wasn't my home, but I didn't have it in me. My head was pounding now, and it was taking everything I had to stay upright.

All I wanted to do was close my eyes.

"No, no, no." Diego's voice seemed so far away. "Let's get you in some shade."

He helped me stand, guided me to another booth, and then placed me in a chair under a canopy. Suddenly, something very cold and very wet was on the top of my head.

"Keep this wet towel here. I'm going to take your things to your car, and then I'll take you home."

I just nodded. He could've told me he was going to take me to the North Pole and I wouldn't have argued. I just wanted to cool down.

It didn't register to me that we had arrived at the house sometime later until Diego said he was going to take me inside and then walk back to the park to get my car.

The house felt at least ten degrees cooler than the outside, but it still wasn't enough.

Suddenly my stomach churned violently, and I wriggled out of Diego's grasp just in time to make it to the guest bathroom and vomit out all the water I'd drunk less than fifteen minutes earlier.

"You're sicker than I thought," Diego said. "I'm surprised. It didn't even reach ninety degrees today."

"I've never been a fan of the heat. So of course I would have to move to the freaking desert," I complained after rinsing out my mouth and splashing cold water on my face.

Diego didn't reply and instead walked behind me. I managed to make it to my bed and collapsed onto it.

"Let me check your pulse," I heard him say, and then his fingers were on my wrist.

"Am I still alive?" I groaned. When he didn't answer right away, I panicked for a second and thought I actually might be dead.

That's when I knew I was probably delirious.

"Yes, you're alive. But your pulse is weaker than I'd like it to be. I think I should take you to the hospital in Santa Fe just to be safe."

"No. No hospital," I protested.

"Gabby, if we don't get you cooled off, you could have a heat stroke."

"Then cool me off."

"It's better if the hospital does it. It's safer."

I reached out and grabbed his shirt. "I don't have insurance, and I still owe money to the credit card companies and my student loans, and I really, really don't like hospitals. Or doctors for that matter. Sorry."

Diego held up his hands as if to let me know he wasn't offended that I didn't like doctors. "You're really sick, and I don't know if . . ."

"Promise me you won't take me to the hospital," I begged, pulling on his shirt again as if to keep him from making the call for an ambulance.

"I can't promise that."

"Fine. Then promise me you won't take me unless you've done everything you can here first."

Even through my haze of confusion, I could see he was conflicted. "Okay. I promise. Let's get you in the shower now."

When you feel like your head is exploding, you don't care about propriety. So when Diego explained he had to help me take off my jeans and shirt and then stay with me in the shower so I wouldn't fall, I didn't balk.

He helped me walk back to the bathroom and sat me on the toilet. I was wearing only my bra and underwear, and then he proceeded to take off his clothes too. And although Diego's naked chest was quite the sight to behold, I still struggled to keep my eyes open.

"Hey, hey, Gabby, wake up."

Diego's voice was muffled as if he were underwater. That's when I realized I was under with him. My eyes flew open as a cold spray hit my face.

"Stay awake, okay?"

"Okay, Mayor Baseball Cap," I whispered, even as I felt my body falling.

"I got you." Strong arms wrapped around my stomach, and I felt Diego's hard chest against my back. In that moment I was grateful for the delirium. Because if I had been thinking straight, I might have cared that he was touching my flabby skin and most likely seeing the stretch marks along my thighs and middle section.

And I might not have cared just how nice it felt to be held by him.

Even though my eyes were closed, I knew it was daytime. Light and warmth teased my eyelids to open and, slowly, they did. The first thing I noticed was that my mouth was as dry as the front yard. My lips stuck together as I tried to swallow. Instead, I coughed.

"You're awake."

I turned my head in the direction of the deep voice and saw Diego sitting in a chair next to the bed. He stood up and brought me the bottle of water that had been sitting on top of the dresser. I sat up, propped one of my pillows behind my back, and took the water from him.

"What happened?" I croaked after taking a few gulps.

"You became overheated at the Sábado Mercado."

"How did I get here?"

"I brought you."

Images of him helping me down from his truck and through the house flashed in my mind.

"And then what?"

"You begged me not to take you to the hospital, so I did what I could to cool you down here."

I trembled from the memory of strong, wet fingers grabbing my hips. "We took a shower together," I said. And then quickly regretted it when I saw Diego's face redden.

He cleared his throat. "I had to make sure you didn't fall."

"And what happened after the shower?"

He shrugged. "I put you in your bed."

"In my wet bra and panties?"

"No," Diego said after clearing his throat. His cheeks were flushed, and I realized that I enjoyed making him uncomfortable. "I took those off and put the nightgown on you I found in your dresser."

"So, you saw me naked and you went through my things?"

I had meant to tease, but it sounded more like I was flirting. My face heated instantly, and it took everything I had not to stick my head under the sheet.

Diego sat up defensively. "I was a doctor, Gabby. I've seen thousands of people naked."

That made me laugh, which made me cough again. "Fine. But you have to forget what you saw, okay?"

"What does that mean?"

"It means erase that image from your memory." I didn't want Diego all of a sudden remembering my naked body in the middle of painting someone's house or, worse, taking out his trash. Just like I didn't want to remember the feel of him holding me in the shower.

"Erase it?"

"Yes. Erase it."

"Okay," he said and closed his eyes.

"Wait. What are you doing?"

"I'm erasing it just like you said. But in order to do that I have to pull it up in my mind first."

I grabbed the pillow next to me and threw it at him. His eyes flew open when it hit his face, and he started laughing. "I'm kidding, Gabby. Kidding. Glad to see you're feeling better."

Maybe I was still delirious, or maybe I was just tired of always feeling so defensive around him. Either way, my voice choked up with emotion, and I struggled to get the words out.

After another gulp of water, I did.

"Listen, Diego. I want to thank you for helping me yesterday. You probably even saved my life," I said softly.

"I wouldn't say that."

"I would. Lots of yesterday is still a blur, but I do remember that you had plans with your friends and you canceled them to take care of me. I know it could've gotten way worse, and if you hadn't stuck around to make sure it didn't, I don't even want to think of what would've happened. So thank you. I owe you big time."

He opened his mouth, and I thought for a second that he was going to shrug it off or make me feel like I was being overly dramatic. Instead he said with a curt nod, "You're welcome."

We sat there for a few seconds just staring at each other in awkward silence. That's when I noticed he was wearing the same clothes from yesterday. He had stayed the entire night with me.

"I'm feeling much better, so if you need to go home and change or take a nap, I'll be okay."

"Oh. Okay. Are you sure?"

I smiled even though a strange feeling of disappointment that he hadn't protested swirled inside me. "Yeah. Yeah. I'll be fine."

Diego slapped the tops of his thighs and stood up. "Okay then. I'll get going and let you rest."

"Thanks again," I said as he walked away.

Two seconds later Diego came back into the room. And why on earth did that please me?

"I almost forgot. Lola brought by some tonics she says will help hydrate you. So try to drink those, and I wouldn't eat too much today. Stay away from anything too heavy or salty, okay?"

"Wait. Did you say Lola? You mean the . . . neighbor?" I'd almost said *witch*.

"Yeah, yeah. Last night after you finally fell asleep, I walked to go get your car from the park. She came over to talk to me after I parked it in your driveway, and I told her what had happened. This morning she dropped off the tonics and told me to tell you that she hopes you feel better."

I didn't know what to say. Since when did Lola care about my feelings?

"How nice," I said, already deciding that there was no way I was drinking any concoctions made by that woman.

Diego put his hands on his hips and nodded. He looked around the room as if he were seeing it for the first time. Then I noticed he was looking at my mom's urn. Panicking that he was going to start asking questions about her, I said, "I think I'm going to try to take a nap." I didn't have the energy or emotional fortitude to talk to Diego about my mom.

"Yeah, of course. You should," he said. Then he added, "I'm going to be meeting Carolina for dinner later, but I can stop by after to check on you or bring you some Gatorade or something to eat."

The mention of Carolina and the fact that he was choosing to spend time with the awful woman heated me up all over again. "You don't have to. I have stuff in the fridge. Plus, I'll probably just sleep most of the day anyway. I'll just see you on Tuesday."

"Tuesday?"

"Yeah, Monday is Memorial Day. I wasn't expecting you to come work on the house that day. Besides, isn't the city doing some sort of celebration or service? I figured as mayor you'd have lots of hands to shake and babies to kiss."

Diego raised his eyebrows. "What?"

"Well, I don't know what it is mayors do. I just assumed you're just like any politician. Always have to be onstage and be everyone's friend."

"You're right. You don't know what mayors do."

I could tell he was irritated. But I didn't care. I was tired and felt as if I'd gotten run over by a truck—not that I had any experience to compare that to. I just felt like shit, and I was pissed that I was pissed that he was going to dinner with a woman who didn't deserve his company.

Not that I did. Or that I wanted to deserve it.

Ugh. I wasn't thinking straight.

So before he could say anything snarky or annoying, I told him to have a good day and lay down with my back facing him.

And when I heard the front door finally close a few seconds later, I screamed into my pillow out of frustration.

Chapter Twelve

Except for a few trips to the bathroom and an attempt to eat some toast, I slept my Sunday away.

By Monday morning I was feeling a little more like myself. So much so that I showered and changed into actual clothes. Then I called Auntie Lily.

"What exciting plans do you have today?" I asked after we'd caught up on the small stuff. And since my almost dying from heat exhaustion was pretty huge, I chose not to bring it up.

"I'm going to a pool party over at the Venetian. A new client invited me."

I had known Auntie Lily all my life. And if there was one thing she loved about her job, it was the perks. So the fact that she was obviously trying not to sound too excited or boastful about being invited to a pool party set off all kinds of alarm bells.

"Auntie Lily," I said slowly. "Who is he?"

"I told you. He's a client."

"Got you! You never said he was a 'he,' and the fact that you purposefully didn't tell me he was a he makes me think he's a special he. Am I right?"

She let out a long sigh. "Fine. His name is Lance. We met a few weeks ago, when I showed him a beautiful five-bedroom villa. We've gone out to dinner twice and now this pool party today."

As Auntie Lily went on to tell me about Lance, I tried to be happy for her. While my mom and Auntie Martha were both widows and had never shown any interest in dating again, Auntie Lily was on all the dating apps. She once told me she was only on them because she hated going out to eat at restaurants or to the movies by herself. But every few months she'd meet a man she really liked, and he would be all she'd talk about until one day she didn't and would refuse to share why. When it came to boyfriends, Auntie Lily loved hard and fast. No wonder her relationships and her marriages always seemed to burn out as quickly as they'd began.

"I'm glad you found someone to have fun with. Just be careful, okay," I told her.

"Always. You know me, though. I'm not looking for another husband. It's just nice to have someone to hold my shopping bags when I need it."

I laughed, but I knew better. Auntie Lily liked to say she was perfectly fine being single for the rest of her life. But she had to be lonely living in her big house all by herself.

We talked for a few more minutes and then hung up so she could get ready for her party. Then Raul called around nine to ask how I was doing and if I wanted Antonio to bring me some breakfast from the restaurant.

"No, that's okay," I said, ignoring the loud rumbling in my stomach. "I'm just going to eat some oatmeal."

He was quiet for a few seconds. "I'm sorry I wasn't here."

His apology surprised me. "You don't need to apologize. It was my own stupid fault. I know how sensitive I am to the heat. I should've taken better precautions. Besides, you were out of town. It wasn't like you knew this was going to happen."

"I know. I just feel bad. I'm the only family you have here in Sonrisa, and I want you to know that you can count on me to be there when you need me."

The conversation had taken a turn I hadn't quite been expecting. I wanted to tell him that he wasn't my family. That the only reason I'd almost called him that day wasn't because he was my dad. It was because besides Diego's, his was the only other number I had in my phone for someone who lived in Sonrisa. He was only a consideration because of his geographic location and nothing else.

But I thought better of saying that much. Instead I said, "It's okay. I'm fine now."

A long sigh came through the phone. "I'm just so glad Diego was there and that he knew what to do. I already told him I owed him dinner on the house for a week."

I bristled at the thought of the two of them coming to some sort of payback arrangement. Was this the 1800s or something—when the father gave his daughter's new husband a pig or a cow as payment for taking her off his hands? But in my case, it was a week's worth of tacos.

"That was nice of you, but I don't think it was necessary. I already thanked Diego for taking care of me," I said through my teeth.

"Chale! It's the least I could do. He also told me not to bother, but eventually he agreed. Because no one ever turns down food from Carlita's Cocina."

I rolled my eyes. "I bet. Okay, then, I'm going to go make my breakfast. Thanks for calling."

"Let me know if you change your mind about getting food from the restaurant. Whatever you want, okay?"

I told him I'd think about it, and then we hung up. My mind drifted back to Diego. I hadn't heard from him since yesterday morning. Not that I'd bothered to reach out. Truthfully, now that my brain fog had lifted and I was thinking more clearly, I was cringing at the memory of how I had acted and what I'd done in front of him. He was my handyman. He was the freaking mayor of the town. And this man had watched me throw up, had taken a shower with me, and seen me naked. It didn't matter that I'd been sick. It wouldn't have mattered if I'd been dying.

Just the thought of him seeing me like that was almost too much to bear. And if there had been any other repair guy in town who could get the projects done at the same cost and in the same amount of time, I would've asked Raul to fire Diego.

But my life never seemed to work out the way I wanted.

A growl from my stomach let me know it didn't appreciate all this contemplating. It wanted food and it wanted it now.

As I heated the water for my oatmeal in the kettle, I opened the fridge in search of something to drink instead of coffee since I was out of creamer. That's when I noticed a wire basket on the top shelf holding six glass bottles. It took me a few seconds to realize that they must be the concoctions that Lola the neighborhood witch had sent over.

I pulled the basket out and placed it on the counter. The glass bottles were nondescript except for their handwritten labels, which read:

BARLEY WATER

CUCUMBER WATER

SABJA COCONUT MILK

When Diego had called them concoctions, I had envisioned weird colored liquids with various solids floating inside. Except for the sabja, I recognized the simple ingredients. I picked up one of the bottles labeled *CUCUMBER WATER* and gingerly unscrewed the cap. Then I brought it to my nose and sniffed. It smelled like cucumber and lime. The liquid was a pale green with bits of dark-green cucumber peel and some transparent seed clumps mixed in with what I assumed to be water.

Even though I remembered being wary of drinking anything that came from the neighbor, it smelled good. Plus, I was so sick of plain water.

I made the sign of the cross and took a small sip. The sourness of the lime and the lightness of the cucumber mixed to create a refreshing combination. And since I hadn't collapsed into a heap on the floor, I decided to take another drink. And then another. And before I knew it, I'd bled the bottle dry.

Thirty minutes later, I drank all of a second one too. It reminded me of the aguas frescas Auntie Martha would buy from a man who pushed a little white cart down the street of her neighborhood in Milagro Gardens. But the ones she'd bring back to the apartment would be super sweet, with Tajín sprinkled on the top. I loved those ones too. My favorite, though, was Jamaica—the one made from hibiscus flowers. It was fruity and tangy and addictive. When I was younger, my mom would insist on sharing one with me because she said it had too much sugar. But when she wasn't around, Auntie Martha would let me have one all to myself.

"Us gorditas didn't get chubby from one agua fresca," she'd tell me and then promptly add to never tell my mom that she'd let me have a full one.

I smiled at the memory.

Later that evening, I transferred the other drinks to two larger pitchers and washed the glass bottles they'd come in. I took them and the basket over to the neighbor's, along with a small note thanking her for the thoughtful gesture. But as I walked up the steps to her porch, I second-guessed my choice to stop by when it was already starting to get dark. Despite the bright moon, the front of her house was covered in shadows thanks to the multitude of plants hanging in pots all over the small space.

I decided not to even knock. Instead, I bent down and placed the basket in front of the door. As I turned to run back down the stairs, I heard, "I see you're all recovered."

A high-pitched scream escaped my lips, and I jumped like a cricket. "Jesus!" I yelled after I realized the voice had come from the figure sitting in a porch swing to the left of me.

That cracked Lola up, and she laughed like a hyena for a solid two minutes.

"Sorry," she finally said after catching her breath. "Sometimes I forget I'm invisible."

Her odd choice of words surprised me. "I just came to return your bottles," I said in her general direction since I still couldn't make out her face. "Thank you for the drinks."

"You're welcome. Don't tell me you drank them all already."

"Uh, no. I poured them into bigger containers for later. I did taste them all. The cucumber was my favorite."

I felt silly talking into a void, so I stepped closer. Finally, Lola's face and body came into view. She was wearing another caftan and shawl, but her feet were bare.

"I'm surprised, actually. I told Diego you were going to think that I was trying to poison you."

Good thing it was dark. That way she couldn't see the guilt that was probably in my eyes. Then I figured she would hear it in my voice. All I could do was be honest.

"The thought had occurred to me. And I'm not saying I still don't think that. But my good sense must have been damaged by the sun because I'm going to drink them anyway."

That made her laugh again. She scooted over to the right edge of her swing and invited me to join her. I wasn't joking about my good sense short-circuiting. Because I did exactly that.

"So what do you want to know?"

Confusion made me scrunch up my brows. "About what?"

"About the house. About Teresa. About Raul," she said. Then she squinted and added, "About Diego."

"I don't know what you're talking about."

"Now come on. Don't get shy on me again. If you're honest with me, then I'll be honest with you. I'm too old to play games. I can see the questions buzzing around you like a swarm of flies. They're not going to leave you alone unless you get answers. So start asking, or go back to the house and keep pretending that you don't care about all of this."

I didn't like her tone or her accusations. I almost called her bluff. I almost stood up to leave.

Almost.

"Fine," I said instead. "Why did you tell me that first night that Teresa didn't want me at her house? She never even knew me."

"I didn't."

"Now who's playing games. You said, 'She doesn't want you here.'"

"I wasn't talking about Teresa."

"Then who?"

At first, I thought she meant Carolina. But that didn't make sense. I hadn't met Carolina until days later.

Lola watched me as if she was waiting for me to give the answer. It came to me just as a cool whisp of air breezed its way through the leaves of Lola's jungle of plants. I shuddered.

"How could you . . ." I couldn't even finish the question. I couldn't finish it because I told myself it couldn't be true. I didn't believe in such things. I didn't believe that Lola could tell me things about my dead mom any more than I believed she was a witch.

"You don't have to believe me, Gabby," she said even though I hadn't shared my thoughts. "It doesn't matter to me either way. I don't say things to be mean or kind. I just say them because they need to be said."

I wanted to tell her that wasn't true. That some things were indeed better left unsaid. However, there were a few questions I did want to ask.

"Tell me about Teresa. I heard you two were friends."

Lola smiled wistfully. "We were. I miss her."

"What was she like?"

"Oh, she was mean. Very judgmental and opinionated. She didn't really like a lot of people. Well, I guess she didn't like anyone except me. But it wasn't like that right away. We didn't get along at all that first year I moved in. Then we both realized we had a lot in common, and

I was very drawn to her. I guess she liked me because I always told her the truth. I was like the granddaughter she never had. But it was very hard to gain her trust. She was the kind of person who always thought the worst of people."

"That's no way to live," I said.

"It isn't. So why are you headed down the same path?"

I winced at her accusation. "Me? What are you talking about?"

"Raul."

"I don't think the worst of him. Honestly, I don't really have an opinion either way at this point."

Lola shook her head and laughed. "That's because you're keeping him at arm's length so you don't have to get to know him. But trying to pretend that Raul isn't your dad is never going to change the fact that he is."

"Biological dad. My dad, my real dad, was Juan Olmos," I said through my teeth.

Lola tilted her head. "One doesn't negate the other, Gabby. Accepting that you are Raul's daughter doesn't erase your love for Juan Olmos. You have no reason to be afraid of getting to know Raul. He says you've never asked him one single question about what happened between him and your mom."

It was true. I hadn't asked because I was afraid of what I would learn. It wasn't that I hated Raul. Even I could admit that he seemed to be really trying to live up to his end of our bargain. But that didn't mean I was ready for anything more. And I really did not like the fact that Raul was talking about me to others—especially this woman.

"Because it's not important," I said. "It's in the past."

"Maybe," she said with a shrug. "But when you don't deal with your past, then you can't move on with your future. Look at poor Teresa."

I was agitated now. Lola didn't know me. She didn't know my family. What an old, sad woman did years ago had nothing to do with me in the present. "This is different. I'm here, aren't I? If I didn't accept

123

that Raul was my biological father, then I never would have accepted his offer."

"Well, we both know why you accepted it. And it had nothing to do with Raul. You should talk to him. I'm not saying you have to love him or even like him. But it will only help you if you find out the truth."

"And what truth is that?"

"Who you are. Where you come from."

Thoughts of my mom, my dad, Auntie Martha, Auntie Lily, and my grandparents floated in and out of my head. Images of birthday parties, Christmases, family vacations, and just ordinary afternoons pieced together to make a picture. It wasn't perfect. But I could still see it. And it didn't matter that Juan had been in my life for only twelve of my twenty-nine years on this planet. He was and would always be the only man I ever called dad.

"I know who I am, and I know where I come from."

Lola sighed as if she was bored with the conversation. "Not if you don't have all the pieces. I think you're beginning to realize what parts are missing, but it's going to be up to you to go find them."

I turned away and stared into the shadows. Not knowing what was hidden in them was a little scary. Didn't mean that finding out would make it less so. "Maybe I'm okay with the missing pieces," I told her. "I've never needed to go searching for them before."

"Knowing where you come from becomes more important as we get older," Lola said. "Whether it's good or bad, you will regret not knowing that part of yourself."

So much of what I'd believed had been proven wrong already. I didn't know if I could handle learning any other truths—especially about Raul. Because then that would mean I might have to forgive the man who had rejected me before I was even born.

Was I that desperate or pitiful? And then what if he rejected me a second time? What if I did let him get to know me and he decided he didn't like who I had become?

My heart was already broken. I would be dumb to let someone destroy it completely.

I let out a long breath. "Or maybe I'll regret letting down my guard?"

"That's always a risk when you decide to trust someone," Lola admitted. "But you seem to have a good head on your shoulders, Gabby. Something tells me you'll know when it's right to take that leap."

That made me laugh. I could think of a ton of times when I'd made the wrong choice.

"And here I thought that you might be psychic. You obviously don't know me at all," I said.

Lola raised an eyebrow at me. "A psychic? I thought everyone believed I was a witch?"

Chapter Thirteen

"Are you sure you want to do this?"

I looked at Diego and nodded. "I'm sure," I told him.

"Because, you know, once we do it, there's no going back."

"I know that."

"So if you want to wait a few minutes and think about it, that's cool with me."

"I'm done thinking," I told him.

"Okay, then. Let's do this."

Using an X-Acto knife, Diego began making slits into the old yellowed wallpaper that lined the kitchen ceiling just above the cabinets. As he made the slits, I sprayed a concoction of liquid fabric softener and hot water into them in an attempt to loosen up the stubborn glue. He was on a step stool, and I was standing on the counter.

"Watch where you aim that thing," he said. "I'm starting to taste lavender."

"Well, why is your mouth open?"

After we wet the area, we needed to leave it for about fifteen minutes so the liquid could seep into the wallpaper and, hopefully, loosen it up so we could pull it down.

"While that's soaking, let's move to the other side of the sink and do that part," Diego said as he got down from the step stool.

I was about to also climb off the counter when something red and flat sitting on top of the refrigerator across from where I was standing caught my eye.

"There's something on top of the fridge," I told Diego. "I want to get it."

He helped me off the counter and moved the step stool to the side of the fridge. I climbed up and raised my hand to try to find the object.

"There's definitely something back here, but I can't reach it."

"Let me try, shorty."

I rolled my eyes at Diego's lame comment and stepped off the stool. It had been a few days since my heat exhaustion drama. And although I could tell Diego wasn't quite sure about how things were going to be between us, he seemed to follow my lead, and we'd gone back to our usual sarcastic exchanges. It was as if we'd both decided to forget what had happened that day of the Sábado Mercado and just move on with finishing the house.

But, even I had to admit that things seemed more comfortable between us. So comfortable that I'd caught myself staring at the way his T-shirt sleeves perfectly wrapped his biceps like a second skin. I wrote it off as just a newfound appreciation for the man who had nursed me back to health and held me almost naked in the shower. I guess near-death experiences will do that to a girl. I knew not to read too much into it, and I was sure the more time I spent around him, the faster I would get back to my usual semiannoyed reaction whenever I saw his face.

Diego stepped on the stool, reached up, and after a few twists and tugs, he pulled down what looked to be a spiral notebook.

He handed it to me, and I dusted off the cover with a paper towel. "What is it?"

"I'm not sure," I said and carefully opened it.

As I thumbed through the pages, though, I had a better idea. "It's a book of recipes," I said. "I guess they must be Teresa's."

Diego took the book from me and began to look through it himself. "I'm not so sure," he said. "I don't remember the restaurant ever having any of these dishes. If they were Teresa's, wouldn't Raul have them already?"

That was true. Based on what I'd seen on the menu of Carlita's Cocina, none of the recipes in the notebook were still being served. They had to be older.

"What if they're Teresa's father's recipes?" I asked him.

He continued to read and nodded. "I think you're right. Wow. These could be the original menu items from Carlita's Cocina. You need to show Raul."

We were both grinning as if we'd just discovered some long-lost buried treasure. I had no idea why I was so excited about an old journal or why Diego was just as excited as I was.

And I had no idea why I was finding it so damn sexy.

Diego handed it back to me. "If you want to go now, I can do the wallpaper myself," he said.

"No," I said way too quickly. "I don't have to give it to him right this second. Besides, he's probably getting ready for the lunch rush right now. I don't want to pull him away from his work. I'll stop by later and show him."

"Okay. I guess let's get back to work then."

I wondered if finding the journal had been a sign. Ever since my conversation with Lola the other night, I'd been thinking of how to start a conversation with Raul about the past. I still didn't know if I could handle knowing everything that had happened between him and my mom. But Lola had convinced me to at least try.

About an hour later, we had sprayed all the surfaces in the kitchen covered in wallpaper and begun on the hard part—scraping it all off.

Diego took the section over by the pantry and fridge, and I took the section by the stove and sink.

It seemed simple enough, but it was definitely giving my arms a workout.

"This reminds me of one of my first jobs in a kitchen," I said. "Every night I had to scrub all the grease and pieces of food off the flattop grill."

"Oh so you have experience?" Diego replied. "Then you should be doing it all so I can tackle some other things."

I waved the scraping tool at him. "Uh-uh, mister. How about you finish it and I can go take a nap. I'm still recuperating, you know."

Diego shook his scraper at me. "First of all, it's barely eleven in the morning. You don't need a nap. Second of all, you seemed perfectly fine yesterday when we went to the hardware store and you begged me to install a ceiling fan in the bedroom, even though that was not on our list."

"That room is so stuffy and dry. I'm surprised I don't wake up with a migraine every day."

"And did you get a better sleep last night? Although that mattress is so old it's like you can feel every spring under the thin padding. I also don't know how you don't wake up with a migraine every day."

The fact that he knew the feel of my mattress threw me for a second. It was personal. Intimate. But the man had seen me naked. We were way past intimate, I guess.

"Anyway, the point is you promised to help me today because I have a council meeting later and need to leave by three."

I brushed off the uncomfortable reminder of the other day. "I only promised because I was shocked you actually had to go do mayorly stuff. I was starting to think you gave that title to yourself."

"Funny," he droned. "I'll have you know that I was elected by the highest margin ever in Sonrisa's history."

"Why?" I asked, trying to sound bored. "Because no one ran against you?"

"Actually, I had a very formidable opponent. Raul."

That made me stop scraping. "Raul ran for mayor and lost to you?"

"Yeah. It was especially hard since he was the one who had encouraged me to run for a city council seat four years ago. I'd been living in town for only about a year, and I would always complain to him about how antiquated the city's building codes and permit system were. It was frustrating trying to help my customers with their home-improvement projects, because the red tape held things up. I told him that he and the other council members needed to hire someone to revamp the process."

This information surprised me. "Wait. Raul was a city council member?"

Diego gave me a look that told me he couldn't believe I hadn't known this. But how could I? Raul and I didn't have long heart-to-heart talks. In fact, most of our conversations were over texts. Despite my new decision to be open to learning more about Raul, right now I was more comfortable asking others about him than the man himself.

"He served several years," Diego explained. "He finally stepped down after losing the mayoral election."

"And even though you two were opponents, you're still friendly?"

"We're friends. Raul is a good guy. He helped me a lot when I first moved here, and I feel lucky to know him."

With that, Diego went back to scraping. It might have been my imagination, but it sounded a lot quicker and more forceful than before.

It was obvious that Diego was a loyal friend to Raul. I figured it had to count for something.

"So what pressing items are on the agenda for the Sonrisa City Council tonight?" I said as I tried to peel off the strips of paper that I'd manage to lift so far.

"The usual stuff. Zoning complaints. Parking issues. Oh, and the record store wants permission to put tables outside their front door on the sidewalk so they can put out crates of albums to look through when people walk by."

"Sonrisa has a record store?" I asked.

"It does. Al, the guy who owns it, has a pretty good collection too. Why? Are you looking to buy some new albums for your nonexistent record player?"

I stopped peeling to look over at him. "No, but I did find a huge box of albums in the room with the sewing machine. It was in the back of the closet, along with a briefcase of cassette tapes."

"So you want to see if you can sell them to Al?"

"Definitely. I had planned on looking up some stores in other cities and taking a day to drive over. But if there's a place here in town, then I want to try it first."

"Yeah, that sounds good," he replied with a nod. "I'm surprised you didn't know about the record store."

"Why would I?"

This time Diego stopped working, then stepped off the stool and walked over to my side of the kitchen, where I was standing on the counter. "Besides Carlita's Cocina and the grocery store, where else have you been in Sonrisa?"

I thought about it for a few seconds. "Well, I've gotten lattes from that nice little bakery—you know the one where I met your *friend* Carolina." I made sure to exaggerate the word *friend* because I still didn't understand why Diego hung out with her. "I've been to the hardware store, obviously. Oh, and I went to the park. How could I forget that fun experience?"

"So you're telling me that you've been in town for what? About a month? And you haven't gone exploring?"

"I've driven to Santa Fe a few times."

"Santa Fe is not Sonrisa."

"I guess I figured I'd do it eventually. I just haven't yet."

He didn't look like he believed me. "What are you doing this Saturday?"

"I thought we were going to paint the kitchen? Isn't that why we're taking off all this wallpaper?"

"We'll paint on Monday. I'm going to give you a tour of the town and also take you to my favorite spot."

"You don't have to do that," I said, wondering why I felt a little nervous about spending time with Diego outside the house.

"I know I don't have to. I want to. I think it will be good for you to get to see Sonrisa the way I see it. It's a special town. And, it's part of your family's history. That way when you go back to LA, you'll remember more about the town than just its lattes."

Even though I wanted to argue, I couldn't. Diego was right. So was Lola. Whether I liked it or not, Sonrisa and Raul were entangled in my roots. It was time for me to start digging.

"Okay, fine. Let's do it."

Now that that was settled, Diego nodded and began to walk back to his side of the kitchen. Then he turned around and pointed a finger at me. "And for the love of all that is holy in this life, make sure you wear sunscreen, a hat, and eat a real breakfast. I'll pick you up at seven."

We continued working the rest of the morning on tearing down the old wallpaper. The kitchen already looked so different. I knew the paint was only going to add to the transformation, and I couldn't help but feel excited about seeing the finished project.

After Diego left for his meeting, I put the journal in a drawer for the time being. What I hadn't mentioned to Diego was that I wanted some time to look through it more carefully. Maybe I would even try cooking one of the recipes myself. Just the idea of making something that required thought, precision, and creativity made me feel excited. More than I had been in a very long time.

For now, the journal and all its secrets would be mine.

Chapter Fourteen

Saturday morning came fast.

For some reason I was still nervous about whatever Diego had planned for us that day. So much so that I almost texted him to cancel an hour before he was supposed to pick me up.

"I know, I know," I said, staring at Mom's urn. "It's just because I'm not the one in control."

She had always told me that my anxiety over the unknown was holding me back from new life experiences and adventures. The summer before my junior year, I had the opportunity to go to Paris with my class. As soon as she heard about it, she began planning outfits and looking for French tutors.

"This is why me and your dad work so hard, Gabby. These are opportunities we never had, and now we can give them to you."

Except she never had asked me if I wanted to go to France. Probably because what teenage girl wouldn't jump at the chance to go to Europe without her parents.

But I was that girl. I had no interest in going to a country I'd never been to before. I didn't speak the language, didn't know the food, and I knew I'd be forced to spend time with the same girls who liked to make snide remarks behind my back about my weight or my unstylish clothes. If my best friend, Jenna, had been going to go on the trip, then

I might have considered it. But she had told me her mom couldn't afford to send her.

Then, a month before the registration and consent forms were due, my dad died.

I remembered being appalled when my mom told me that he would still want me to go. I was grieving. The last thing I wanted to do was go to Paris and pretend like my entire world hadn't just been turned upside down. So the day everything was due, I conveniently forgot all the paperwork at home. My mom found out weeks later that I had never turned it in, and the trip was already fully booked. I wasn't going to Paris.

She was big mad about it too. It was the first time that she went a full two days without speaking to me. It was awful, and when I couldn't take it anymore, I called Auntie Lily in tears and begged her to come get me and take me to go live with her in Vegas. I was already struggling being in our house without my dad there. Everything reminded me of him. Everything reminded me that he would never be in our house again. And the fact that I couldn't talk to my mom about it made me feel even more alone. I was so desperate that I told Auntie Lily I was going to run away if she didn't come get me.

She showed up that night.

But instead of taking me and my packed suitcase with her back to Vegas, she and my mom had a screaming match in the living room. It wasn't the first time I'd heard them fight. But it was the first time I was worried that they would stop being best friends. All because of me.

It must have been about two hours later when my mom finally came into my bedroom and collapsed into my arms. She apologized for giving me the silent treatment and for being so wrapped up in her own grief that she hadn't tried to help me through mine. She admitted that part of her had wanted me to go on the trip so she could just stay in bed all day and not have to worry about taking care of anyone else for that week. Mom told me she had hoped she'd be better by the time I got back and we could move on without Juan.

All my anger disappeared when she told me the truth. It was the first time I'd seen my mom as a human being. She had lost the man she loved, and now she was lost and in pain. I offered to still go with Auntie Lily to Vegas to give her space and the time she needed to herself. But she told me she didn't want me to go.

"How about this? We'll both go to Vegas this summer during the same week you would've been in Paris. We can even invite Auntie Martha. We'll make it a girls' trip. Just the four of us, like it used to be."

And we did exactly that. The trip didn't change the fact that my dad was gone, and it didn't fix the issues between my mom and me. But for one glorious week, all had seemed right in our world again.

When I'd gotten my first sous-chef job, I opened a savings account and began transferring whatever I could afford from my weekly paycheck. The goal had been to save up enough to take my mom to Paris for her fiftieth birthday.

Instead, I was using that money now to pay off credit card bills and my student loans, and just to live.

So, yeah, adventure wasn't for me.

Maybe that's why I nearly had an anxiety attack when it knocked on my door at exactly 7:00 a.m.

Besides his four reminders about making sure to wear sunblock and a hat, he hadn't given me any other hints as to what he had planned for us. But I was relieved when I saw he was basically wearing something similar to what I was—jeans and a T-shirt. But while he wore boots, I had on my favorite pair of Converse tennis shoes.

"Is this okay?" I said and waved a hand in front of my body. "Or should I change into shorts or different shoes."

Diego's eyes scanned me from top to bottom and then bottom to top, lingering just a few seconds longer on my cleavage peeking out from the top of my V-neck. I tried not to read too much into it or, worse, imagine him remembering my naked boobs.

"Eyes up here, buddy," I said, hoping the humor would deflect whatever it was I was feeling in the pit of my stomach.

"I wasn't . . . ," he stammered.

"I'm joking, Diego. Seriously, though, do I need to change?"

His eyes were back on mine. "You're fine. I mean you look fine. Just bring a sweater or sweatshirt just in case. And don't worry about water. I brought enough for the both of us."

"Why are we going to need water if we're just going around town?"

Then he did something I had never seen him do. Diego winked at me. "I'm taking you somewhere else first."

That somewhere involved about an hour's drive to what he told me were the Jemez Mountains inside the Santa Fe National Forest. During the ride, we talked about what he always talked about: the list. This time, though, it was exciting news. The new countertops were scheduled to be delivered in about a week, and he wanted to take me to a warehouse on Tuesday so we could pick out the tile that would go in the kitchen, living room, hallway, and both bathrooms. He had already bought the laminate wood flooring for all the bedrooms.

"Lola says she knows a place where we can get a good deal on hand-woven Navajo rugs," I told him. "We should go check them out next week. I think they'll bring some personality and color to the rooms."

Diego looked over at me as he continued driving. "Are you two friends now? I thought you thought she was trying to poison you so you'd move back to LA."

I scrunched up my face. "That was forever ago. Where have you been? And I don't know if she would call me her friend, but I think she's interesting. And I like hanging out with her. Well, most of the time I do, anyway."

He turned his eyes back on the road. "Why sometimes?"

I hesitated telling him the reason. It was true that I had grown fond of Lola. And I didn't want to be one of those gossiping wenches like Carolina and spread rumors. Still, I was dying to talk about it with someone, and my gut told me I could trust Diego.

"All right, I'll tell you, but you have to swear you won't mention it to anyone, especially Carolina."

He looked at me again. "Why not Carolina?"

"Because she, like a lot of people in this town, doesn't like Lola. And I don't want them to have any additional ammunition to use against her."

I thought he would defend his friend, but he didn't. "Okay. I swear."

"Lola has this ability to look into your soul and tell you things about yourself you sometimes don't want to hear. She knows things before you even tell her. It's cool, but it also makes me uneasy. She says she can't help it, that all this stuff just spills out of her on its own."

"Like a psychic?" Diego asked.

"No, not like that. She's not a fortune-teller. Personally, I just think she's a very empathetic person and can connect to others on a very deep level. So that, combined with all of the healing remedies she makes at her house, people can get the wrong idea about her."

He nodded. "We've gotten the few odd complaints at city hall about her property. The Sábado Mercado organizers actually wanted to deny her application when she first asked to have a booth. But there was no good reason to. Now she's one of the most popular vendors there."

"I'm sure she is. She knows a lot about plants and herbs. And it's not because of witchcraft. She's a botanist. Did you know she teaches at a community college in Santa Fe?"

"I didn't," he admitted.

"I told her she should teach psychology, too, based on how much she analyzes me. I realize now, though, that when she tells you things about yourself, she's not doing it to be mean or hurtful. But it can be a little disconcerting."

"Yeah. She told me some stuff when I first moved here. It's not the best feeling."

That piqued my interest. "What did she tell you?"

Diego shifted in his seat and continued staring straight ahead. "Just some stuff. I didn't really understand most of it. It doesn't matter now."

Translation: it did matter, but he didn't want to talk about it. I got the message and decided to change the subject.

"So are we almost there or what? I need to pee."

He glanced over at me, obviously surprised. "What?" I asked. "I made sure to drink an entire bottle of water before you picked me up."

Fortunately for me and my tiny bladder, we pulled into a campground area about fifteen minutes later.

"Don't tell me we're going camping," I said, even though I knew that couldn't be true. I'd only seen a backpack behind our seats. Then another thought came to me. "And please, please don't tell me we're going on a hike."

Diego's face fell. "You don't like hiking?"

"It's more like hiking doesn't like me. In case you haven't noticed, I'm not exactly an athletic kind of girl. And need I remind you that I almost died just sitting on my ass at the park during Sábado Mercado?"

He laughed at that. "It's not a steep hike. It's less than a mile, and the end will be worth it, I promise."

I gave him a skeptical look, put on my LA Dodgers baseball hat, and got out of the truck.

After we'd both visited the public restrooms, we found the entrance to the trail and began our journey. Although I was still apprehensive, I had to admit that being outdoors like this felt nice. It helped that the lush green forest provided lots of shade and picturesque scenery. We didn't talk much on the short hike, mainly because I was trying to conserve my oxygen and energy so Diego wouldn't have to carry me back to the truck. But he was unusually quiet, and I started to feel bad that maybe I had ruined his excitement about bringing me here.

"Can we stop for a second?" I said.

He looked concerned. "Are you okay?"

"Yeah, yeah I'm fine. I just want to take some photos for my Instagram." I pulled out my phone and began shooting. It really was beautiful.

"Do you want me to take your guys' picture?" a voice behind me said.

We turned around and saw an older man and woman standing in the middle of the trail.

"No, that's . . . ," Diego began.

"Yes, please!" I said at the same time. I gave my phone to the lady and went back to stand next to Diego. "And you better smile," I whispered.

"I'll do better than that," he whispered back. Before I knew it, Diego had wrapped his arm around the back of my waist and pulled me up against his side. His fingers curled into my flesh, and I gasped. He bent down and leaned so close to me that I could feel his breath on my ear. It tickled and felt good all at the same time.

The lady told us to smile, and I tried to remember how. Because having Diego hold me like this again was bringing up all sorts of emotions I wasn't prepared for. Especially when he didn't let go even after the woman stopped taking pictures. I was the one who broke our contact to get my phone back from her.

"I think you'll like the pictures," she told us. "You two look good together. Have a great afternoon."

I was about to tell her that we weren't together like that. But Diego replied with, "Thank you—you too," before I said anything.

I looked at the pictures, and the woman was right. We did look good.

"Well, are they Instagram worthy?" he asked over my shoulder.

"I guess," I said nonchalantly. "All right, let's keep moving before it gets dark."

"Gabby, it's only eight thirty, and we're almost there anyway."

He started walking, leaving me alone to find my bearings. But then I lost them again when I finally caught up to Diego and saw the reason why we were here.

The army of trees that had dotted the trail opened up like a theater curtain to unveil white-and-blue water spilling over two tiers of a majestic rock formation that seemed to touch the heavens.

"It's a waterfall in the middle of the desert," I announced.

"Technically, we're in the mountains now," he corrected.

"Whatever. It's pretty cool either way."

"It is," he said. "But this isn't the best view. Come with me."

Diego grabbed my hand and led me to a section of nearby rocks. Slowly we climbed down and stopped about halfway. He pulled a towel out of his backpack and laid it on top of a flat boulder. He motioned for me to sit down and then took the spot right next to me.

"It's Jemez Falls."

"It's breathtaking," I said.

"I think so," he said softly. I glanced over and noticed he was watching me.

"What? Do I have a bug on my face or something?" I asked, brushing the top of my nose and forehead with my fingers.

He chuckled and shook his head. "No. I'm just glad you like it."

We sat there in silence for a few minutes just enjoying the view and the cool mist coming off the waterfall. I closed my eyes and listened to the low rumble of the water as it flowed off the edge of the rocks and onto a small pool below us.

When I opened them, Diego was watching me again.

He smiled at being caught and then looked away. My face warmed, and I was grateful for the umbrella of trees all around us. If I wasn't careful, I'd get overheated again. This time for a way different reason.

"So this is your favorite spot in New Mexico?" I asked, trying to distract myself from thinking too much.

"Mm-hmm. When I first moved here, I ran into a couple of campers at the bakery. They had just spent a few days up here and were headed home to Texas. They're the ones who told me about it, even showed me their pictures. On my next free day, I decided to make the drive and come see it for myself. Now, I try to make it out here every few months."

"Why do you think you like it so much?"

Diego chuckled. "How about you guess?"

I looked over at him, and I could tell he was challenging me. "Okay. Well, for one, no one's asking you to fix things here."

"That's true," he said after a loud laugh.

"I mean it's definitely something beautiful and wonderful to look at. It forces you to take a breath and pause for a minute. It's almost like it gives you permission to just be, to just exist. All those worries and struggles you have in your life can be put aside because none of them matter here."

I hadn't expected to go that deep. But it was how I was feeling about being in this place. The water, the trees, even the rocks were reminders that there was more to this planet than just my little complicated corner of it.

"That's exactly it," he said softly.

I smiled and inhaled the fresh mountain air. I turned to him and said, "You're going to regret bringing me here."

"Why is that?"

"Because this is now my favorite spot in all of New Mexico too."

Diego shrugged. "I don't mind sharing. Guess that means you'll have to come back here again, you know, after."

"Yeah," I said, nodding. "I guess so."

I knew right away that I had meant it. I wasn't just agreeing with Diego because I wanted to make him feel like the trip had been worth it.

"And so what's the grand plan, Gabby?" he said after a minute or so. "What's next after you leave Sonrisa?"

It was the million-dollar question. The one that kept me up at night trying to find the answer. "Not sure," I admitted. "I'm still thinking about it."

"Do you want to keep working as a sous-chef?"

"I do, but the more I'm away from it, the more I don't miss the bad stuff that came with it."

"Like what?"

Immediately, I thought about the night in Chef Dean's office. But I still wasn't ready to tell Diego about that.

Instead, I said, "Being a female sous-chef isn't easy to begin with. But throw in being a Latina? I have to prove I deserve to be in a kitchen even before I cook a single meal. Everything I do, everything I say is dissected and judged. It took me years to get to my first position, but to do it, I had to be smart—but not too smart. I had to be nice—but not too nice. I had to be tough—but not too tough. I had to be attractive—but not beautiful. Do you understand? Saying the wrong thing to the wrong chef or food critic could overshadow the most important thing about me—I'm a fucking great chef. So, yeah, not having that pressure right now has been kinda nice."

"Do you miss cooking for people?"

"I do. That's why I know I still want to do something in the food industry. But I don't know if that means I stay in Los Angeles or go somewhere else." My own words surprised me.

It must have shown on my face since Diego then asked, "What?"

I shook my head. "I would've never even considered moving out of LA a few months ago. After the doctors told us that my mom didn't have that much time left, I was so focused on the end that I never really thought about the after, you know? I thought the worst thing in the world was going to be having my mom die. But it's not. The worst thing is learning how to live without her."

Diego nodded as if he understood exactly what I was talking about. I wanted to ask him why, but I didn't feel like I deserved to know. He barely knew me. Hell, he barely even liked me.

Then why was I baring my soul to him?

Suddenly, a rush of embarrassment came over me. Diego hadn't asked me to come with him today so I could tell him about my problems or feelings.

"So, what's next on this warped tour of yours?" I asked, obviously changing the subject.

"Back to Sonrisa," he said. "There are a couple of places I want you to see and even meet a few people. It's not going to kill you to get to know a few of them while you're here."

Maybe not. Didn't mean I had to like it, though.

"Fine," I groaned. "But then you owe me a nice lunch for making me hike and climb and basically exercise on a Saturday."

"Deal," he said, meeting my eyes with a huge smile.

And for the first time since I'd met Diego, I wondered what his lips would feel like against mine. The thought startled me. Made me dizzy.

"All right," I said, jumping off the rock. "I think I've had enough naturing for today."

I didn't miss the wave of disappointment that crossed his face even though it was gone as quickly as it had appeared. But I couldn't afford to worry about that. We were going to be together for several more hours and working together for several more weeks. It would do neither of us any good if I spent most of the time acting like a silly teenager with a crush.

Whatever feelings Diego was starting to stir up in me had to go away and go away fast.

Maybe Lola had a concoction for that?

Chapter Fifteen

"I have exactly what you need."

I wanted to tell Lola that I doubted that she did. Because she had no idea what that was, and I wasn't about to tell her. And owing to the fact that she always seemed to know exactly how I was feeling or what I was thinking, I debated about even coming over.

But I was a woman on a mission.

I'd been going through the journal Diego and I had found on top of the fridge and earmarked a couple of recipes I wanted to test out. The more I read, the more convinced I became that these were probably the original recipes for Carlita's Cocina when it first opened over a hundred years ago.

The only reason I hadn't tried cooking them yet was because all the instructions were in Spanish. So yesterday, after we'd come back from exploring Sonrisa, Diego and I sat down at the dining room table and he translated while I typed up the two recipes I wanted to test first.

It had been a really good day. Probably one of the best I'd had in years. I kept telling myself it was because my mom's sickness had cast a shadow over so many things for so long. It had felt nice to not worry about having to rush home to take care of her or getting a call that would make me drop everything I was doing because she needed me.

But I also knew it was because of who I had spent the day with.

And that was the main reason why I'd been hesitant to go see Lola when she'd invited me to come over and pick the chiles I needed for the recipes.

Because what I really needed was something to shake these new feelings for Diego out of me. He was Mayor Baseball Cap, for God's sake. He annoyed me. He pissed me off sometimes.

Not to mention the fact that he'd made it clear on the day we met that he would never be attracted to me. I was mistaking a budding friendship for romance. And I had to stop.

I just didn't know how to at the moment. And I wasn't going to ask Lola to help me either. I didn't mind her help with my cooking experiment, but no way was I going to involve her in my love life. Or lack thereof.

Instead, I followed her to her backyard garden and let her show me all her chile plants.

"You said over the phone you needed jalapeños and poblanos, right?" she said, pointing to two large pots in the corner of her patio.

"Yeah. And some serranos and cactus."

"I'll go pick those and you pick the others. Then we'll take them inside and wash them, and then you can tell me why you're so pink."

I touched my warm cheek. "Oh I'm probably a little sunburned," I told her.

"The heat coming off you isn't that kind of heat, Gabby."

I was sure my face reddened with embarrassment. I spun around so she couldn't see whatever it was she was seeing and began picking what I needed.

Fortunately, when we were back in her kitchen, Lola didn't bring up my pink cheeks again. She was too busy asking me questions about the journal of recipes I'd found.

"How exciting," Lola said as we wiped off the chiles and sorted them into containers. "I wonder if Teresa even knew the journal was up there."

"I don't know. The layer of dust was pretty thick, and the pages are already tinted yellow. It had definitely been years since anyone had opened it. Did she ever cook for you when she was alive?"

Lola looked up at her ceiling in thought. "Now that you mention it, no. I can't remember her ever cooking me anything. If we ate together, it was usually at the restaurant or over here. I wasn't a chef like her, but I'm a pretty good cook. But I'm also a vegetarian, so maybe that's why she never offered? And then these last few years, Raul was the one who cooked for her."

I nodded. It made sense, especially if she'd been sick or not able to get around like she used to. I had cooked for my mom too. That reminded me that there was another question I'd been wanting to ask Lola.

"Did you know her daughter, Raul's mother?"

"No," she replied with a shake of her head. "I've never met Regina. But I feel like I know her, based on everything Teresa told me. Poor thing. She's such a lost soul."

It felt strange to talk about my paternal grandmother, whom I had never met. Until that moment I hadn't even known her name. I had never asked and Raul had never told. In fact, he never talked about his mother at all. Part of me kinda assumed she was no longer alive. But Lola had used the present tense.

"Where is Regina now?" I asked.

Lola shrugged. "Who knows? Like I said, she's a lost soul."

I wasn't exactly sure what Lola meant, but it didn't sound good. "I'm assuming Teresa and Regina didn't have the best mother-daughter relationship?" I thought of my own mother and the fact that despite our differences, I was there for her at the end. Did Regina even know that Teresa had died?

"No. In fact, after Regina's brother died, they had no relationship at all."

"Wait. Teresa had a son? And he died?"

I watched as Lola shivered, even though the temperature hadn't changed. "He got really sick during a visit to see some of Teresa's relatives in Mexico, and he passed away over there. He was only four. Anyway, Lencho, that was Teresa's husband, had stayed here in Sonrisa to work at the restaurant, but she had taken the kids with her. Teresa was so distraught that she just wanted her son buried immediately and didn't tell Lencho until she and Regina returned. He never forgave her for that, and their marriage was never the same. Regina, who had been ten at the time, also was never the same. It didn't help that the only way Teresa could cope was to basically make every reminder of her son disappear. She took down all of his photos and forbid everyone from even mentioning his name around her."

My heart rate was racing as if I'd taken a jog around the block instead of sitting there listening to the tragic story. "What was his name?" I asked, somehow already knowing the answer.

"Raul," she said.

I gasped.

Lola nodded knowingly. "It was bad enough when Regina told her that she was pregnant at sixteen, but when she told Teresa it was going to be a boy and that was going to be his name, it was too much. She kicked her out. Sent her to LA to go live with some cousins."

"And what about after Raul was born?"

"She says Regina would bring him to visit every once in a while— usually when she needed money. And then, well you know this, he came to live here when he was in his twenties."

I hadn't known, but I nodded just the same. "Did they have a good relationship?"

"Um, I don't know if I would say good. I mean, Raul always tried to be a good grandson. He worked at the restaurant like she had wanted him to. After he got his own place, he still came over to cook dinner for her once a week and help her with things like groceries and cleaning the house. But she always kept him at arm's length, and I don't think he ever really knew why."

"That's sad," I said, surprised at my feelings toward what Raul must have gone through with a mom like Regina and an abuela like Teresa.

"It was sad," she said after a long sigh. "But we all deal with grief in our own way. Unfortunately, Teresa's way was to try to pretend like the death never happened. Out of sight, out of mind and all that. But that meant also pretending like her life before the death—the good life she'd lived with her husband and daughter and son—never existed. And, eventually, they stopped existing to her as well. That made her bitter, resentful, and lonely."

I couldn't help but think of my mom and how she'd been after my dad had died. She could've turned into Teresa.

"Do you think Raul knows all of this?"

"I never said anything to him. Maybe Regina told him?"

I remembered the photo I'd found in the hatbox. "There was a photo in Teresa's closet—well, it was stuck inside a hatbox—and I think it was a picture of her family. There's a little boy in it who looks like it could be Raul at that age."

"You should give it to him," Lola said.

"Maybe. Or maybe all of this is none of my business."

"Oh, but it is. You know I believe everything happens for a reason. Maybe this is the real reason why you're here in Sonrisa, Gabby. You might not see it this way, but you and Raul are more alike than you think. You're both grieving."

I stopped sorting. "Teresa died over a year ago, and his mom is still alive, apparently. Who did he lose?"

"You. Or rather, the daughter he never got to know. When you think about it, Raul has never had a real family. Sure, he had a mother, but from what I've heard, she never really acted like one. He had an abuela, but she was a stranger and, basically, stayed a stranger up until the day she died. He's never been married, doesn't have any other children that he knows of, and lives by himself. I think Raul is stuck. Like you. Neither of you can move on until you get the answers you've been looking for your entire lives. Now, you can give that to him. And he can give that to you."

The weight of what Lola had just unloaded onto my shoulders was too much. Tears welled in my eyes, and my throat burned with emotion.

"Don't wipe your eyes with your fingers," Lola said before getting up from the table. She pulled a paper towel from her dispenser and handed it to me. "The chiles," she explained. I nodded and patted my face with the towel.

"I'm sorry. It seems like I cry at everything these days."

"That's understandable. Like I said, you're grieving. Remember when I told you that first night about someone not wanting you in the house and you thought I had meant Teresa?"

I nodded. "You meant my mom, didn't you?"

"No, Gabby, I didn't."

"I'm confused now. Then who?"

"It was you . . . or the past you, anyway. In your heart, you felt guilty about moving here because you felt like you were betraying your mother. But that was the grief talking, honey. Being here and letting Raul into your life has nothing to do with your relationship with your mother. I know this is going to sound harsh, but you need to stop trying to make her proud. I think deep down you know she was proud. Of course she was."

Lola's words made the tears come rushing back, and this time I couldn't stop them.

Chapter Sixteen

As I walked into Carlita's Cocina, I couldn't help feeling like I was about to take an important test. And even though I'd studied and done the work, there was no guarantee that I was going to pass.

The restaurant had just closed for the night, but I'd texted Raul earlier and asked if I could meet him there. I also told him not to eat any dinner.

"What's going on, everything okay?" he asked after I set the bag down on the counter. "What's that?"

"I'll show you. But first I need to show you this." I handed him the journal. "I think these are your great-grandfather's recipes. I think they're the original recipes for Carlita's Cocina."

Raul's eyes grew big as he opened it up to the first page. "Where did you find it?"

"On top of the refrigerator. Diego and I were removing the wallpaper, and I saw it sitting up there when I was standing on the counter."

Raul continued to flip through the pages without saying a word. Sometimes he'd stop and read something. And sometimes he'd just stare at the page. When he finally closed it, he looked as if he'd seen a ghost.

"I think you're right. I think these are my great-grandfather's."

"Really?" I asked, not able to contain my excitement anymore. "How do you know?"

"The handwriting. My abuela's was the worst. I could barely decipher her grocery list. This writing, though, is neat, almost purposeful. No way is it my abuela's."

"That means this journal is at least a hundred years old, right?"

Raul nodded. "Yeah, at least. My great-grandparents were one of the original families of Sonrisa. They opened the restaurant in 1921. This journal is a piece of the town's history. I can't believe it's been sitting in my abuela's kitchen all this time."

"Do any of the recipes look familiar? Do you still serve any of them?"

He opened up the journal again. "There are a few here that we still make, but they're a little different now. Some of these ingredients aren't really sold in the market or restaurant-supply store anymore. And then there are others that I don't recognize at all."

I couldn't wait any longer. "Well, before I gave this to you, I wanted to try out a few of the recipes." I reached into the bag and pulled out two foil containers. Then I removed the lids and pushed both toward him.

"This one is chiles en nogada," I explained, trying to pronounce it as Diego had taught me. The plate held four poblano chile peppers covered in a white cream sauce dotted with chopped walnuts and dark-red pomegranate seeds. I'd followed the original recipe by stuffing the peppers with picadillo but changed up the usual mixture of ground meat, stewed tomatoes, and potatoes by adding diced apples and jalapeños.

The other container was a vessel for a cold mixture of thinly sliced cooked cactus, jalapeños, onion, cilantro, and tomatoes. I'd substituted the recipe's queso fresco for crumbles of feta cheese and made my own version of a dressing.

"And this one is a nopales salad. Lola helped me with the nopales, since I'd never cooked with them before and didn't know how to clean and prepare them."

Raul clapped his hands in excitement. Then he pulled out two forks from behind the counter and handed one to me. He looked at me before taking a piece.

I laughed. "Go ahead. Dig in."

First, he tried the chiles en nogada. "Is the picadillo made with ground pork or ground turkey?" he asked after swallowing the first bite.

"Both. And the recipe called for something called bisnaga? But I couldn't find any, so I just used some dried pineapple."

"I can taste it. This is amazing, Gabby. Really."

Pride swelled inside me. It had felt so good to be cooking again. But to have someone taste your food and enjoy it was on another level. I continued watching Raul as he tried the nopales next.

"The recipe in the journal was more for like a warm side dish. But I thought the salad might go better with the chiles en nogada," I explained. "Oh and the dressing has cider vinegar and Dijon mustard."

"I love the tanginess of it. It just tastes so bright, so fresh. I love it."

Between the two of us, we made a good dent in both containers. Raul said he would put away the leftovers for Antonio to taste in the morning.

"Although if he knows you can cook like this, he's going to be asking you to bring him lunch instead of the other way around," Raul said.

"Hey, I'm willing to make some sort of trade arrangement with him. Tacos for nopales salad sounds perfectly fair. So, what are you going to do with the journal?" I asked after taking a drink of my Coke.

"Oh, don't you want it back? You should try out some more of the recipes."

"Are you sure? I mean it belongs to you."

"It belongs to both of us."

I wasn't sure how I felt about that. "How about this? I'll take the journal back for a few days and type up the rest of the recipes. Then you have it and do whatever you want with it."

Raul considered this. "There is a history display at the library. Maybe they would want to display it there?"

"I think that's a great idea. In fact, I'll mention it to Diego the next time I see him and find out how we can make that happen."

"You two seem to be getting along better," he said with a raised eyebrow.

I willed my cheeks not to flush. Raul wasn't Lola. He couldn't see what I didn't tell him. And I wasn't about to talk to him about Diego or these strange new feelings. We were getting along better. Much more than better, to my dismay.

"Yeah, I guess." I decided to change the subject to one just as touchy. "So, I didn't just come over tonight to give you the journal or have you taste the food I made."

Raul straightened in his chair. "Oh, okay. Do you want to go over the list again and make some changes?"

"No this isn't about the house. Well, I mean, not exactly." I took a breath. "God, this is harder than I thought it would be."

"You can tell me anything," he said and reached out to cover my hand with his.

Instinctively, I pulled my hand away. But then I remembered my conversations with Lola. As difficult as this was about to be, I knew that we both had to go through it in order to keep moving forward.

"What happened between you and Mom? I'm ready to hear the story. I want to know the story . . . if you want to tell me."

"I do want to tell you, but I'm also afraid. You have to know that I honestly had no expectations when you agreed to move here to Sonrisa. But part of me did hope that if we could have a fresh start, then maybe we could find a way to build some sort of relationship. Do you think that's going to be possible after I tell you?"

How could he know that was exactly what I was wondering?

"I can't promise that. But what I can promise is that I'll listen."

Raul looked away as if it was hard to face me. Maybe it was. I knew I had kind of sprung this on him. And I wouldn't blame him if he wanted to talk about it another day.

"That's fair. So where do you want me to start?"

"From the beginning."

He told me basically what Auntie Martha had already told me on the day of Mom's memorial service. They had all been friends, he said. And then he and Mom were more than that.

"The summer before your mom's senior year—I had just graduated—your grandparents decided to move out of the projects. They bought a house about thirty minutes away in the city of El Monte. She was so mad about having to leave Lily and Martha, and me. She begged them to let her stay so she could finish out her senior year with all of her friends. But they wouldn't hear of it, and they also told her she had to break up with me. They never liked me. Never thought I was good enough for her. They were right, of course."

"Because she got pregnant."

"Bingo. Anyway, she had just turned eighteen, and we talked about getting married and getting our own place. But I knew she wanted to finish school. She had big plans for herself, you know. She always believed that she deserved the better things in life. I believed that, too, and I wanted to give them to her. Eventually, your mom thought she deserved better than me too. So when she told me she didn't want to get married anymore, I let her go."

"But you were still going to be a dad," I said as if I didn't already know how the story ended.

He shook his head. "I was a punk back then, Gabby. I could barely take care of myself. I didn't know how to be a dad. How could I? I never knew mine. I figured I'd be a crappy one just like him. Back then I thought the both of you would be better off without me."

"Then why didn't you let Juan adopt me?"

He flinched at the question. "You know about that?"

I nodded my head. "Auntie Martha told me. But I'd like to hear it from you."

"After you were born, I stayed away," he said, leaning back into his chair. "I got a job at a warehouse and was doing okay for a while. But I never stopped thinking about Sandra or you. So when I ran into Martha, I told myself this was my chance to check in and see how you both were doing. But then your mom told me about Juan wanting to adopt you, and I lost it. You have to believe me. I really thought I was ready to be your dad at that point. That's why I told Sandra I was going to take her to court."

"But you never did," I said. It was as if he'd disappointed me all over again.

"No, I didn't," he said and hung his head. "My mom had promised me that she was going to help me pay for a lawyer because she wanted to get to know you. At least that's what she told me. But two days before I was supposed to pay the retainer, I came home from work and the cash I'd been saving in an envelope in my sock drawer was gone. And so was Mom. She'd left me a note saying she was borrowing the money to take a quick trip up north to visit a friend and that she'd pay me back the following weekend."

"Did she?"

"Nope. In fact, I didn't see her for two weeks. By that time, the lawyer told me that if I didn't pay by a certain date that he wasn't going to take my case. So, my stupid ass decided to get the money another way."

I was almost afraid to ask. But I had to. "How?"

"I started stealing rims off cars and then selling them at the local swap meet. But then I got busted and had to spend a few nights in county jail. I hated it so much that I bit the bullet and called my abuela and asked her to send me money to bail me out. I hadn't talked to her in years, but she agreed on one condition. I had to move here to Sonrisa and pay off my debt by working in her restaurant."

The realization that he'd been here in Sonrisa all this time disappointed me. If he'd stayed in jail, maybe his explanation would've been easier to swallow. But there was no real good reason that had prevented him from being a part of my childhood. Or my teen years. Or any timeline until now.

"So then what? You became the owner of Carlita's, became a city councilman, made a nice life for yourself here, and decided it's finally time to introduce yourself to your only kid?" I said, not caring if I sounded bitter. I was bitter.

Despite my harsh tone, Raul didn't balk. "Maybe you never saw me or talked to me, but I was around, Gabby. I kept tabs on you through Martha in the hopes that one day I could be there for you for real. So, yeah, I used my abuela's house for a chance to finally get to know you."

It was a lot of information to take in. But it was still a hard pill to swallow knowing that a parent didn't want you, especially when you had never done anything to bring it on. I was four years old when Raul decided he could live his life without me as a daughter.

How was I supposed to get over that?

I got up. "It's getting late. I better go."

"Gabby," Raul said. "Please. Let's keep talking."

I had told myself I would listen, and I'd done just that. I didn't want to talk anymore. I needed time to digest and think.

I shook my head. "No. I think I've heard enough for one night. I really do have to go."

Then I grabbed my purse and left.

Chapter Seventeen

I'd never known I could be excited about tile shopping, yet here I was.

A few days ago I'd decided to add a backsplash to the kitchen wall behind the sink. It was not on the project list, but I thought it would add some personality to the space. Raul, of course, had immediately agreed, so Diego and I were going to go tile shopping.

Things between Raul and me were off kilter again after the night he told me what had happened to him after my mom had gotten pregnant. I wouldn't say we were back to square one in terms of our relationship, but it definitely seemed like we'd taken a few steps in reverse. It was all on my end. I knew that. For his part, Raul still invited me to dinner at the restaurant or offered to bring me lunch, but I had declined his offer the last few times.

"I thought you were giving him a chance to make things right," Diego had said yesterday after we'd scrolled online to pick a backsplash design.

"I did. I am. But it has to be on my own time," I had explained. "In my head, I know that he's not the same person that he was back then. I just need to reconcile that in my heart and figure out how he fits in my life."

Luckily, Diego hadn't pressed the issue anymore.

I had to admit one of the reasons I had put up a wall again was because of the growing guilt I'd been feeling about withholding some details from Auntie Lily and Auntie Martha about Raul. Whenever they'd ask about him, I gave them only the basics, and it all had to do with the house. I didn't tell them about the journal or the fact that I'd started to become more interested in knowing about him and his family—my family.

Auntie Martha probably would've been pleased in her own way, but Auntie Lily would've been hurt. After all, it was exactly what she had been worried about and why she hadn't wanted me to come to Sonrisa in the first place. So if I couldn't tell Auntie Lily, then I couldn't tell Auntie Martha.

The practical side of me knew I had nothing to be ashamed about. But the emotional side of me couldn't help but feel like I was betraying everyone who had loved and supported me before he was even in the picture. Correction. *After* he had voluntarily left the picture.

Needless to say, I was confused. So, I focused on what I could control—a new kitchen backsplash.

◆ ◆ ◆

Diego's text that morning had said to meet him at noon for lunch before we made the drive to Santa Fe. But when I arrived five minutes early, I thought I'd typed the wrong address into Google Maps since it had led me to a house and not a restaurant.

I was about to call him when his truck parked behind my car.

"What are we doing here?" I asked after we'd met on the sidewalk in front of the one-story house. It wasn't adobe like Teresa's. It was more modern. Well, if you could call a dark-brown roof and white stucco modern.

"I told you," Diego said as he began to walk up the driveway. "We're going to have lunch."

Even though I was still puzzled about why we were at someone else's home for lunch, I followed him anyway. My confusion only grew when Diego didn't even knock on the front door and, instead, let himself inside.

"What are you doing?" I whispered, careful not to alert an angry homeowner in case Diego actually didn't know what he was doing.

He winked at me and then called out, "We're here!"

"I'm in the kitchen," a deep male voice yelled back. I recognized the voice immediately.

We were inside Raul's house.

I abruptly stopped in the small foyer. "Diego, what's going on?"

He turned to look at me, rolled his eyes, and grabbed my hand. "It's just lunch, Gabby."

We walked a few feet down a tiled hallway and then turned into an open arched doorway. Raul was standing at the stainless steel stove and stirring something inside a big black pot. The aroma of garlic, oregano, onion, and tomato filled the space, and instantly my stomach growled.

"You guys are right on time. The meatballs are just about ready." Raul waved us over to the small kitchen table in the corner.

"Meatballs?" I asked as I took a seat next to Diego.

The older man shrugged and then proceeded to take plates out of a nearby cupboard. "I figured we'd change it up. Seems like we eat Mexican food almost every day. I thought we could do Italian today."

I didn't miss the "we" part of that sentence. Had the three of us become a "we" now?

"I don't mind," Diego offered. "I could eat tacos every day."

"You *do* eat tacos every day," I said, stretching the truth just a little bit.

Diego ignored my teasing. "So, what did you make?"

"My famous meatball sliders," Raul said proudly from across the kitchen.

"Awesome. Sounds delicious," Diego said just before his phone dinged with an incoming text. He glanced down, scrunched up his eyebrows, and then put his phone down again. "Mrs. Ramirez's AC is acting up again. I'm going to have to skip lunch."

I froze. "Are you serious? You have to leave right now?"

Although I knew my glare would have no effect on him, I still tried to burn a hole in his smug expression. Judging by the way Diego refused to meet my eyes, I knew that he had absolutely planned this.

Diego stood up. "She's almost ninety, Gabby," he said with a tone that was clearly fake offense. "Do you really expect me to let her sweat it out just so I can eat some sliders?"

"No," I said, gritting my teeth. "Of course, you need to go. And what about the tile?"

"We'll go tomorrow instead," Diego said matter-of-factly. "The tile will still be there."

Raul walked over with a foil-wrapped bundle and handed it to Diego. "For the road," he said.

Diego nodded in appreciation and left Raul and me alone in the kitchen.

"I can make yours to go, too, if you want," he said. I nearly agreed, but then felt guilty for even considering it.

"No, it's okay. I can stay," I said.

His face immediately brightened. "Good. I'll serve us now."

A few minutes later, Raul presented me with a plate carrying two meatball sliders. The buns were the perfect shade of toasted brown. In between, a bright-red and thick marinara sauce oozed down the sides, taking along swirls of white cheese. I couldn't tell yet if it was provolone or mozzarella. I'd have to take a bite to find out, and I couldn't wait.

"They look amazing, Raul," I said truthfully. "They smell amazing."

"Hopefully they taste amazing too," he said.

Eagerly, I picked up one of the sliders and bit down. The combination of the bread, sauce, cheese, and meatball exploded into a blast of flavor inside my mouth. It was hearty and comforting.

"Is there provolone and mozzarella in here?" I said after swallowing my first wonderful bite.

"Yeah. And the bread has parmesan. Why? Do you think it's too much cheese?"

"There is no such thing as too much cheese," I said before taking another bite.

We continued eating for several more minutes, only talking here and there. It wasn't because I didn't want to. It was just that the food was too good.

"Thank you for lunch," I said after pushing away my empty plate.

Raul nodded with a huge grin. "You're welcome. I'm glad you let me cook for you."

"What are you talking about? You've cooked for me before at the restaurant."

"I know. But, this was different."

I knew what he had meant. The meatball sliders weren't anywhere on Carlita's Cocina's menu. And even though he didn't say it, I guessed that Raul didn't make them for just anyone.

"You'll have to give me the recipe for those meatballs," I said after a few seconds of silence.

"Definitely. I can't wait to see how you make it your own," he told me.

I shook my head. "No way am I changing anything. They are awesome just the way they are."

He gave me a sheepish smile. "It's taken me a few years to get the recipe just the way I wanted. But that doesn't mean you couldn't take it further and perfect it."

"You give me way too much credit." I was surprised by the emotion welling up in my chest. His words—his praise—sounded genuine.

Raul leaned back in his chair, and his expression turned serious. "You really are a talented chef, Gabby. Are you going to try to find another sous-chef job when you go back to LA?"

I shrugged. "I don't know. It's a competitive field, especially in LA. Also, part of me wishes I could just be my own boss so I can cook the food I want to cook using my recipes."

"So do that. I know restaurants are hard to open, but what about a food truck?"

"A food truck?" I asked.

Hadn't Chef Dean tried to intimidate me into thinking that was the only job I could get? Was I really going to consider doing it on purpose?

It wasn't something I had ever wanted for my career. My dream had always been to be the executive chef for a high-class, award-winning restaurant. The kind that had waiting lists three months long. I'd always thought a food truck was more suited for hustlers—people who thrived on the challenge of going to where the customers were instead of waiting for the customers to come to them.

I didn't think I had that kind of chutzpah. My mom used to say there were people who were go-getters but I was more of a go-give-it-to-me. And I didn't even deny it.

"Food trucks are risky," I added.

"Sure, everything good in life usually is. But food trucks have low overhead, and they're mobile. You don't even have to do it in LA. You can open one anywhere you want in the country."

I shrugged. "I don't know."

"Well, you don't have to decide now. You got some time."

Did I, though? I was going to be thirty years old in a few months. The three years I'd spent at Sky Grill had been two years longer than any other job I had ever had. Mom used to tell me that I was running out of time to get my shit together and become an adult with a real career and make something meaningful out of my life.

On the other hand, time could open doors that you thought had been closed forever.

I cleared my throat and shifted in my chair. "About the other night . . . ," I began.

Raul held up his hand. "We don't need to talk about it."

"Yeah we do."

He sat up straight and took a long breath. "Gabby, I need you to know that I will accept whatever you think of me. I know I deserve it. I have no excuse for abandoning you and your mom. And I'm going to regret doing that for the rest of my life."

I heard the break in his voice, and a wave of sympathy rolled through me. It finally dawned on me. All this time I'd been focused on what my mom and I had lost because of Raul. It was clear now that he had lost a lot too.

So where did we go from here?

"I'm just not sure what you want from me," I told him.

He seemed to consider my question for a few seconds. Then he shrugged. "How about we just take it day by day?"

It wasn't what I had expected. But it was exactly what I needed to hear.

"Sounds good to me," I said and gave him a genuine smile. "Could we start with another slider too?"

Chapter Eighteen

Tequila is dangerous.

Especially when you haven't had it in a while. And especially, especially when it was this good.

"So smooth," I purred after downing my third shot.

Diego laughed. "Don't tell me you're a lightweight."

I couldn't help but be offended. "Excuse me? I'll have you know that I could outdrink every bartender in every single restaurant I ever worked in."

"I'm impressed. Well, I would be if that was actually something to be impressed by."

"You're a mean drunk," I muttered.

"I'm not drunk."

"Then you're a mean . . . sober? I don't even know what I'm trying to say anymore."

The alcohol had warmed me up and made me feel all sorts of good. I was relaxed and happy. So of course that meant I had to keep on talking.

"This is nice," I admitted.

Diego nodded, probably thinking that I was talking about the cool evening or the fact that we were enjoying our tequila on the newly cleaned up and restored backyard patio. He'd washed and repainted a couple of chairs and a small round table, while I'd found some inexpensive cushions at Walmart. It didn't seem like much at first, but it had really transformed the area. So much so that I'd insisted we break in the new set that night.

He had brought the tequila as a peace offering for his little stunt the other day. As I'd expected, it had been his idea for Raul to make us lunch and then he'd faked an AC emergency. I still wasn't happy about him leaving me. But what I hated the most was that his plan had worked. Raul and I were back on track to figuring out how to be in each other's lives. And I had a renewed interest in learning as much as I could about the restaurant's history through the recipes from the journal.

Along with the tequila, Diego and I were nibbling from the impromptu charcuterie board I'd thrown together with some deli meats, cubes of pepper-jack cheese, pretzels, and olives. Based on how much tequila I'd already had, though, I probably should've tried to make an actual meal since we hadn't stopped at the restaurant for our usual weekly dinner. That's when I realized that I couldn't remember the last time I'd eaten dinner on my own. If I wasn't grabbing food with Diego, then I was over at Lola's enjoying wine and takeout.

"If you're still hungry, I can make some spaghetti or something. I think I still have some tomatoes. But you'll have to settle for the noodles from the box. I haven't made fresh pasta in months."

"Well, I only eat fresh pasta, so . . ."

I must have given him a look, because he immediately started laughing. "I'm kidding. I'm fine with what we already have. But I'll take a rain check on having you cook a real dinner for me, though. Raul hasn't shut up about the dishes you made for him the other night."

I hesitated for a few seconds and then decided to tell him about part of my conversation with Raul. "He doesn't think I should go back to being a sous-chef. He thinks I should open a food truck and be my own boss."

Diego whipped his head in my direction. "Here in Sonrisa?"

"What?" I scoffed. "No. Back in LA. He thinks that's what I should do with the money I get from selling the house. Invest in myself."

Diego nodded. "That's actually pretty smart."

"I don't know. Food trucks are a pretty risky business, especially since everyone and their mother has been starting one lately. And LA is a very competitive market. Customers aren't going to follow you all over just for the same tacos or burgers they can get from the truck that's parked outside their office building. You have to offer them something different, something they can't get anywhere else."

"So make that."

I laughed. "Yeah, because it's going to be that easy."

"Didn't you once tell me that you were a realist and that you would always do whatever it took to get what you wanted?"

"I hate when you quote me," I said with a groan.

Diego straightened his back. "All I'm saying is that if it's something you want to do, then do it. In the meantime, I'll happily volunteer to taste test anything you make. I was serious about that rain check because you are going to have to make me real food at some point. Otherwise I'm going to start doubting that you're a real chef."

"Fine. I guess that's only fair since you've proven to me on more than one occasion that you're a real doctor."

As soon as I said it, I regretted it. Especially since Diego didn't laugh.

"I'm sorry. I didn't mean to . . ."

He held up his hand. "It's fine. I know you didn't mean anything by it. I guess I owe you some answers, don't I?"

"No. No, you don't owe me anything, Diego," I rushed. "I'm sorry for bringing it up."

"It's okay. I don't mind. What do you want to know?"

I thought about the question and answered truthfully. "Everything."

He chuckled and poured himself another shot of tequila. "Fair enough. I used to be an ER doctor back at a hospital in San Francisco. Technically, it was a trauma center, so I saw the worst of the worst."

"Wait. You're from California too?"

"I am. I grew up in Bakersfield, but moved to the Bay Area for college and medical school."

"Are your parents still alive?"

He nodded. "Yep. And married for almost forty years now. They still live in Bakersfield in the same house I grew up in. My mom was pregnant with me when my parents immigrated to the US from Jalisco. In Mexico, my dad was a science teacher and my mom had worked for her parents in their market. But over here, she could only find work as a housekeeper, and my dad worked in construction. He was the one who taught me how to fix things around our house and build things. They both retired a few years ago but are threatening to go find part-time jobs somewhere because they say they're bored."

"Any siblings?" I said with a laugh.

"One. I have a younger sister who lives in Seattle with her husband and my niece and nephew. She and her husband own their own furniture business. I guess you could say she's pretty good with a hammer too."

"So are you the only doctor in your family?"

He nodded and bowed his head. "I am. My parents were so proud the day I graduated from medical school. It was a big deal for them . . . and for me."

I could hear the wistfulness in his voice. Even regret. "So what happened?"

Diego held up a finger to let me know he needed a second. Then he downed the shot. "A woman," he said and then sighed.

"Oh. Ohhhh." I was definitely intrigued, but also a little jealous. Okay, a lot jealous.

"Yeah. Exactly. She came in one night with a black eye, some bruises, and a sprained wrist. She had a story about tripping over her cat, but I didn't believe her. But I had no proof that someone had hurt her, and since she wasn't admitting it, I had to discharge her. I gave her my card and told her to call me if she ever needed anything."

Guilt washed over me. No wonder Diego had reacted so seriously to the bruises on my arm. "I'm guessing giving a patient your information wasn't exactly allowed."

"So not allowed," he said. "But I kept telling myself that I just wanted to help. Anyway, she called, and before I knew it, we were dating. She finally confessed that it was a boyfriend who had hurt her, but that she'd broken up with him after that night we had met. He'd called her a few times and shown up at her work. But I'd believed her when she said she hadn't seen or heard from him in weeks."

My gut roiled with dread. "Oh no. I don't think I'm going to like what comes next," I admitted.

Diego looked away and just stared into the night air. "It was a slow Tuesday night in the ER. I was just about to go on a meal break when we got the notification that two ambulances were on their way with gunshot victims. I took the first victim—it was a woman. There was so much blood on her face that I didn't recognize her at first. But then I noticed the tattoo on her shoulder, and I knew."

I reached out and touched his hand. He didn't pull away. Instead, he turned it so he could grab on to me.

"Her ex had ambushed her in the parking lot of her apartment complex. He shot her and then shot himself. He was dead on arrival. I did everything I could to save her, but I couldn't. I had lost patients before, but this was different. It messed me up. I couldn't eat. I couldn't sleep. Eventually, the hospital suspended me. And I just never went back."

"How did you end up in Sonrisa?"

"I had gone to high school with Carolina, and we were friends on Facebook. About two months after I'd decided I didn't want to be a doctor anymore, I saw a post of hers about a house for sale in town. She'd already been living here for a few months, but I never paid much attention to what was going on with her. The house was a fixer-upper, but there was just something about it that called to me. And when I scrolled through Carolina's other posts about Sonrisa, I knew I had to come here, especially seeing that slogan: 'Where Smiles Grow.' I figured if I wasn't going to use my hands to fix people anymore, then I'd used them to fix a house. And that's basically the story of how I ended up in Sonrisa."

"I'm so sorry you had to go through all that."

He let out a long sigh. "Yeah, it was a really dark time. Even when I moved here, I still felt like something was pulling me down. Almost like I was drowning. Remember how I said Lola had said some stuff to me? She looked me in the eye and said, 'You have the power to pull yourself back up. All you have to do is let go of the guilt.' And she was right."

A chill ran through me. "Yeah. She usually is."

He looked over at me and gave me a small smile to let me know he was okay.

"What about you? Any tragic stories about exes you want to share? I'm sure you've broken a couple of hearts in your time."

That made me yelp. "I wish. And the only tragic thing about my exes is the fact that there aren't that many. And the tiny few I do have dumped me, not the other way around."

"Then they were the stupid few," Diego said. "Their loss will be someone else's gain."

"I'll drink to that," I said and poured myself another shot.

"I'm serious, Gabby. Those guys, those boys, have no idea who they let get away."

I wanted to laugh again, but I saw how his eyes seemed to be searching every inch of my face for some unattainable answer. The warm evening air danced with anticipation. It was as if every plant and every creature were holding their breath, waiting for something to happen between us.

I was waiting. Hoping now, even. Because the butterflies that had been growing in that cocoon of denial were now free and fluttering around inside me. Something had changed between us. I accepted that now. The only question was whether Diego felt it too.

"Oh, I almost forgot to tell you something," he said, breaking whatever hold he'd had on me. And also answering my question. "Carolina might already have a buyer for the house."

"What?" I asked, careful not to let him see how deflated I felt. "How is that possible? It's not even on the market yet."

"I know. But she called me earlier to say that someone had called her office, wanting to know if she knew of any homes in this neighborhood that were going to be for sale in the next few months, and she mentioned this one. The man said he was definitely interested. In fact, he was willing to buy the house as is because he needs to relocate soon."

"As is? That doesn't sound like we'd even get close to market value then."

"No, that's the thing. He told Carolina that he would be willing to pay whatever the most recent comp sale was."

I should've been happy. Ecstatic even. But my mom always told me that if something sounded too good to be true, then it was probably the worst-case scenario.

"Wow. That is amazing. Can you do me a favor, though? Can you get the man's information from Carolina for me?"

It was a long shot, but I was going to see if Auntie Lily could do a little research to make sure the guy was on the level.

"Yeah. Yeah. Does that mean you'd consider his offer?"

"Maybe? But that doesn't mean I think we should stop moving forward with the repairs. Just in case this guy doesn't work out, I don't want to lose time or slow down our progress."

Diego nodded. "I agree. Okay, I'll get the information for you. But it will be business as usual as far as our checklist."

"Perfect."

"Hey, Gabby," he said softly.

I almost thought—I almost hoped—that the next words he said would be the ones I had been waiting for days to hear.

Of course they weren't. Instead, he reminded me to call the hardware store in the morning and order more paint.

I chided myself for reading into everything Diego said as if his kind words were somehow code for romantic feelings. Why hadn't I learned by now that men like him would only ever see me as a friend?

Chapter Nineteen

There are many things in life that I don't recommend doing.

One of them is waxing your face with a kit you found at the dollar store (thanks, paramedic, for that tip . . . after the fact). And another is getting your water turned off in the middle of your shower.

At first, I thought Diego had shown up early and decided to work on replacing the water heater today instead of starting on the countertops like we'd discussed. I yelled out the bathroom's tiny window for him to turn it back on. But when nothing happened, I wrapped my shampoo-covered hair in a towel, put on my robe, and stomped out of the bathroom. Diego was nowhere to be found. Then my phone rang. It was him.

"One of the city's water mains sprang a leak," he said as soon as I answered. "You're not going to be able to use the toilet or take a shower."

"Too late." Then I quickly added, so he would know exactly what I meant, "My hair is full of shampoo. How long is it going to take to get fixed?"

He sighed. "It's hard to say. We've got a contractor coming out to take a look. I'm not going to be able to come over until we get this mess sorted out."

"Fine. But call me back as soon as you know something."

A few minutes later, Raul called. "Is your water out too?"

"Yeah. Diego says a water main broke. I guess we're both part of the affected area. What about the restaurant?"

"No, all of the businesses on Main Street are connected to a different line. So I'm going to head over there now. If people can't cook, then they're going to come out to eat."

"Look at you," I teased. "Ready to take advantage of people's misfortunes."

"Yeah, if I wanted to do that, then I'd raise all the menu prices. Hey, actually, that's not a bad idea."

I was about to tell him that it was when my phone beeped. "Raul, I gotta go. Diego is calling."

We said our goodbyes after I promised to check in with him later. Then I clicked over to the other line. "Is there news?"

"Kind of. But it's not good. The contractor says he can't get here now for at least two hours. I guess some of his equipment is not working."

"Two hours? What am I supposed to do with no toilet and no shower for two hours?"

Diego was quiet for a few seconds, and I thought he'd hung up. But then I heard him sigh.

"Go to my house."

Now it was my turn to be stunned into silence.

"Gabby? Are you there?"

"Yeah. I'm here. Did you just tell me to go to your house?"

"I did. You can stay there until your water gets turned back on. I can't go anywhere, so you'll have the place to yourself. Take your shower; make something to eat. I have a spare key hidden in a ceramic frog by the water hose in the front."

"A frog?"

"Do you want to go to my house or not?"

"Yes, please. Thank you. I really do appreciate it."

"You're welcome. And, Gabby?"

"Yeah?"

"No snooping."

"That's not fair. I seem to recall a time you snooped through my drawers when I was basically unconscious."

"That was a medical emergency. Would you have preferred I let you sleep naked while I watched?"

"Of course not," I told him. Even though now, I probably wouldn't mind it.

"I'll be home as soon as I can."

"Okay," I said weakly. "Bye." His words had hit me in my feels. I liked the way they'd sounded.

Dear Lord, I was in trouble.

◆ ◆ ◆

When I first walked through the front door of Diego's home, I cursed.

Not because it was awful. But because it was perfect.

From the colors on the walls to the tile on the floor, I could see Diego's touch. Everything in the house told me a story about the man I was getting to know. He was thoughtful. Creative. Humble.

I knew that the place had been a fixer-upper when he'd bought it. It was clear just how much work he'd put into it to make it his own. But instead of feeling like an interloper, I felt comfortable in these surroundings. And I knew it was because I was comfortable with him.

A few hours later, I'd reshowered, made myself an omelet, and watched some TV. Since there was no television in Teresa's house, except for in her bedroom, I usually streamed stuff on my laptop or phone. I forgot how nice it was to watch shows on a screen that didn't fit inside a backpack. Eventually, though, even the real housewives couldn't make me keep my eyes open. I decided I needed some caffeine.

Since Raul had told me that all the businesses on Main Street still had water, I drove over to the bakery. It was way busier than a usual weekday afternoon. Although I had wanted to drink my coffee there, I couldn't see an open table anywhere. Then I saw a hand waving at me from the back of the shop. It was Lupe the town librarian.

"Hello again," I said when I walked up to her table.

"Hi, Gabby. I saw you scouting for a seat. You're welcome to join me if you'd like."

"Definitely. Thank you."

"No problem. I don't usually like drinking alone, even if it's just a coffee."

"Same here," I told her.

We chatted for several minutes. I told her about the house improvements so far, and she told me about the latest library gossip. I was impressed by all the minor scandals going on in Sonrisa.

"Is it just me, or does it seem like a lot of people move here because they want a new start out of life?" I asked her. "I mean, that was me in a nutshell."

"It's not just you. The stories I could tell you, just about the people sitting in the bakery."

I laughed. "Remind me to never do anything to get on your bad side."

"Oh no, it's not like that. Would it make you feel better if I told you my story?"

I took another sip and settled into my chair. "I would love to hear it, but only if you're comfortable sharing."

Lupe's smile faltered. She lowered her eyes, but not before I saw the raw emotion reflected in them. I instantly regretted pushing the question.

I held up my hand. "Never mind. You don't have to do this."

She looked up, and whatever emotion had been there before on her face was now gone. "It's okay. It's good for me to talk about it, at least that's what my therapist says. Anyway, I moved here after my fiancé called off our engagement a month before the wedding. Apparently, he decided that being a husband wasn't for him."

"How so?" I asked.

"Well, for one, he didn't want to have to give up his girlfriends."

"Girlfriends? As in plural?"

She shrugged. "Yep. It was weird that I didn't see the signs, because looking back, I know there were a ton of them. But we had been dating for five years, and I just wanted to have a wedding and be a wife. It was almost like it was a box to check off, you know? It was almost like the groom could've been anyone. He just happened to be willing . . . well, after five years he was finally willing. And then he wasn't."

"Wait. When we first met, you told me that Carolina had helped you and your husband buy a house. Doesn't that mean you went through with the wedding after all?"

Lupe laughed. "God no. Samuel, that's my husband, was my fiancé's best friend."

I roared like a hyena. Here I had been worried about pushing Lupe to divulge all her secrets, and she wasn't hiding anything at all.

"So, tell me, why did you pick Sonrisa of all places?"

"I grew up in the RGV down in Texas, and I guess I kind of missed that small-town community feeling. So when I saw the job posting for a librarian here, I applied."

"What's the RGV?" I asked since I had never heard that term used before.

"Oh. It stands for the Rio Grande Valley. It's the area of Texas that sits adjacent to the Mexican border and along the Rio Grande river."

"Well, Sonrisa is definitely a small town, so I guess you moved to the perfect place," I said.

Lupe nodded excitedly. "And most importantly it's a small town filled with people who look like me and my family. It's quite something to live in a place where your heritage is the town's heritage."

I hadn't ever thought of it quite like that. Lupe was right. There were small towns all across America where I would've stood out like a sore thumb. Not just because of the color of my skin. My body, my hair, my clothes, all would've been one big flashing neon sign that screamed *outsider*. Even if Raul's family—well, my family—hadn't helped found Sonrisa, I somehow knew I still would've been accepted here.

"You're right," I told Lupe. "Although, isn't it funny that the one thing all small towns have in common is the love of gossip?"

"Definitely. The chisme around here flies fast and furious. You can't walk ten feet without someone stopping you to ask, 'Did you hear?'"

I laughed because I knew exactly what she meant. I'd been spending more and more time at Carlita's Cocina, either eating with Diego or going over the journal's recipes with Raul. And since the restaurant was one of the town's main gathering places, I had overheard story after story about people I didn't even know, and some I did. It was almost as entertaining as one of my reality TV shows.

After a few minutes, I noticed that I was doing all the talking now and Lupe was only nodding her head. She was obviously troubled about something. She bit her lip, and I knew she was debating whether to spill her guts.

"What's wrong?" I asked. "Do I have foam on my face?"

"I have to tell you something," she finally said.

"Oh-kayy."

"Carolina really has her eyes set on Mayor Paz. She is obsessed with the man."

I relaxed. "I figured. She isn't very subtle about it, is she?"

"Not in the slightest. I just wanted to make sure you knew. I'm not saying he would ever cheat on you, but Carolina could be a problem if you're not on your guard."

"Hold up," I said, raising my hand. "Diego—Mayor Paz—is not my boyfriend. We're not together. Like at all. Do people think that?"

Lupe shrugged. "Some people do. You're always together at the restaurant, and his truck is always at your house."

"Because he's working on it. And the only reason we're always at the restaurant together is because both of us get free food there. We are not dating."

"Oh, okay," Lupe said. I didn't think she believed me, though.

"And feel free to share that with your fellow librarians too." It bothered me that people thought something was going on between Diego and me. Bad high school memories I had worked hard to suppress threatened to bubble up to the surface. Memories like the time I had been in a bathroom stall and accidentally overheard a group of girls saying in one breath how they felt sorry for me because my dad had died and then in the next breath making rude comments about what I had worn to school that day.

I hated when people talked about me behind my back.

Not only that, Diego was the mayor. I'm sure he had some sort of reputation to protect.

It wasn't lost on me that once I left the bakery, I would be headed right back to his house.

Maybe I should park my car down the street?

By five that evening, the pipe still hadn't been fixed. Diego came home, and we agreed we'd have dinner there while we waited for an update. While he was in the shower, I cooked us some sirloin steaks with crispy diced potatoes and made a simple garden salad of romaine lettuce, cherry tomatoes, sliced cucumbers, and my go-to lemon vinaigrette dressing.

I was setting the table when I heard, "Damn, that smells good."

I looked up to see Diego walking into the dining room shirtless. His hair was still damp from the shower, as was his chiseled and tanned chest. Thank God he at least had his jeans on.

"Do you eat naked or something?" I joked, turning away to go into the kitchen.

"Sorry," I heard him say. "I'm used to not having anyone else here."

When I came back with the food, he'd put on a T-shirt and was decent again. It was disappointing, but I knew it was for the best.

"How about some wine?" he asked as he walked over to a wine rack on the counter.

"Sounds good. I saw you had a cabernet, so how about that one?"

Diego walked back to the table with two glasses and a bottle. "I thought I told you no snooping," he said as he poured us both some wine.

"Excuse me? The wine is right there on the counter in plain view."

He sat down across from me and raised an eyebrow. "Fine. But I still don't believe that you didn't go through my drawers or closets."

I lifted my glass and tilted it toward him. "Believe or don't believe. But I guess you'll never know for sure either way."

We ate and chatted for several minutes. Diego talked about how the contractor planned to fix the water main. I decided to tell him what I had found out about us.

"Well, I think I made a new friend today," I started.

He arched an eyebrow. "Who?"

"Lupe from the library. I don't know her last name, but that's what I'm going to call her from now on."

He cut another piece and nodded. "Her last name is Cantu, and I'm glad you made a friend. She and her husband are good people."

"Glad you approve, Mayor Paz," I quipped.

Diego didn't respond, because he was chewing. Or because he didn't have a comeback.

"Anyway," I continued. "Lupe told me something disturbing, and I'm not sure how to handle it."

"What did she say?"

"She says that people in town think we're dating." I made sure to raise my voice so he understood the importance of what I was telling him. But Diego only responded with a shrug. "Why aren't you horrified?"

"Because it's just gossip. I'm used to it. Rumors are launched any-time I'm seen with a woman. Plus, I already knew some people thought that. A few of them have actually come right out and asked me."

"Why didn't you tell me?" I asked, surprised no one else had said anything to me.

"Why would I? Like I said, it's just gossip."

"And it doesn't bother you?"

"I already said it didn't. Does it bother you?"

"Yes! It does."

Diego put down his fork and set his elbows on the table. "Why? Are you embarrassed to be seen with me? Is the idea of being with me—even though it's not true—that revolting?"

I squinted at him. "What? No, of course not." Then I quickly corrected myself. "Not that I've thought about it. I just don't like being the subject of strangers' conversations, especially when they don't know the truth and just start to assume things about me. That's all."

"You can't control everything, Gabby."

I knew that already, of course. I had my old nemesis Lana Moran to thank for that.

"I know," I explained to him. "But high school wasn't the best experience, especially after my dad died. And rumors didn't help. I just hate being the topic of other people's conversations. Especially when they have no idea what they're talking about."

Diego nodded. "I get it. And if I'm asked again, I'll make sure to deny it."

"Thank you. I appreciate that."

We ate in silence for a couple of more minutes until I decided I didn't like the silent chewing anymore. "I bet you loved high school. You were probably Mr. Popular and had all of the girls following you in the halls like little lovesick puppies."

That made him laugh. "Okay, first of all, I didn't love high school. I mean, what teenager does? And while I did have a lot of friends, I was not the most popular guy in school. That was Josh Sherman. He actually won homecoming king. The only thing I ever won in high school was first place in the science fair."

I gasped. "Diego, are you telling me that you were a nerd in high school? Oh my God, please tell me that."

"I was not a nerd. I was just smart and I liked science."

"You were a nerd."

"Whatever. And what were you? Let me guess. Goth chick? Drama queen?"

"Neither. I was just me. I kept my head down, hung out with a very small circle of friends, and was an average student. Super boring."

"I doubt that. And what about boys? Did you have your own—what did you call them—lovesick puppies?"

I scoffed. "Yeah right. I was invisible to high school boys. They would walk right past me and straight to my skinny blonde friend Hannah."

"I would've noticed you," Diego said.

"Only because I probably would've done something to make you grumpy. Trust me, I am not, nor will I ever be, the type of girl that guys like you notice voluntarily. You basically said so that first day we met, remember?"

He looked down at his plate and was quiet for a second. I really wasn't sure what he could say after that. Maybe the conversation had made him uncomfortable and he was trying to figure out how to change the subject.

"What I said that day wasn't true—it was a knee-jerk response," he finally said. "I'm the bachelor mayor. People around here are always trying to set me up. So I told Antonio what I tell anyone who wants me to go out with a woman I barely know. I say she's not my type."

I scoffed. "Yeah right. Plus, um, I also remember the words *opinionated* and *judgy* used. Do you say that about all women too?"

"Nope." He nodded before finishing his wine. "Just you."

"You're such a—" Before I could call him a name, though, he interrupted me.

"I'm kidding!" he said with a laugh. Then he cleared his throat. "You're right. I was a jerk that day, and I should've apologized to you a long time ago. I'm sorry, Gabby. I judged you way before you even walked through the restaurant's front door. That wasn't fair. I really am sorry."

His words stilled me. It took me a few seconds to digest his admission. "But why?"

Diego shrugged. "I guess I was just being protective of Raul. He had told me that you had made it very clear that you didn't want a relationship with him, and I saw that as a character flaw. It wasn't until I got to know you that I began to see things from your side and I understood where you were coming from."

The validation was unexpected, but it was still nice. "Thank you for saying that," I told him. "Apology accepted."

"Good. I'm glad." I smiled at him and refilled our glasses. But right before I could take another drink, he spoke again. "And just for the record? I was telling the truth before."

"About what?" I asked, putting my glass back on the table.

He met my eyes, and the heat behind his gaze immediately warmed me. "You are the kind of girl I notice, Gabby," he said. "I notice you all the time. I notice when you wear your hair up in that ponytail thing. I notice when your eyes get tired, because you start fidgeting with your glasses as if you're trying to focus. I notice when you talk to one of your aunts on the phone that you like to doodle on whatever paper is nearby. You're not invisible, Gabby. Trust me. I see you all the time."

All I could say was, "Okay."

I was reeling from the intensity of Diego's eyes on me and his words. Feelings swirled inside me, and I wasn't quite sure what to do with them. And just when I was starting to wonder if he was going to make some grand confession, he finished off his wine and said, "That steak was phenomenal."

"I'm glad you liked it," I said, still trying to act as if his words to me were perfectly normal.

"I can't remember. Was that another recipe from the journal?"

I laughed. "God no. I actually learned that from the chef at the last restaurant I worked at. It was one of the first things he taught me when I became his sous-chef."

"Well, it was delicious. So I guess he was a good teacher. Do you miss working for him?"

Images from the last night in Chef Dean's office came rushing back, and my stomach churned, threatening to evict the beautiful steak I'd just gobbled up.

"Are you okay?" Diego said. "You look like you're going to be sick."

I tried to smile to let him believe I was fine. Then I downed the rest of my wine in an attempt to settle my nerves.

"Yeah," I rushed after putting my glass back on the table. "I think I might have eaten too much, that's all."

"I don't believe you."

I met Diego's eyes, and I could see the concern. I knew I couldn't come up with another story fast enough. I also didn't want to lie to him.

"Um. Let's just say I didn't leave that job on very good terms. So the answer to your question is, no, I don't miss working for Chef Dean."

"Why? What did he do?"

"Diego . . ."

"Gabby. What happened?" I noticed how tightly his lips pressed together then and the sharp tick of his jaw. I couldn't handle the weight of his gaze and pretended to study my empty wineglass.

"When my mom's cancer came back, I decided to quit so I could be there for her for whatever time she had left. Chef Dean was furious—he saw it as some sort of insult since he was the one who had handpicked me for the position. After she was gone, I begged him to give me my job back. I told him I would do anything. Well, on my first night back at the restaurant, I found out that he had a very different idea of what I would be willing to do."

"Did he?"

My eyes shot up to meet his furious ones. "No. I got away before he could."

"The bruises . . . ," he whispered.

I tried to laugh off the thick tension coming at me from across the table. "Well, I'm sure I left a pretty good mark on his face, so I guess you could say it was a draw."

"That's not funny, Gabby. I can't believe your boss assaulted you. Did you at least call the police or file a complaint?"

"Diego, Chef Dean is the most influential and powerful chef in LA right now. He threatened to ruin my reputation in the industry if I said anything. It would've been my word against his, and I would've never been able to find a job at another restaurant in the city. And honestly I just didn't have another fight in me. So I did the only thing I could at the time. I took Raul up on his offer and moved here."

"It's still not right. That asshole deserves a lot more than a mark on his face."

"Definitely," I said. "But I just want to put that night in the past. I only told you because I didn't want to lie to you a second time."

He nodded. "Thank you for telling me the truth. I know that was hard for you."

"All right, buddy. That was the most intense dinner I have ever had—and that's saying something with a mother like mine. So we are even now. You told me about why you're not a doctor anymore; I told you why I'm not a sous-chef anymore. There are no more secrets between us, right?"

"Right," he said and then finished his wine. I couldn't put my finger on it, but something seemed off about him now.

We were washing dishes when Diego got a call from the head of the city's water district. Judging by his pacing back and forth and the way he kept rubbing his head, I knew the news wasn't going to make me happy.

He came back into the kitchen several minutes later. "They're saying it won't be fixed until at least tomorrow morning. They're going to work through the night, though."

"Dammit. This sucks," I said.

"It does. The water district is going to be calling everyone in the dry zone to let them know what's going on. Do you want to call Raul?"

"I just texted him while you were on the phone to warn him that it probably wasn't going to get turned on tonight. He's going to go home with Antonio after the restaurant closes—I guess he's going to sleep on his couch and then head back to the restaurant early in the morning."

"Good. And, of course, you can stay here tonight."

I shook my head furiously. "What? No. Didn't we just have a conversation about not adding fuel to the rumors about us? It's fine. I'll get a room downtown."

"Polly's B & B and the Garden Inn are in the dry zone. And I talked to Nate earlier today because he was worried the contractor was going to turn off the other main because he's fully booked for the weekend."

"Oh, okay. Then I'll just drive to Santa Fe and get a room there."

Diego put his hands on his hips and gave me a look—the look that always told me his patience was razor thin. "Don't be ridiculous. I have a guest bedroom. Why are you going to spend money you don't have?"

That bothered me. How many times had I heard the exact same thing from my mother? It made me feel like I was some irresponsible flaky teenager all over again. I stepped closer to make sure he could see that I was pissed. "Hey. Don't be worrying about what I do with my money. I appreciate the offer, but it's not necessary."

"You're being unreasonable, as always."

Heat burned the back of my neck. "And you're being bossy, as always."

"I'm being bossy because I'm trying to do you a favor, and instead of being grateful, you're being stubborn. The world's not going to end, Gabby, if you accept someone else's help. You're not proving anything to anyone by always making things harder for yourself."

"I'm not trying to be difficult. I'm just used to taking care of myself, that's all."

"How? By pushing people away who only want to make things better for you?"

"Why are you so upset?" I finally yelled.

"Because this is too hard," he yelled back, motioning to the both of us. "I can't do this anymore."

I froze. Of all the things I thought Diego was going to say, that was definitely not one of them. I was stunned.

"Are you quitting?" I asked.

He whipped his head around. "No, that's not what I meant."

"Then what are you so worked up about?" I asked.

Diego dragged his hand down his face in very obvious frustration. "I want to kiss you so bad. All the time. Actually, I want to do more than kiss you, and it's killing me because I know that's not what you want."

His words shook me to my core. I couldn't move. Or speak. I could only watch as Diego took a deep breath and stepped closer.

"There. *Now* there are no more secrets between us."

Had I heard right? Had Diego just confessed that he wanted me? I had been wrong. Every time I had convinced myself that I was reading too much into his lingering looks or arguing with me when I'd make some dumb remark about my looks, I had been completely and gloriously mistaken.

It felt amazing to know that Diego had these feelings about me. It also was fucking terrifying.

But instead of running away or shutting down like I always did when things got to be too much, I met his hard stare and made an admission of my own.

"Who said I didn't want that?"

"Don't say things you don't mean."

It was a statement. Yet it was also a challenge.

I knew that. He knew that. It was what we'd done to each other ever since we'd met. One of us pushed. The other pushed back. It was a test of wills to see who would back down first.

I wasn't about to fail. Not when the stakes were so high.

"I could say the same to you. But I'm warning you. If you're going to start this, then you better be prepared to finish it."

Diego's eyes flashed with desire. In an instant, his lips were on mine, hard and desperate. I bit his bottom lip, and he groaned again, then thrust his tongue inside my now-open mouth. His hands were all over me, squeezing and caressing whatever he touched.

"You make me crazy," he rasped after moving his mouth to one side of my neck and then the other.

"You make me even crazier." I could still smell the soap on him, and it made me drunk with lust. This man was all I wanted, and I would never be satisfied until I had him.

Diego walked me backward until I was pressed against the front door. He moved his hands to pull my shirt over my head, and I moaned with utter pleasure as his hungry mouth found my breasts. My own fingers worked quickly to find the buttons on his shirt and undo them. When his heated skin touched mine, we both gasped.

And then he pulled away.

"Why are you stopping?" I complained and tried to find his lips again, but I stopped when I saw the seriousness in his eyes.

"I just want to make sure you're sure about this," he said between panted breaths. "We still have to work together. You still want to leave."

They were both good points, and maybe if I hadn't been so lost in the pleasure of finally having Diego—even if it was for one night—I might have given in to the realistic, practical side of my brain.

But once I felt the softness of his lips and the touch of his hands on my bare skin, my brain was no longer in charge.

"I'm sure. This doesn't have to change anything."

He nodded, and then he took me by the hand and led me to his bedroom.

Chapter Twenty

"So, how long do I need to wait before filing a missing person report?"

Diego looked up from the counter he'd just installed. "What are you even talking about?" he asked with a laugh.

"Auntie Lily said she was going to text me when she left Albuquerque, and she hasn't, and my last three phone calls went straight to voice mail. So I either report her missing or strangle her when she gets here."

He shrugged as he collected his tools. "That's too bad. I was kind of hoping to meet her," he teased.

I set my phone down on the counter and folded my arms. "You think I'm joking, but I listen to at least ten different true-crime podcasts. I could totally get away with it."

That made him laugh again. "Most true-crime podcasts are about crimes that were solved. That means the murderers didn't get away with it."

"Exactly. So I would know what not to do."

Diego looked at me. "You know that's probably not something you should be proud of or admitting, right?"

I didn't answer right away and instead walked over to the kitchen table and picked up two cucumber slices from the tray of fruits and veggies that I had already seasoned with Tajín and lime juice. Auntie Lily always told me it was proper etiquette to have snacks ready for any visiting guests. But I was on the verge of tossing the tray into the garbage.

"Fine," I said after popping them both into my mouth and picking up two more. "I won't kill her," I mumbled. "But only because I really hate those orange jumpsuits."

"Good to know," he said.

I picked up the tray to store it in the fridge before I stress ate my way through the jicama and pineapple too. "I'm still furious, though," I continued after a long sigh. "She was the one who insisted on this last-minute trip. The least she could do was keep in touch."

Despite my objections, Auntie Lily had announced last night that she was going to drive to Sonrisa and make sure the renovations were on track. She still didn't trust Raul as far as she could throw him, and she didn't know Diego—other than the limited information I'd given her when I'd first arrived.

Needless to say, I had not yet told her about us sleeping together. So much for that one-time nonsense. We'd been together every night the past week. Mostly at his house since the twin bed I was sleeping on was neither big enough nor comfortable enough for Diego. And we both agreed that we would never have sex on Teresa's bed.

It was weird, but the more I was with him, the more I missed him when he wasn't around. Maybe that's why I was always hungry for him. He told me he felt the same.

Which was why Auntie Lily showing up out of the blue was going to be very, very inconvenient.

Diego walked over to me and took me into his arms. Even after a week of him touching me and holding me, it still felt surreal to be with him. But other than this new level of intimacy, not much else had changed between us. Some days it felt nice that we could still be so comfortable with each other and continue working together on the house. Other days, I couldn't help but feel that something was missing.

"Gabby, stop being so dramatic. Based on everything you've ever told me about your auntie Lily, it seems like she does what she wants when she wants. Sounds like someone I know, actually. I'm sure she made a detour or just had a late start. She will be here."

I groaned into his chest. "I know. I'm just nervous about her being here. The whole thing with Raul and the house . . . it's going to be weird."

As already evidenced by the exchange at Mom's memorial service, Auntie Lily pulled no punches when it came to dealing with people she didn't like. I remembered the time she had taken me shopping in the juniors' section at Nordstrom for a dress for my eighth-grade graduation, and the salesgirl couldn't be bothered to help me find ones to try on. In fact, whenever Auntie Lily would pull one from the rack, the sour-faced lady would say it didn't come in my size. Then, when she finally suggested we go look in the women's section, Auntie Lily ripped her a new one. I'd been mortified and proud at the same time.

So I didn't even want to imagine what she would say to Raul now that she'd had weeks to stew over the fact that he was back in our lives. I wouldn't be surprised if she'd even practiced it like a speech.

Diego kissed the top of my head. "It's going to be fine. But just to be safe, I'll get out of here before she shows up. That way you two can have some alone time and you can start to feel more comfortable. And, hey, I don't need to meet her if you don't want me to. I was just kidding."

My heart warmed at him being so considerate. But I also felt a little guilty. "Actually, I was thinking that maybe it wouldn't be the best idea for her to meet you right now. I have no idea how she's going to react to being here, and I really don't want to add to that. I'm sorry."

If he was disappointed or if I'd hurt his feelings, Diego didn't show it. Which wasn't out of character since I never knew how he felt. Especially about me. The last week had been one of the best in my life. I didn't want to tarnish it with doubts or unanswered questions. Obviously, he enjoyed kissing me and having sex with me. But we never talked about our feelings or where this thing between us was going. After all, we both knew it couldn't go much further if I was in LA.

So, the both of us kept our mouths shut when it came to talking about ourselves.

"It's fine. I promise," he said. "I'll take off. Just give me a call tomorrow and let me know when the coast is clear, and I can come back and finish up the other counters."

"You're the best," I said, wondering if that was too much, too transparent.

"I know," he said with a wink.

I guess that was my answer.

Auntie Lily arrived in Sonrisa two hours later in a hail of shopping bags.

"What's all this?" I asked as she walked through the front door.

"Samples we can use for staging the house," she said, as if she always brought me throw pillows and candles. "They had these amazing shops next to the hotel I stayed in, and I did a little shopping before driving over here."

After setting the bags down on the floor, Auntie Lily removed her sunglasses and gave the living room a once-over. "Dios mío. It's worse than I thought. I'm going to call my assistant and tell her to bring more throw pillows."

I laughed until I realized she was dead serious. "Auntie Lily, you are not going to do that, okay? Besides, the house isn't even ready to be staged yet. I still need to paint in here and the bathrooms. Not to mention, I've barely touched Teresa's bedroom."

"Who's Teresa?"

"My . . . Raul's abuela. You know the lady who died so I could sell her house?"

Lily put her hands on her hips. "See? This is why I needed to come. We need to start fast-tracking some of these last projects. There is no way you're staying here past the summer."

"And what if the house doesn't sell by then? Then what?"

"It's going to sell. I know it."

I sat down on the couch and began to look through the bags. "Hey, did you ever find out anything about the guy who was interested in buying the house as is?"

"Oh, yeah. Well, I mean I found out that Mr. Steven Chambers is a real person, so that's that. He works for some finance company in Florida. He doesn't own any other homes. And that was about it. Why? Did he call again?"

I ignored the hopefulness in her voice. Something still sounded off to me. If he lived in Florida, then why was he so interested in buying a house in this particular neighborhood?

"I know you've been looking at updated comp sales. Are there any pending right now?"

"Yeah, actually there's two pending on this street. Both, though, were sold at around the three hundred thousand mark—just like the others."

"Do you think it's strange that this street has lots of recent movement?"

Auntie Lily shrugged. "Not really. It's off a main highway, close to downtown, and these houses are some of the oldest in town. It's a prime location. Naturally buyers are going to be attracted to it."

"I guess," I said.

"What's going on? What are you thinking?"

"Nothing."

Auntie Lily moved so I would have to look her in the eye. "Are you having second thoughts about selling the house? Are you considering staying here?"

"No, of course not," I said defensively. "It's just that we are putting in a lot of work, and I want to make sure that's going to be reflected in the final price."

"Okay, that makes sense. But I promise I'm not going to let you get cheated out of what you deserve."

"I'm so glad you're on my team."

"Always."

After showing Auntie Lily the rest of the house and reviewing our checklist, we took her car in to town so she could check in to Polly's B & B. I had offered to sleep on the couch and let her take my bed, but she'd insisted on staying at a hotel so she wouldn't get in the way of Diego and his repairs.

I knew, though, that it was more about the B & B offering espressos and turndown service.

We dropped off her luggage set—yes, set—and decided to grab dinner at Luigi's. One, it was the most expensive restaurant in town, and two, it wasn't Raul's restaurant.

"Are you really going to try to avoid him while you're here?" I asked once we were seated.

"Why on earth would I need or want to see that man?" she said.

"I just thought maybe you were curious, maybe you wanted to catch up?"

"I'm not Martha. I couldn't care less about making small talk with Raul. As far as I'm concerned, the only person I need to spend time with in Sonrisa is you."

I rolled my eyes, but at the same time I understood. Auntie Lily only knew what she knew from the past. If she wasn't willing to talk to Raul and decide if he was worth getting to know as the man he was now, then there wasn't much I could do to change her mind.

Fortunately, the sore subject known as Raul was not brought up again for the rest of the night. Dinner was amazing, and the wine was even better. We laughed like we used to laugh—before everything happened with Mom. Before we felt guilty being happy.

"So tell me about this Diego? Is he good with his hands?" she asked over our shared hot fudge sundae.

I nearly choked on a spoonful of vanilla ice cream. "What did you say?"

"I asked if he was a good handyman. Is he doing what he's supposed to, or is he one of those guys who starts something but never finishes it?"

Graphic images of Diego bringing me to orgasm flooded my mind, and I nearly choked again. "Oh, he definitely gets the job done," I said, trying not to grin like the Cheshire cat.

"Good. When you told me he was the only handyman in town, I thought the worst."

"And he's the mayor."

"Who is?" Auntie Lily asked.

"Diego. The handyman. He's the town mayor."

"Why would a handyman be the mayor?"

"Because people here like him and he helps them. Oh, and get this, apparently he beat Raul in the election."

Auntie Lily polished off her glass and then clinked it against mine. "I like him already."

We stumbled out of the restaurant after eleven. Luckily we had walked there from the B & B. Still, Auntie Lily wanted to drive me back to the house.

"I can walk," I insisted.

"Absolutely not. These streets are dark. It's not safe."

"It is safe. Plus, the house is literally only two blocks away."

"How about you just come back to the hotel with me and spend the night? I'll take you back in the morning."

"Auntie Lily, you're being ridiculous. I promise you I'll be okay walking. I've done it lots of times."

"I don't like it," she said. "Just stay with me."

That's when a thought popped into my head. "Okay, how about this? I'll call for a ride."

She contorted her face in confusion. "They have Uber out here?"

"Sort of. It's more of a local service."

Ten minutes later, Diego pulled up in front of the B & B. I made sure Auntie Lily got to her room safely and then hopped into his truck.

"Hello, Uber driver," I said before leaning in to give him a long kiss.

"Mmm. You taste like a merlot," he whispered after I pulled away.

"It was Italian."

Diego laughed. "Seems like you had a nice dinner with your aunt."

I couldn't help but smile. "I did. I hadn't realized how much I had missed her. It felt good to be around family again."

"I get that. I'm glad you enjoyed your dinner and your wine. So, you called for a ride. Does that mean you're ready to go home, or are you up for taking a little detour?"

"A detour?"

Diego curved his hand around the back of my neck and pulled me closer. He gently brushed my lips with his over and over again. "How about going to my house?" he asked in between kisses.

I could blame the wine or my exceptionally good mood. But spending the night with Diego sounded like the perfect end to a perfect evening.

"Yes please," I whispered.

Chapter Twenty-One

The first question that popped into my head was whether it was still a walk of shame if you were driven to your final destination?

Because when Diego pulled his truck into my driveway the next morning and I saw Auntie Lily's car already parked on the street in front of the house, I cringed. How on earth was I going to explain that I was sleeping with the town's mayor, who also happened to be a very good friend of Raul's?

I realized when I'd woken up that my phone had died. I panicked that Auntie Lily might have been trying to call me and made Diego drive me home as fast as he could. But it was too late.

"Shit," I whispered as I watched her get out of her car.

"Do you want me to go talk to her?"

"Are you kidding me? Of course I don't want you to talk to her. Let me handle this. How about you go pick up the supplies without me, and I'll text you when it's safe to come over?"

"Good luck," he said and then kissed me on the cheek.

Quickly, I got out of the truck and headed to the front door. Although I didn't look back, I knew she was behind me. At first, I thought about making up a story that we'd had to get up early to go to the hardware store. But it was already after nine, and I was still wearing my same clothes from last night.

Then I remembered I was an adult. I didn't have to explain myself to anyone.

"Do you want some coffee?" I asked over my shoulder as I walked into the kitchen.

"No thanks," she said. "I grabbed a lovely macchiato at the hotel's coffee cart. And then I had to drink a second one to calm my nerves after thinking you must have been kidnapped by the guy who picked you up last night."

I poured water into the coffee maker and scooped grounds into the filter. As it percolated and brewed, I had no choice but to finally face her.

"I'm sorry I made you worry. My phone died, or else I would've called you as soon as I woke up this morning."

For a moment, I thought she'd give me a pass. I was wrong.

"Now I know why you didn't want to spend the night with me at the hotel," Auntie Lily said and plopped her purse onto the dining room table.

"I wasn't planning on spending the night with Diego. If I had, I would've at least taken a change of clothes . . . and my charger."

Auntie Lily's eyes widened in shock or horror. Or maybe both. "Diego? As in your handyman Diego?"

"Technically he's not my handyman . . ."

"Gabriela. Don't play coy with me. What in the world have you been doing here?"

I tried not to let my irritation bubble over. "I'm getting this house ready to sell. What's happening with Diego was unexpected, but I'm enjoying it."

"And what's going to happen after the house sells?"

"I'll move back to LA and probably never see him again."

"It's going to be that easy?"

"Why wouldn't it?"

"Because I know you, Gabby. You don't do casual sex or no strings attached. You feel everything. All you have are strings. I just don't want to see you get into a painful and tangled mess. That's all I'm saying."

I walked over to Auntie Lily and grabbed her hands. "I won't. I know what this is with Diego, and so does he. We went into this with our eyes open, and we know there's an expiration date."

"As long as you're sure," she said and hugged me.

"I am," I replied, realizing I might have been trying to convince myself more than her.

An hour later, I was showered, changed, and going over everything with Auntie Lily. I even told her about the journal. She wasn't as excited as everyone else had been.

"Why would you try to make some of the recipes?" she asked.

I shrugged. "I guess to see if I could. It felt so good to cook like that."

"Like what?"

"With purpose. I was thoughtful about every ingredient, every step. It was a thrill to challenge my cooking abilities like that—to cook something new to me but familiar and traditional at the same time. And that's what's going to make me a better chef in the future. Raul even wants us to cook one recipe together. He wants to challenge himself too."

Auntie Lily plopped onto the living room couch. "So now you're cooking together? What's next? Does he want you to stay in Sonrisa and help him run his restaurant?"

"Of course not. He just wants to learn his family's old recipes, and I want to help him."

She shook her head. "I knew this was a bad idea, Gabby. I told you not to trust the man. He's manipulating you into staying."

"I don't think that's what this is. Why must you think the worst?"

"Because when someone shows me who they are the first time, I don't need a second example to believe it. Raul Esparza is not a good man. I just don't want you to fall for his lies like I did."

I had known that Auntie Lily had strong feelings about Raul. I had chalked it up to her being hurt on my mom's behalf when he'd abandoned her. But the emotions written all over her face now were telling me a different story. One that had everything to do with a broken heart.

I was stunned. "Wait a second," I said. "Did you two date?"

Auntie Lily's face went white. She stammered for a second and then shut her mouth again. But it was too late. The cat was out of the bag.

"Auntie Lily . . . ," I pressed.

"Okay," she heaved and put her head in her hands. "We went out a couple of times. Before he dated your mom. But he was only one in a rotation of many, and eventually, I blew him off. Then he and Sandra . . . well, you know."

"How did that make you feel?" I couldn't quite get my head around the fact that Auntie Lily had dated the man she'd once called a liar. Maybe I should've been angrier on my mom's behalf. But honestly I just wanted to know the truth—even if it was going to be hard to hear.

She laughed. "I told myself I didn't care. Sandra asked me a thousand times if I was cool with it before she went out with him that first time. I told her I was."

"But you weren't?"

Lily picked up the picture of my mom I now kept on the side table next to the couch. "I was. But then one night Raul called and told me that Sandra had broken up with him. This was before she got pregnant. They were always breaking up and then getting back together. But this time he was distraught and asked me to pick him up so we could talk. So I did."

"And?"

She set the photo down and turned her head so I could only see the right side of her face. "And we had sex."

"Oh," I said after a small gasp left my lips.

"They were only broken up for a day, and Raul begged me not to tell Sandra what had happened. Obviously, I wasn't itching to confess, either, so we both kept our mouths shut."

"Did she ever find out?"

"Nope. She never knew about that night . . . or the other nights."

"Other nights?"

Lily still wouldn't look at me. "Every time they'd get into a fight, he'd come running to me. I told myself it was just sex and was convinced that that time they'd stay broken up, so it wasn't a big deal. Then Sandra would take his sorry ass back, and I'd feel horrible and swear I'd never do it again. But I did. And I honestly could never figure out why. Until Sandra told me she was pregnant."

"I don't understand."

"When she told me she was carrying you, I was devastated. Like Martha, I was upset because I knew how hard it was going to be for her, and I also knew that Raul was sure as hell not going to step up. But it was more than that. It felt like my heart shattered."

"Because you were in love with him." The realization stung my heart. I felt sorry for teenage Lily. I realized now why she reacted to Raul the way she did.

Lily shook her head furiously in denial. And then she dissolved into tears. She covered her face with her hands and let out a long guttural cry. "Yes," she sobbed. "And that's when I knew that Raul and Sandra were going to be connected forever and that I was the worst friend in the world."

After her cries died down, we sat in silence next to each other on the couch for several minutes. My heart broke for her. I could see the pain she'd been living with all these years. Not only had she lost her first love to her best friend—she'd had to grieve that loss in silence.

"Are you still in love with him?" I asked.

That's when she finally looked at me. It was as if I had just asked her to go outlet shopping. "God no," she blurted.

"Oh. I just thought, you know . . ."

Lily wiped away her tears. "I got over Raul years and years ago. What I have not gotten over is how I betrayed your mom." Her voice still creaked with pain, and I thought the tears would come back.

I reached out and grabbed her hand. Auntie Lily had punished herself enough. I knew now that you couldn't betray someone who was no longer here. Both of us had been so hung up on protecting my mom that we couldn't allow ourselves to move forward, because we felt like we didn't deserve to. Mom wasn't here to absolve us. We had to do it all on our own. "You were my mom's best friend. Whatever happened back then is in the past. You proved to her over and over again that you loved her, especially these past few months. She may never know what happened, but she knew that."

Auntie Lily hugged me. "I hope so."

"And can I say one more thing?"

She nodded.

"I know that Raul hurt you, but that's between him and you. I need to decide for myself if I want him to be a part of my life after I leave Sonrisa. And if I do, then I really need you to respect that. You don't have to like it. You don't even ever have to be in the same room with him. But I need you to let me figure this one out on my own."

She didn't say anything for a while. I was worried she might even storm out of the house.

Instead, she seemed to study me. Sat back and said, "I blinked, and suddenly you're all grown up."

"It's about time, right?" I said with a laugh.

Chapter Twenty-Two

I began cooking Sunday's dinner on Saturday.

Mole negro was the next dish I was going to attempt to make from the journal. And, this time, I was going to have a sous-chef of my own—Raul. After Auntie Lily had left to go back to Vegas, I'd spent the rest of the morning shopping for ingredients in Santa Fe—the ones I couldn't find either at the Sonrisa grocery store or in Lola's backyard. The afternoon was reserved for all the prep work and whatever I could precook. The plan was for Raul to come over on Sunday afternoon, and we'd finish the dish together and then enjoy it for dinner with Diego and Lola.

When I'd copied the recipe from the journal, I was amazed by the number of ingredients alone. Like the name suggested, this mole was going to have a dark—almost black—sauce made from dried chiles, dried fruit, nuts, assorted spices, and chocolate. The sauce would then be poured over cooked turkey legs and breasts.

It was a complex dish with rich flavors and usually involved a two-day process.

Mole is a labor of love, Raul had explained.

Maybe that's why my dad had always enjoyed my mom's. It was probably his most favorite meal in the world. But Mom would only make it for him on special occasions because she used to say it was hard work and took forever. When I moved out on my own for the first time,

I wanted to try to make it and looked up recipes online. I saw what my mom had been talking about. And there were so many different versions. Since I wanted to learn how to make the one she used to make for my dad, I finally asked for her recipe.

That's when I realized her big lie.

Her recipe was basically sauce that came from a jar. I mean, yeah, it still wasn't a quick dish because you had to keep stirring the paste while it cooked on the stove in order to get the right consistency. But it hadn't taken two days to make like this one.

I started by separating the seeds, stems, and veins from dried pasilla, ancho, and chilhuacle negro chiles. After crisping them up in a frying pan and letting them cool off, I added the chiles to a pot of boiling water to soften. As that was happening on the kitchen stove, I took the bowl of seeds out to the backyard, where I had a comal heating up on the barbecue grill. I had already warned Lola that she might want to stay inside her house for this part. Wearing a bandana over my nose and mouth, I began to toast the seeds, and soon I could smell the fumes even through the material. My eyes were watering, but I was determined to keep moving the seeds around so they would blacken, but not burn.

When I thought they were toasted enough, it was time for the next step—the one I'd had to ask Raul about because I hadn't believed Diego when he'd translated it for me.

"*Quemado* means 'burned,'" Raul had confirmed. "You're supposed to burn the seeds by lighting them with a match."

"So set them on fire?" I'd asked, still not thinking that was true.

"Yes. But they won't be on fire long. The seeds will burn themselves out."

And I whooped with laughter when they did just that.

The prep continued the next day, with Raul in charge of heating tomatoes, onions, bread, sesame seeds, raisins, almonds, walnuts, nutmeg, cloves, cinnamon, and ginger—separately—on the comal outside.

Diego was out there, too, keeping him company and handing him ingredients as needed.

Meanwhile, I stayed in the kitchen to monitor the turkey parts I had put to boil in the biggest pot I could find in Teresa's pantry.

About an hour later, it was time to start making the mole sauce. We blended the chiles, seeds, and everything else together and then added them to a little bit of hot oil in another stockpot and let them cook for twenty minutes.

"I still can't believe there are so many ingredients in this thing," Diego said after I announced it was time to add the turkey broth.

Raul nodded. "But all of those flavors are going to be layered and enhanced, so when you take that first bite, you'll be able to taste every single thing."

"Exactly," I added. "You almost have to understand chemistry to know how each ingredient pairs with another to come up with such a thoughtful and complex sauce."

I noticed Diego staring at Raul and me with a weird grin.

"What's so funny?" I asked.

"Not funny. Just interesting. You two really are a pair of food nerds."

Raul looked over at me, and we both couldn't help but laugh because it was true.

Another thirty minutes later and it was time to add the star of the sauce—Mexican chocolate.

"It smells so decadent," I said as I broke the brick into chunks and then tossed them into the pot.

"It is," Raul agreed. "But the smell is deceiving. I remember being so excited when I found a leftover chunk lying on my tía's counter. I popped it in my mouth before anyone could see and then promptly spit it out because it was so bitter. I'm surprised I still liked chocolate bars after that."

I laughed. "Ah, so you're a chocoholic?"

"I am. What about you?" he asked.

"Definitely. I could never understand why my mom didn't like it. My dad used to buy a bag of the bite-size Snickers and hide it in the garage. He'd sneak me a few pieces after dinner when my mom wasn't paying attention."

Raul laughed, and I wondered if it bothered him when I called Juan my dad. But even if it did, I knew I would never stop. I had to admit, though, that it felt good to talk to Raul like this and get to know more about his life and love of food.

He leaned over the pot and inhaled. Judging by the way he closed his eyes and smiled, I knew the sauce was going to be a hit. When he stepped back, he saw me staring at him. "It smells amazing, Gabby."

I nodded my acknowledgment of his approval and went back to stirring.

"Yeah, I never understood why Sandra didn't like chocolate either," Raul told us. "There was this guy back in the projects who used to drive through the neighborhood after school got out, and he'd sell all kinds of sweets and snacks to all of us kids. His name was William, but we called him Winchell, like the doughnut chain back in LA, because he had the best doughnuts. He even let families run a tab with him during the week, and then he'd come back around on paydays—usually Fridays—and collect. One time, I got a dozen doughnuts from him and told him to put it on my tía's tab. I was so proud when I showed up to the playground with doughnuts to share. But Sandra was the only girl who didn't take one."

"Let me guess. They were all chocolate," I said with a laugh.

Raul nodded. "They were all chocolate. So the next week, I showed up with a dozen glazed doughnuts, and I think that was the first time she ever talked to me."

"Did you like growing up in Milagro Gardens?" I wasn't sure why, but I really did want to know.

He put down the rag he'd been using to clean up and leaned against the counter. "Sure. I guess. But it's hard to want something you don't know exists, right? That neighborhood was my entire world back then. The only time we really left the projects was to go to the doctor or to go to the little shops on the other side of the freeway. And people were afraid to come into the neighborhood because of the gangs. For a long time, we couldn't even get pizza delivered to our apartments. But if you lived there, you had nothing to fear. These mean-looking gangbangers would drop everything in a second to help some abuelita with her groceries or help a little girl find her lost dog. So, yeah, I liked living there when I was a kid. But when I got older, it wasn't the same place and it was better for me to leave than to stay."

"You were a troublemaker, weren't you, Raul?" Diego teased.

"Nah. I was more like a trouble finder," he said, making us all laugh. "I never hurt nobody, of course. But, yeah, I'm sure I gave my tía lots of white hairs back in the day, God rest her soul."

"Is your tía the one who taught you how to cook?" I asked.

"No way. I didn't learn until I came to work at the restaurant. Before that, the only thing I had ever made was a peanut butter and jelly sandwich. And sometimes we didn't even have the peanut butter, so it would be jelly only." Raul watched me as I continued stirring. "What about you, Gabby? Who taught you how to cook?"

I set the spoon down on a ceramic holder and turned to face him. "Me? I mean Mom showed me how to cook simple things like fried eggs and spaghetti. But I didn't really start following recipes until I was in junior high, I think. Since both my mom and dad worked, I'd come home to an empty house after school. I used to watch the Food Network while I did my homework, and I'd see these chefs using ingredients I had never heard of, and I wanted to taste and smell everything I saw. Then I just decided one day that I was tired of eating pizza on Friday nights when my parents would go out with their friends, so I started cooking some of those dishes I had seen on TV. Of course, we didn't have some of the ingredients, and my mom refused to buy them because she said she would never use them. Looking back, I'm sure whatever I made didn't even come close to what it was supposed to taste like. But to me, they were delicious."

"Did you ever try making those recipes again when you were older and could buy the ingredients yourself?" Diego asked.

I shook my head. "No. Because I know I wouldn't really enjoy eating them anymore because I'd be too focused on what I had done wrong back then. I prefer to keep those memories untainted."

"Sounds like you were putting your spin on recipes even back then," Raul told me. "That's pretty remarkable."

Heat rushed to my cheeks, and I knew it had nothing to do with the steam rising from the pot in front of me. It wasn't that I didn't like compliments. It was just that I'd never really learned how to respond to them.

"All this talk about food is making me hungry," Diego said. I was thankful for the change in subject, and I knew it had been purposeful. "Is this thing going to be ready soon, or do you have to add like fifty more things to it before it's ready?"

"I think someone is a little hangry," I said with a laugh.

"No need to think. I definitely am."

"Fine. Can you wait—what? Like fifteen more minutes?" I said, looking over at Raul for confirmation.

"Yeah, I think fifteen minutes should do it," he replied.

"Thank God," Diego announced.

When the mole negro was finally ready, I dipped a spoon into the pot and brought it up to my face and inhaled. All the spices immediately tickled my nose, making my mouth water with anticipation. I took a small careful sip so I wouldn't burn my tongue. The rich flavor danced across my taste buds, and I closed my eyes as if to memorize the moment in my mind with every one of my senses. I was exhausted, but proud. And I could tell that Raul felt the same.

I texted Lola that dinner was ready, and she showed up five minutes later with a six-pack of my favorite beer and another six-pack of the beer I knew that Diego and Raul drank. She also brought her drink of choice—sun tea.

Raul served everyone, and then we finally began to eat.

Silence at first. And then came the "oohs" and "mmms."

The warm spices mixed in with the bitterness of the chocolate perfectly. The hint of smokiness helped to balance the richness of the sauce, allowing you to savor each bite.

"Wow." Diego was the first to speak. "You guys, this is fucking amazing."

Raul wiped his mouth with a napkin and added, "Thank you, but Gabby did most of the work."

"Thank you both. Let's just say it was a group effort," I said, enjoying the compliments but also not wanting to take all the credit. Sure, I had made small tweaks to the original recipe from Raul's great-grandfather. But I couldn't have done anything without Diego's translation and Raul's explanations. Even Lola did her part by providing a majority of the ingredients.

"You should bottle this sauce and sell it at the festival next month," Lola said, finally coming up for air after nearly finishing her bowl.

"What festival?" I asked and took another drink of my beer.

"It's called the Feast of St. Adelita, and it's always held the last weekend of July," Diego explained.

"St. Adelita? Hmm, I don't think I know her, and I've had twelve years of Catholic school."

The three of them looked at each other as if they knew the punch line to a joke and I didn't.

"She's not a real saint," Raul said. "In fact, she's not even a real person. St. Adelita is more of an embodiment of a group of women."

"I'm not following."

Lola sighed. "Ay, Raul, let me tell the story," she yelled, shaking her napkin at him. "Gabby, have you ever heard of a soldadera?"

I hadn't, but I was able to translate the word in my brain. "A female soldier?"

"Yes, but these women soldiers specifically fought in the Mexican Revolution. And when I say fought, I mean they went to battle alongside Pancho Villa and his troops. Some of them even dressed as men so they would be treated just like the other soldiers."

"Like Mulan?"

They all laughed, but Lola nodded. "Kind of. Anyway, when the revolution ended, a lot of these women were expected to go back home and just fall back into their old lives. But a lot of them found themselves ostracized either because their families questioned their virtue after fighting alongside men or it was just difficult for the women to find satisfaction in traditional roles like homemakers and mothers. So, a group of these former soldaderas decided to leave Mexico and start their own town where they could do whatever they wanted with their lives. That town was Sonrisa."

I looked over at Raul. "Wait. Does that mean Carlita was a soldadera?"

"She was," he said, beaming with pride. "There's a picture of her in her uniform on the wall of the restaurant. I guess you never noticed it before."

I hadn't because I hadn't ever bothered to look.

Lola continued. "Anyway, the festival is called the Feast of St. Adelita because it's to mark the founding of Sonrisa. *Adelita* is the nickname given to a soldadera. It's taken from a famous Mexican corrido, 'La Adelita.' Although, nowadays the name refers to any strong woman who fights for what she believes is right."

I couldn't believe that I had never heard the story behind how the town was founded. It made me proud to know that my ancestor was an honest-to-goodness soldier. It was kind of cool and very inspiring.

"I love all of this," I told them. "And I especially love that the town celebrates their female founders, like Carlita. So, tell me more about this festival and how I can be a part of it."

Raul cleared his throat. "Actually, I already have an idea about that. I think it would be great if we sell your dishes at the Carlita's Cocina booth this year—the ones you've made from the journal. It would be perfect for the festival. After all, those recipes are part of the town's history too."

I stopped drinking my beer and set the bottle on the table. I glanced over at Diego, and I could tell by his shifty eyes that he'd already known about Raul's idea. In fact, I'd be shocked if he hadn't brought it up to Raul in the first place.

"Before you say anything," he continued, "there's one other piece to this idea. I thought it would be great that we also offer the dishes as weekly specials leading up to the festival to kind of give people a sneak taste of what you'll be selling."

"You want to add my dishes to your menu?" I couldn't have hid my shock if I'd tried.

"Yes. And, like I said, it will only be until the festival, and we can feature just one dish each week so you're not having to cook twenty-four hours a day."

It was one thing to cook for the three of them. It was quite another to cook for the whole town. Especially since they would know it was me who was doing the cooking. I'd always expected that my dream to be a head chef was several years down the line. But here was an opportunity for me to take center stage. Was I ready to put myself and my cooking out there to be judged? Old familiar self-doubts began to creep up to the surface.

"I don't know—it sounds like a lot of work. Plus, I've been helping Diego around here. I don't know if he can handle things without me," I said, trying to disguise my uneasiness with my usual sarcasm.

"Funny," Diego droned and went back to eating.

But Raul wouldn't give up. "Although I'm very sure that Diego depends on your help, I think we can work out a schedule where you really only need to cook one day a week."

Part of me wanted to say yes. I was excited about more people trying my food. Another part of me wondered if I should just concentrate on doing what I had come to Sonrisa to do. It was a tempting distraction, for sure.

"Can I think about it?" I said.

"I'll pay you, of course," Raul added.

I told him I would do it.

Chapter Twenty-Three

I snapped a photo just as Diego licked one of his fingers.

"Really?" he muttered with his mouth full of food.

"What? It's for the restaurant's Instagram. I'm trying to build anticipation for the festival. We only have two weeks left, and I want to give people a sneak peek of what they'll be able to eat. Plus, it's publicity for the restaurant. It's a win-win."

Diego cleaned his hands with a napkin. "Aren't you supposed to ask someone's permission before you put their photo all over social media?"

I shrugged. "Usually. But you're a public figure. Besides, think of it as supporting a small business."

He couldn't argue with that, so he rolled his eyes instead.

As Raul had promised, my dishes were added to a special Adelita weekend menu for the restaurant. Last weekend, we'd offered the nopales salad and mole negro, and both had been a hit. This weekend was going to be the vegan sopes, with jackfruit, which Diego apparently had found finger-lickin' good. The small thick tortilla-like vessels had turned out even better than I'd expected. I was still testing out a couple of more recipes for the last weekend before the festival. Part of me wanted to try a dessert. I had never been much of a baker, but there was one recipe for a candy in the journal and another for something called a jericalla.

"Raul really needs to step up his social media game," I said as I reviewed the few posts on the restaurant's account.

"Why?" Diego said. "He always tells me that business is good."

I waved my hand at the handful of customers considered the lunch "rush." "Obviously if you're one of the three restaurants in town, you're not ever going to be hurting for customers. But that doesn't mean you shouldn't want more. And because Sonrisa is a tourist stop, social media can help attract the foodies."

"Foodies?"

"Yes, the people who live for trying new foods. And not just the tourists—food bloggers, reviewers, influencers, and even other chefs look to social media to find out what's hot and where they need to go next. I've known people who have mapped out their entire cross-country road trip based on places they want to eat."

"So how are you going to attract these foodies here?"

"With lots and lots of pictures. I'm also going to tag some of the major food bloggers in the posts so they see them. And tonight when I'm testing another recipe, I'll make a video and post that too."

I looked over at Diego and noticed how he was watching me. "What's up with the goofy smile?"

"It's not goofy. It's just a happy one."

"If sopes are all it takes to make you happy, then I'm going to make them every day so you're not always so grumpy."

He made a face at me. "See," I said. "That's what I'm talking about right there."

"I was going to say something nice to you, and now you've gone ahead and ruined the moment."

I laughed and hugged his arm. "I'm sorry. Go ahead. Say something nice about me."

Diego shook his head but then chuckled. "I was just going to say that I like seeing you so excited about something. And it's nice that you're trying to help the restaurant at the same time. That's all."

"Thank you. That was nice. Okay, you can finish your sopes now."

He took another bite and then held one up. "I still can't believe I'm eating a vegan sope."

"I told you that you wouldn't miss the meat," I said proudly. "The recipe in the journal called for just beans, but I thought that was too simple."

"Honestly, what really makes these delicious is the salsa. It's freaking tasty," he said with his mouth still full.

That got my attention. "Let me see."

I pulled Diego's plate toward myself and examined the half-eaten sope. I noticed a green sauce mixed in with the onions, cilantro, beans, queso fresco, and jackfruit. "Hey, that's the sauce I brought Raul to taste yesterday. I didn't know he was going to use it on the sopes too."

"It's fantastic," Diego said as he started eating his second one.

"Thanks. It's another recipe from the journal. I tweaked it and added a few more seasonings."

Antonio came out of the kitchen with the box of supplies I'd come to pick up since I was doing a lot of the prep work this week. I was so busy that I was taking my tacos to go. Diego had some city business to deal with, so he'd only worked at the house for a few hours in the morning and was now eating his lunch. And my sauce, apparently.

"Antonio, did you put the hot sauce I brought Raul on the plate with Diego's sopes?" I asked with a laugh.

"Sí, sí. Raul let me taste it, and it was so delicious. I wanted to see what Diego thought of it."

"Wait, so I'm the guinea pig?" Diego replied with fake offense.

"Don't you always volunteer to be the guinea pig when it comes to tasting food?"

He laughed because he knew it was true.

"Gabby, bring me a jug of that sauce next time you make it," Antonio said. "I'm going to add it as a side salsa for all of our taco plates. I bet you it would also be good on our chilaquiles and tostadas too."

"Really? Okay," I said. I was surprised by Antonio's and Diego's reactions to the simple sauce I'd made in less than an hour. Well, technically, drying the New Mexico chiles from Lola's garden in the sun had taken a few days. But once I had ground them up in my molcajete into a nice powder, the actual making of the sauce with vinegar, water, and other spices hadn't taken that long at all.

"What's it called?" Diego asked.

"The sauce? Well, in the journal, the recipe was named 'salsa picante,' but it's not really a salsa, is it?"

"*Salsa* means 'sauce' in English," he explained. "So, pedantically, it is."

"Yeah, but this isn't what I would normally refer to as a salsa. To me, a salsa has fresh-cut vegetables like tomatoes, onions, and cilantro. This is mainly a combo of spices, water, and vinegar. It's a sauce. You pour this on top of food. Salsa is for dipping your food in."

Diego scrunched up his face in thought. "I don't know. I sometimes pour Antonio's salsa over my rice."

I rolled my eyes. "Now you're just complicating everything."

"What is he complicating?"

All three of us turned to see Raul emerging from his office.

"Everything," I droned. "Always. All the time."

Antonio shook his head and laughed. "They're arguing about whether that is a salsa or a sauce," he said, pointing to the green remnants in the small plastic bowl next to Diego's plate.

"Pues, that's easy," Raul said with a shrug. "Es un hot sauce."

I slapped my hand on the counter. "Thank you! See? I win."

"Fine. Because it's so important to you, you win," Diego conceded.

With that decided, I went back to Instagram to check the accounts of my top five favorite food bloggers. Some of them were chefs; others were well-known critics. At one time, Chef Dean's page would've been up there. Now he was blocked on everything.

"Oh my God!" I yelled after a few minutes.

"Qué pasó?" Raul asked.

"What?" Diego said and got up to look over my shoulder.

I pointed to my screen. "Harry Ross is doing a tour of the Southwest!"

"I don't know who that is," Diego admitted. "Is he a singer or something?"

The rush of adrenaline coursing through my veins was too much. I opened my mouth, and it all came out in a flood of near gibberish.

"Harry Ross was the guy who wrote those TV law shows back in the nineties. You know, the ones that always focused on a group of good-looking lawyers who also acted like detectives because they would figure out the real murderer in the middle of the trial and then trap them into confessing on the witness stand. Anyway, he once said in an interview that he would've become a chef instead of a television writer but he would rather eat other people's food instead of cook for himself. That's how much he loves food. Anyway, now he also has this very popular show on Netflix where he visits restaurants all over the country and tastes dishes that are unique to that specific region. It's already going on its third or fourth season, and he even has two books out based on the show. He probably has over a million followers on Instagram because people trust him for restaurant recommendations, and he just posted his first picture from his annual summer road trip. And guess what? He's here! Well, he's here in the Southwest. Do you know what this means?"

I didn't even let any of them answer. "It means if I can get a message to him, he might make Sonrisa one of the stops on his trip! It means maybe Harry Ross might even come here to Carlita's Cocina."

"And that would be a good thing?" Raul asked.

"Yes!" I explained. "Every restaurant that Harry Ross has ever promoted has gone on to be named as a destination spot in all of the major food blogs and magazines. This could be a game changer for Carlita's Cocina and for Sonrisa."

Antonio slapped Raul on the back. "Can you imagine, Raul? Que fantástico."

Diego leaned down to kiss the side of my forehead. "If this Harry guy does come here, I know he is absolutely going to fall in love with the food and with you."

Since he was standing behind me, I couldn't see Diego's face. But I could see Raul's, and there was a big question written all over it. Of course, Diego and I hadn't announced that we were sleeping together. The only other person who knew was Auntie Lily. So I'm sure this little exchange had been a surprise to Raul, and I wondered if he would ask me about it later. In the meantime, I was more thrown off by Diego's comment and the way he'd said it. Maybe he was just trying to be sweet? Or maybe there was something else behind it? Because I wasn't quite sure how to take in what he had just said. And then, just when I thought Diego might actually be feeling something real for me, he walked back to his seat to finish eating.

After a few seconds, Raul asked, "So how are you going to get a message to this Harry Ross?"

My chest tightened with a pang of dread at the thought of what I had to do. "Let's just say I know someone who knows someone."

Later that night, I was completely exhausted from all the cooking prep I had been able to get done after coming back from the restaurant. I heaved a long sigh as I sat down in front of my laptop and opened up my email. There was one last thing I had to do before I could go to bed.

I typed in Andrew's email and began to write:

Hey, Andrew. Hope you are well and everything is going great at Sky Grill. Sorry I didn't reply to your texts after that last night. I guess I wasn't ready to go back or see everyone. I needed to get away from LA for a while, so I moved to this little town in New Mexico called Sonrisa. My biological dad owns a restaurant here, and I've been experimenting with some new dishes that I'm really proud of. In fact, that's the reason why I'm reaching out. I know I don't deserve this, but I wanted to ask a favor of you. I remember you telling me that you have a chef friend who works on Harry Ross's show as a consultant sometimes. I saw that Harry was traveling through the Southwest, and I wondered if you might be able to connect with your friend and have him send Harry the information for the restaurant here in Sonrisa. I would love for Harry to try out some of the dishes I've been working on—plus the other food here is pretty damn great and right up Harry's alley. I know he would love everything here at Carlita's Cocina. Anyway, I'm attaching a sample menu of what we have to offer and some photos. Feel free to call me, too, if you have any other questions. I would love to hear from you and catch up. Take care, Gabby.

Chapter Twenty-Four

"When in doubt, go with white."

That was what Auntie Lily always told homeowners when they were getting ready to put their houses on the market. She would tell them that bright-green walls in the living room could scare away potential buyers because if they didn't like the color, then repainting those walls would just be another thing to do after they moved in.

So, when it came time to pick a paint color for the interior of the house, I always knew it was going to be white. I'd had no idea, though, just how many shades of white existed.

"Just pick one," Diego said as we looked at the sample paint-chip cards he had laid out on the dining room table.

"I'm trying. I like the Antique White, but this Snowbound shade is also calling to me," I said.

Today was the day to paint the bedroom I had been sleeping in and what I now referred to as the sewing room.

Both Lola and Raul were going to be coming over to help as well. At first, it was only going to be Raul, but when I'd mentioned to Lola that he was going to be helping, she'd also volunteered. That had raised some suspicions, of course. I figured, though, that it wasn't my business, and if Lola wanted me to know if something was going on between them, then she would tell me.

Diego dragged his hand over his face. "You've had three days to decide, Gabby. Now you've got three minutes. I'm going to start clearing the furniture out of the bedrooms. Did you get your stuff already?"

"Uh, almost," I said, holding up one of the sample cards. "I'll go help you once I choose."

It was at least another five minutes before I made my final decision: Antique White.

I grabbed the sample and triumphantly walked out of the kitchen to go tell Diego. I stopped in my tracks, though, when I entered the bedroom. His back was to me, and at first I thought he was looking at something outside through the window. Then I realized he was staring at my mom's urn box.

"Everything okay in here?" I said after a minute or so.

Diego spun around at the sound of my voice. "Yeah. Yeah. I, uh, I was going to take down the curtain rod, but I wasn't sure where you wanted to put . . ."

I walked over to stand beside him. "I'll put her in the living room for now."

"Why don't you ever talk about her?" he asked softly.

I shrugged as I took a long breath. "I don't know. I guess I figured since no one here knew her, then nobody would be interested. Even Raul didn't know her as long as I did."

Diego grabbed my shoulders to turn me to face him and then let go. "But she was your mom. She was a part of you. You don't have to lock her memory away just because we didn't know her. Talking about her is what keeps her alive in there."

Diego pointed to my chest, and my heart leaped. This man was doing everything he could to make me rethink everything I ever thought about him and this town.

"I talk to her sometimes," I said before thinking.

He raised his eyebrow. "What do you say?"

"I'll tell her about my day or vent if something or someone made me mad. Mostly, I just tell her that I miss her and I wish she was here."

"Have you told her about me?"

Warmth spread everywhere inside me. And it was more than just slight embarrassment because I very much had talked to Mom about Diego. It was affection and fondness at realizing that Diego cared about what I thought about him.

"Maybe. Just a little."

"Why just a little?" he pressed.

"I never really talked to my mom about the men I was"—I almost said *dating* and then corrected myself—"seeing. Because as soon as I mentioned a name, then it was twenty questions, twenty pieces of advice, and twenty more questions after that."

He chuckled and glanced back at the wooden box still sitting on the windowsill. "She sounds like quite the character."

"That's the perfect way to describe her," I told him, surprised by my sudden rush of emotions. My body began trembling. It was taking everything I had to keep myself from breaking apart. I wasn't ready for Diego to see this side of me—the side that couldn't contain my grief.

So when I felt the tears threaten to spill as forcefully as Jemez Falls, I turned away and tried to leave the room. But a hand grabbed mine, and then I was in Diego's arms. Just like the day of our first shower together, he held me so I wouldn't fall.

"I'm so sorry she's not here anymore," he whispered into my hair.

"Me too," I squeaked against his chest. "I think she would've liked you, actually."

He pulled away from me, and I looked up at him. "Why is that?" he asked with a smile.

"Because you call me out on my bullshit. And because you're a doctor."

"I used to be a doctor," he corrected.

"Trust me. It wouldn't make a difference. Once my mom found something she liked about a person, even if it was wrong, you could never convince her otherwise."

Diego smiled at me and then wiped away the tears I had failed to hold back. "You know you can talk about her, right? Whenever you want. I would love to know more about her when you're ready."

I hugged him tighter. "Ugh. If you keep saying things like that, I might just forget that you used to be a very grumpy man."

"Oh, I'm still grumpy. In fact, I'm starting to get a little irritated that it's been hours since I've kissed you."

"Well, then. We can't have that, can we?" I whispered.

Diego lowered his head and brushed his lips against mine. It was a soft and gentle kiss. Not timid or unsure. I knew that it was his way of asking if it was okay . . . if I was okay.

I opened my mouth, and that was my answer.

He groaned as our tongues finally met. Our kissing became frantic, just like our hands. Diego grabbed my ass, nearly lifting me off the ground. Meanwhile, my hands slipped underneath his shirt and explored the tightness of his abdomen and hips.

"Why can't I get enough of you?" he rasped as he moved his mouth to my neck and collarbone.

I didn't know the answer because I had the same question for him. But I knew now that my need for Diego went far beyond a physical one. Only a few minutes ago, I had been afraid of falling into a hysterical abyss. Now, I was falling for a whole different reason, and it absolutely terrified me even more.

"Hello!"

Lola's greeting from the front of the house brought me back from whatever edge I had been teetering on. I looked up at Diego, and we both smiled after unclenching from one another. He knew as well as I did that we had only been minutes away from ripping each other's clothes off. Lola's timing had been impeccable.

"In the bedroom," I yelled, quickly rubbing my lipstick off Diego's lips with a shirt hanging on the bedpost.

The woman had the nerve to walk through the door with her hand over her eyes. "Do I need to give you two a few minutes to compose yourselves?"

I rolled my eyes at her, even though I knew she couldn't see it. "Behave, Lola. We're not doing anything."

"Too bad," she said with a shrug and then lowered her hand.

Diego laughed. "All right then. I'm going to go get the paint from the hardware store and pick up some groceries for dinner. I have a feeling our painting party is going to go a little late."

I handed him the sample card for Antique White and watched as he walked out of the bedroom. Then I turned my attention to my neighbor. "This is what you wear to a painting party?" I asked, motioning at her floor-length black velvet skirt and black velvet tank top.

"I have two more of these skirts and probably at least four of the same tanks. If I get paint on them, then I can just toss them in the trash. Or, depending on the splatter pattern, I might still keep them."

"You are too much, Lola," I said with a laugh.

"And you are way too tense and blocked off for a woman who gets to kiss that gorgeous man on the regular!"

I rolled my eyes. "How did you . . . ?"

"Mauve Sunset is not really his shade."

Instinctively, my hand touched my lips, and Lola nodded knowingly.

"Must you always notice every little thing?" I asked.

"I must. Now tell me why you're so knotted up? Are you two having some issues?"

I walked over to the bed and sat down. Lola took the chair next to me. "No, actually the opposite. Things are really, really good right now. And that both makes me happy and also super anxious."

"Tell me why," she said softly.

It felt foolish to even voice the thoughts running through my head. "I feel like I'm losing control," I confided to Lola. "I don't like it."

"Mijita, that's what love is." She laughed. "Losing yourself in someone else."

I held up my hand. "Whoa. Who said anything about love?"

"You did. It's written all over your face when you look at him," she said.

I touched my cheek as if to check to see if anything was on it. "No, it's not. Is it?"

Denial was trying to be my friend in that moment. I clung to it at first because part of me knew admitting the truth would sweep me off balance. Then the more I thought about all the feelings I'd been questioning over the last few weeks, the more I began to consider the possibility that I was falling in love with Diego.

Lola reached out and touched my knee. "See? Acceptance brings peace. I can already sense you relaxing."

"Well, then your signals, or whatever it is you see, are off. Because I am definitely the opposite of relaxed. I am absolutely not in love with Diego. This thing between us was only supposed to be temporary. I'm going back to LA."

She laughed her head off. "Look at you trying to think you can control your heart. We don't choose who to fall in love with or whether it fits into our plans. Love just happens. And it usually happens when we least expect it."

"You don't understand, Lola. I can't be in love with Diego, especially when I have no idea how he feels about me." I could admit that obviously Diego was attracted to me—but that had nothing to do with him seeing me as someone he could love.

"Well, judging by the way he looked at you before he left just now, I think he's definitely feeling some type of way."

"Sure, but that's today. What happens when he wakes up one day and doesn't look at me like that anymore?"

"Gabby, why must you always look for the bad—el malo? Why can't you just enjoy what you have now?"

I was surprised by Lola's words. Despite her intimidating presence and penchant for matter-of-fact analyses, was she really a hopeless romantic at heart? And did Raul have anything to do with her optimistic outlook on love?

"Why do you look so surprised?" she said, reading my mind again. Or maybe I just wore my confusion all over my face. "Yes, I've been in love. And yes, I've had my heart broken. But I would definitely do everything all over again to experience that kind of deep connection with someone."

"Who was he?" I couldn't help but ask.

At first, I didn't think she was going to answer me. But then she sighed and looked away. "His name was Richard. I met him while I was teaching in Buenos Aires. He was so handsome. Very intelligent. I think I was in love after only our second date. We dated for three months, and then he was transferred by his company back to their New York office. I was devastated, of course. But he promised to call and text and visit at least once a month. And he did, but then just six weeks after he'd left, he went radio silent. I couldn't get ahold of him on anything. I panicked. I honestly thought he had died or was in the hospital in a coma. Because those were the only two reasons in my mind that I could think of to explain why I hadn't heard from him. I never ever expected a third possibility."

I gasped. "No," I said, my heart already breaking for her.

"Yes. He was married."

"How did you find out?"

"His coworker. I went to his office in Buenos Aires, and I was hysterical, demanding for someone to tell me what had happened to him. That's when the man—I had met him before at a dinner at Richard's house—took me to a conference room and told me the truth."

"I'm so sorry, Lola. I can't even imagine how betrayed you must have felt."

"*Betrayed* doesn't even begin to describe it. I mean I had never ever wanted to get married until I met this man. He made me want kids, the house with a yard, the whole rose-colored suburban-dream package. It's still hard to believe sometimes how much I loved him."

"Did you ever hear from him again?"

"No. But I don't think I needed to. Eventually, I got over the hurt and decided to make a change. I had read about Sonrisa in some travel magazine years earlier. And the town slogan about smiles growing stuck with me. I even cut out the article and kept it in one of my journals. I figured I needed to get my smile back, so what better place to find it than in a town named Sonrisa. And that's how I ended up here."

"And you really don't regret falling in love with someone who hurt you like that?"

"How can I? It brought me here."

"But didn't it scare you that someone else had that much power over your heart?"

"Of course it was scary. But it was also thrilling at the same time. Love isn't supposed to be a power play or some game where there has to be a winner or a loser. Real love, true love, is about two people entrusting their hearts to one another so that together they can become something much more wonderful."

Instead of soothing my fears, Lola's words left me feeling anxious. Every day I was with Diego was another day I knew he was closer to taking control of my heart. And I still wasn't sure if I was ready to give that to anyone right now. It had suffered so much already.

I didn't think it could survive another loss.

Chapter Twenty-Five

The fifth time my phone rang, I knew something was going on.

Still, I didn't answer, because my hands were full. I had just taken a pan of foil ramekins out of the oven and was carrying it over to join the others on the counter. I had spent most of my Friday morning baking up several batches of jericallas, the custard dessert I'd discovered a recipe for inside the journal. Although it was similar to flan (which I still didn't like very much), it didn't have a caramel sauce. Instead, it had a burned top similar to a crème brûlée.

The first time I tried them, I thought they were fine. I knew I wanted to do something different, to make the recipe my own, and came up with the idea to make them vegan. I liked them so much better this time that I told Raul to add them to the Adelita menu for this weekend.

After I turned off the oven, I walked over to my phone, which had been charging on the table. But before I could look to see who had just called, there was a frantic knock on the front door.

"Gabby! Gabby! It's Lola, open up!"

I ran to the front door in a panic. "What's going on?" I yelled as soon as I opened the door.

"Why aren't you answering your phone?" she said and walked right past me to the dining room table. "We've all been trying to call you."

"I was in the middle of cooking. And who's *we?*" I closed the door and followed her. Lola had opened up my laptop and typed something. Then she turned the laptop toward me and pointed to the screen.

"Look!"

I wiped the sweat off my forehead and bent down to read. As soon as I saw the headline, I screamed. "Oh my God! Harry Ross was at Carlita's Cocina! When? How?"

The post on Harry's travel blog featured photos of the restaurant's sign and what must have been the dishes he'd tried during his visit: one of them was my mole negro. Based on that, I figured he must have been in sometime last weekend. Did that mean Andrew had sent the information to his friend after all? I had never received an email back, so I assumed either he'd never received it or he'd deleted it.

I fell into a chair next to the table and brought the laptop closer to me so I could read.

"He says that your mole had an 'amazing aroma and taste,'" Lola said as she pulled up a chair next to me.

"You already read it?" I asked.

"We all read it."

I raised both hands. "Again, who is *we?*"

"Me, Raul, and Antonio, who else? That's why we've been trying to call you."

"Start from the beginning," I told her. I wanted to read the post, but I knew Lola. She was going to keep interrupting me until I let her tell her story.

She nodded excitedly. "Well, I stopped by the restaurant just before noon, and right away I noticed that it was a little busier than usual. But I didn't think much of it, because it's summer and business all over town usually picks up anyway. As I was leaving, though, I noticed a couple taking pictures outside by the sign. I made some joke about the park being a better place for a photo shoot, and the guy said they wanted a picture just like the one on Instagram. Then he showed me on his phone, and there were at least ten others from different accounts. That's when he told me about the restaurant being featured on some food blog. I went back inside and told Raul, and he immediately knew which blog because you had showed it to him, and that's when we saw the article. You should've seen Raul. He was so proud of you and immediately tried calling you. And when he couldn't reach you, I told him I'd come tell you."

I was still getting used to hearing that Raul was proud of me, only because I wasn't sure how to feel about it. It was nice, of course. But it was also strange. It was a fatherly reaction, and I was still getting used to the idea of having that kind of presence in my life again.

"Well, what are you waiting for? Read it," Lola said.

I wanted to tell her she was the one keeping me from reading, but I shut my mouth and turned my attention back to the screen.

The post began with an intro paragraph recapping the towns that Harry Ross had already visited. Then he mentioned that he had heard about the town of Sonrisa from a friend and about the restaurant offering special menu items celebrating its own culinary history:

The town is gearing up for its annual founders' festival known as the Feast of St. Adelita. To celebrate, and to also get residents excited about what the restaurant will be offering at the festival, Carlita's Cocina came up with the idea to offer a special Adelita weekend menu. The limited dishes were created by guest-chef Gabby Medina based on one-hundred-year-old recipes from the restaurant's founders. When I visited, the special Adelita menu item was mole negro. I first had mole negro in Mexico some twenty years ago. Because it's a very complex dish that can feature up to thirty different ingredients, it's traditionally reserved for special celebrations, such as weddings, baptisms, and even Día de los Muertos. I can honestly say that Carlita's Cocina's mole negro turned my regular Saturday afternoon into a very special day indeed. While the turkey was moist and perfectly cooked, it was the dark, smoky, slightly bitter, and incredibly rich sauce that was the real star. Its amazing aroma and taste are the result of a wonderful layering of ingredients that serve to enrich the sauce while helping to keep its authentic flavor. It's a meal of ancient origin with a twist of modern interpretation.

It was also suggested to me to taste Carlita's carne asada tacos—a year-round menu item. I was pleasantly surprised by the tang of the meat, a true testament to a good marinade. It was perfectly paired with a tasty salsa verde that I enjoyed so much that I asked if I could buy a container of it to take with me. The town of Sonrisa and her secret hot sauce are enough to lure me back to Carlita's Cocina someday soon.

I don't think I could have floated any higher. Harry Ross had tasted my food and hadn't just liked it—he had loved it. Then Lola told me something even more amazing.

"Mijita, check Instagram. Your food is everywhere."

I grabbed my phone and opened up the app. Immediately, I searched for the name of the restaurant and there they were. Picture after picture of my mole negro, the hot sauce, even pics of empty plates with posts about how the person was so excited to try the food that they had forgotten to snap a photo.

It was so surreal to see something I'd created being shared by strangers. Even though I'd found pictures of plates I'd helped prepare as a sous-chef back at Sky Grill, no one knew it was me who had placed those perfectly symmetrical dots of cream along the rim of their plate or that I was the one who had diced up the zucchini and carrots for their salads. They didn't know my name because those weren't my dishes. They belonged to Chef Dean, and that was the only name they cared about. Which was how it was supposed to be and I had accepted that. But now, to see my name in those posts alongside those vibrant and beautiful photos, it meant so much. It was validation that I hadn't racked up all those student loans for nothing. I was good at this. All those long hours of being on my feet and putting up with people like Chef Dean had been worth it.

Of course, I knew this didn't really change my situation. Nor was it magically going to put me on the cover of magazines or win me any awards. But it was the sign I needed that those things weren't entirely out of my reach.

Lola patted my shoulder. "Raul wants to know how he can get copies of the article. He wants to buy as many issues as he can so he can hand them out at the restaurant, and he's going to frame one and put it on the history wall."

"It's not like this was in the newspaper," I said with a laugh. "It's a blog on the internet. There are no copies to buy."

"Pues, it's on the computer, so we can print it ourselves, no?"

"I guess," I said with a shrug.

"Perfect. I'm going to go back to the restaurant and tell Raul."

I was still smiling, even though I'd begun to float back down to earth. A forgotten memory weighed heavy on my heart.

When I was a freshman in high school, I'd won third place in our local grocery store's Thanksgiving recipe contest. It was for a cranberry-relish side dish that I had worked on for weeks. Fortunately, or unfortunately, the store took a picture of me holding my white ribbon and posted it at every cash register, along with the other winners. I remembered being a little disappointed that my parents didn't seem as excited as I was when I won the award. They gave me a hug and told me congratulations, but that was it, and I never brought it up again. Then, a few weeks after my dad died, his job sent over a box of the personal things he had kept on his desk. At the bottom of the box was my picture from the grocery store in a pretty gold frame. When I showed it to my mom, she said she wasn't surprised. "He was so proud of you for winning. I think he told every person he knew about it."

I had been stunned. "But he never really said anything to me. I just thought he thought it wasn't a big deal," I had said.

"Juan didn't know how to talk about his feelings. You know that. He liked to show them instead by doing things or giving gifts. He was always so proud of you, Gabby. If you remember anything about him, always remember that."

Looking back now, I knew it was true. My dad hadn't expressed himself with words. He rarely said "I love you," but I knew how he felt by the things that he did for me and with me. Like our annual trip to our city's Fourth of July celebration. It was a tradition for only him and me to go because my mom said she would rather pluck out her eyelashes than go watch a parade. Still, she would get up early with us and pack our water bottles and breakfast burritos and slather sunscreen on my face because even back then, the sun wasn't my friend. Then we'd be off with our camp chairs and little ice chest in tow to find a spot along the parade route. The city would block off one of the bigger main streets, and businesses would stay closed just for the morning. I was always so excited, and my dad would watch as I waved to every float that came by. It didn't matter that it was always the same high school bands or council people riding in convertibles. I loved every minute, as if I had never seen anything like it before, especially the grand finale—the fire department's big red engine. And if they happened to be throwing out candy or little toys, that's when my dad would get off his chair and help me catch one of the prizes. It didn't matter what it was; he always made sure I never left empty handed.

When the parade was over, we'd walk hand in hand to visit the booths set up at the end of the parade route. They had food vendors and people selling handmade items like hair bows and beaded bracelets. We always stopped at the booth selling sparklers and fun Fourth of July headbands. I would wear it later that afternoon, when we went over to a friend's house for a barbecue. And, of course, we always got ice cream cones, even if it was only ten in the morning. One year, we even both got our faces painted. My dad picked a bright-blue lightning bolt for his cheek, while I chose a colorful butterfly. When we got home, Mom said she loved them and immediately took a picture of us. I still had the picture tucked away in the keepsake box I'd made after his funeral. The box also held the charm bracelet he gave me for my twelfth birthday, a picture of us from my First Communion, and other miscellaneous photos and cards. The photo with my award ribbon that he'd kept on his desk was also there. I realized now that every item in that box was an "I love you" from my dad.

"Oh, Gabby," Lola said. "Are you okay?"

I began wiping my tears and tried to laugh it off. "Yeah, yeah. I didn't think I would get this emotional over a blog post."

Lola's raised eyebrow told me she knew I wasn't telling her the whole story. But she didn't press. Instead, she gave me a hug and told me she'd be back later with wine so we could properly celebrate.

My phone rang about half an hour after Lola had left. I thought it was Raul again trying to tell me about the article. But it wasn't him.

It was my second surprise of the day.

"Hey, Andrew," I said as soon as I answered.

"Gabby! Hi! Um, thanks for not hanging up on me."

I laughed. "Why on earth would I do that?"

"Because I wouldn't blame you if you did. I should've called sooner."

"I could've called too," I said and sat on the edge of the bed. "I know I have you to thank for Harry's post. Thank you so much."

"Congratulations," he said. "That was an amazing write-up. I'm ready to drive all night just to taste that mole. I gotta know how in the world you ended up in a small town in New Mexico?"

I sighed. "It's a long, complicated story that I'm sure you don't want to hear. How are you?"

"I'm really good. In fact, I'm pretty great. I left Sky Grill."

I nearly fell off the bed in shock. "What? I can't believe it."

"Yeah, it was time. Especially after I figured out what Chef Dean must have done to you."

I clutched the comforter in my fist. "What . . . what are you talking about?" I asked, trying not to panic. Had he been talking about me this whole time? I didn't want to imagine Chef Dean trying to spin the story so it sounded like I had done something willingly with him.

"Jessica told me. Well, kind of."

My heart fell. "Oh. Um, what did she say?"

"I was at work when I got your email. And, I know this is on me, but after you kind of dropped off the face of the earth, I wasn't exactly happy to get it after all that time. Anyway, I guess I must have said or done something in front of her, and she asked me what was wrong. I just told her that I'd gotten an email from you. So she rolls her eyes and starts making comments about how she knew Chef Dean should've never hired you back and how everyone knew that you two were sleeping together. When I told her that wasn't true, she said that she saw you running out of his office that night with your lipstick smeared and hair a mess. Jessica insisted that she probably had interrupted something. And that's when I knew what had happened, and it all made sense. I'm so sorry, Gabby."

I wiped my eyes and cleared my throat. "You have nothing to be sorry about, Andrew. You've been nothing but a friend."

He scoffed. "Some friend. You couldn't even tell me what happened."

"I didn't tell anyone . . . for a long time." I shifted in my seat. Even though I had told Diego, I wasn't ready to talk about it with Andrew. In fact, I'd resolved to push it out of my mind. What happened that night wasn't ever going to define me or limit me. I was thankful every day that I'd been able to get away before something worse happened. But if I let myself get bogged down in thoughts of "What if?" then I would never be able to get past it.

There was silence for a few seconds on the other end of the phone. "Well, after that, I knew I couldn't stay working for that asshole. I quit the next day."

"You quit!" I exclaimed. "Wow. I'm really proud of you. Chef Dean might be a great chef, but he is not someone who should be managing people. That place was toxic, and I'm so happy you got out of there."

"Me too. I only stayed as long as I did because I had no other options. But sometimes you've got to take a leap even when you don't see the bottom. Otherwise, you may never find something better."

Andrew had no idea how true his words were. It was hard to believe that only a few months ago, I had been standing on a cliff of my own, afraid to jump off because I wasn't sure where I would land. Sure, maybe it had been desperation that finally kicked me off. But once I'd stopped falling, I made myself take the next step. And look at where I was now.

"Well, you're an amazing chef," I told Andrew. "I know you'll find something soon."

"I already have," he told me with a chuckle. "I decided to go through with opening my restaurant. In fact, I already lined up the only investor left in this world who couldn't care less about Chef Dean or his threats. I'm headed to Vegas next week to look at potential sites."

I was so thrilled for Andrew. I knew how hard he had worked for this. "Congratulations! I'm so happy for you."

"Thank you. Look at us! Finally making our dreams come true."

"Yeah. Yeah. It's kind of amazing." I wanted to sound more excited. While having a well-respected chef enjoy my food had always been on my bucket list, I wouldn't exactly call it my dream.

And that's when it hit me. I wasn't sure what that was anymore.

Chapter Twenty-Six

The Feast of St. Adelita finally arrived on a warm Saturday morning in July.

It hadn't even started yet, and I was already exhausted. I'd spent the last two days precooking whatever I could. I also made dozens of batches of the hot sauce and poured them into eight-ounce glass bottles. Lupe from the library also helped me print out cute labels that read: *Sonrisa Secret Sauce.* The sauce had been in high demand ever since Harry Ross's blog post, so I knew we had to take advantage of the buzz and sell it at the Carlita's Cocina booth.

I met Raul and Antonio at the restaurant at the crack of dawn, and we loaded up all the supplies and containers into Diego's truck. It was a short walk to the park, but no way were we going to lug everything on foot. Especially since it took three trips to get everything there.

The three of us spent the next two hours setting up and then cooking. Diego was in full mayor mode, but he'd stop by in between crises to check on us and offer moral support. Of course, he volunteered to be the taste tester for whatever was ready for him to taste.

By the time the festival opened at eleven, we had a line at least fifteen people deep.

"I hope we made enough," Antonio said.

Raul clapped his hands in excitement and gave me a huge smile. "It's going to be a good day. I can already tell."

I scanned the crowd waiting for us to start taking orders, and I felt the same anxious—but happy—nerves I'd had on opening night of Sky Grill. Carlita's Cocina wasn't my restaurant. Still, people were lined up to taste my food. It was either going to be the best day ever. Or a total fail.

As far as I was concerned, there would be no in between.

Luckily for me and Raul, best day was the winner. All the dishes seemed to be a hit. Even the Sonrisa Secret Sauce was selling as fast as we could bottle up more batches.

"Wow, I can't believe how many people turned out for the festival. Is it always this packed?" I asked Raul as we fulfilled the orders Antonio was taking.

"Oh yeah," he replied. "I told you. The town looks forward to this every year. Even former residents come back just for the festival."

We worked without stopping for the next few hours. When I wasn't cooking or serving, I was chatting with customers and taking pictures with them. Lots of them even tried to get me to give them the recipes.

I'd point to Raul and tell them they had to ask him. To which he always responded, "You'll just have to wait for her cookbook."

Then I'd have to explain that he was kidding and that, no, I was not publishing a cookbook anytime soon.

When there was a lull in the line, Raul insisted I take a break to cool off.

"I'm fine. I've been drinking water, and the canopy is enough shade. I just need to sit down for a few minutes."

"Why are you so stubborn?" Raul asked, as if he didn't know. "Oh, look, there's Diego. I'm going to tell him to take you for a break."

"Raul, no. I'm sure he's busy being the mayor. I don't want to bother him."

"Diego!" he yelled out anyway.

Right away, Diego jogged over to the booth. "What do you need?"

"I need you to take Gabby away. She needs a break, and of course, she's being stubborn about it."

Diego looked at me. "Of course she's being stubborn."

"I'm not being stubborn. We're very busy and—"

"And nothing," he said and walked around the table to grab my hand. "Come on. The show is about to start."

I tried to protest, but it was two against one. I was being forced to take a break.

He led me through the crowd to the far west side of the park. The trees opened up, and we came upon a small amphitheater.

"I had no idea this was here," I said as we climbed down a few steps. Most of the concrete benches were already full of people, so I scanned the area for some open spaces. But it turned out there was no need. The front row had been cordoned off, and I noticed that a piece of white paper with *Mayor Paz* written on it was taped to one section.

Diego waved and nodded to some people in the crowd, and it felt like a million eyes were on us. Watching. Whispering. Especially since he still held my hand as we sat down.

"The concerts in the park are held here in August," he explained. "We should come."

I nodded. It was the first time he'd mentioned us doing something together since our hike that wasn't eating or working on the house. I tried not to read too much into it. But it was becoming clearer that our relationship had changed over the past couple of weeks.

Then he let go of my hand.

"I'll be right back," Diego told me.

I watched as he walked over to the amphitheater's stage and took a microphone from a man I didn't recognize.

"Good afternoon, vecinos. Welcome to the Feast of St. Adelita!"

Cheers and applause erupted from the crowd.

"I'm so excited and proud to be here with you. This is my first time officiating as mayor, and it amazes me just how much work goes into planning this event every year. But it's worth it, right?" More hoots and hollers answered him.

"Now, before we begin the show, I just want to remind you to visit as many booths as you can. We want this to be the most successful festival ever in the history of Sonrisa, okay? All right, then, it gives me great pleasure to welcome Señora Gutierrez up to the stage to introduce her folklórico group. Señora, please come up."

A petite woman with short silver curly hair walked up and took the microphone from Diego. He waved again to the crowd and then came back to his seat.

"How did I do?" he leaned over to ask.

"Great. Don't tell me you were nervous?"

He shrugged. "Emceeing the Feast of St. Adelita festival is perhaps the most important responsibility for the town mayor. I didn't want to mess it up."

I was touched by how seriously he had taken his role. I reached over and grabbed his hand. "You really were great."

Diego leaned toward me and kissed my cheek. "Thank you."

Hundreds of eyes were probably on us again. But I didn't care this time. I squeezed his hand and turned my attention to the show that was already starting.

A line of female dancers stomped onto the stage from both sides, each wearing a white peasant blouse, colorful flowy skirt, and dark boots. But perhaps the most eye-catching parts of their costumes were the cartridge belts crisscrossed against their chests in an X formation and the rifles they carried in their hands.

"Why are they wearing those ammunition belts across their chests? Seems out of place, given their colorful skirts and blouses," I said.

"They're supposed to be soldaderas, Las Adelitas," Diego explained. "They're going to dance La Revolución."

The music started, and the women danced in formation. Given that it was named La Revolución, I had expected the song to be heavy and serious. But it wasn't. And when the male dancers, dressed all in white, joined the women onstage, it seemed as if the couples were dancing at a party. Their feet tapped in perfect rhythm with the buoyant, almost festive music. Even the crowd contributed to the lively energy by clapping from their seats.

The whole show, from beginning to end, was so entertaining. I loved all the songs and the dancers' costumes. But I especially loved the fact that Diego, who had probably seen these dances several times, seemed just as excited as I was. Every once in a while, he'd lean over and explain the lyrics or the symbolism behind the dancers' props.

It was the most fun I had had in a long time.

As we walked hand in hand back to the Carlita's Cocina booth, I couldn't help thinking how happy I was. What a difference a few months had made. What a difference finding something—and someone—I was passionate about had made. It was almost too good to be true.

"How's it going?" I asked Raul after taking my spot back behind the table.

He and Antonio were packing up a box with several bottles of Sonrisa Secret Sauce. "It's going great. In fact, we just sold all these bottles to your friend."

"What friend?" I asked, thinking that except for Lola, everyone I regularly hung out with in Sonrisa was under this canopy.

"Hi, Gabby."

I turned and saw Andrew standing on the other side of the table.

"Andrew?" I asked, even though I knew that's who it was.

For some reason, my brain summoned all my nerves to attention like good little anxiety soldiers. They were alert and at the ready. But I had no reason to be nervous. Andrew was a friend.

"Sorry to show up out of the blue like this. I was going to call you this morning but thought I'd surprise you. Surprise!"

I let out a tittering laugh. "Um, well, it sure is."

That's when Diego stepped forward and held out his hand. "Welcome to Sonrisa. I'm Mayor Diego Paz."

Andrew shook it. "Good to meet you. I'm Andrew Dane. I used to work with Gabby in LA."

Diego nodded and glanced over at me. I knew he would have questions later.

"And I'm Raul Esparza," Raul said, shaking Andrew's hand next. "I'm a . . . I'm the owner and chef of Carlita's Cocina."

I couldn't help but smile at Raul calling himself a chef. He'd never used that around me before.

"I thought you were going to Vegas this weekend to look at properties?" I said after the introductions were made.

"I was. I am. I just thought I'd take a little detour to come check out the festival. When we talked earlier in the week, you made it sound like it would be fun."

"That's quite the detour," Diego said.

Andrew shrugged. "I don't mind driving."

The nervous laugh was back. "Well, it's great to see you, Andrew. And, wow, you're buying up half of our bottles of sauce too?"

"Yeah. Raul gave me a sample to try, and when he told me that you made it, well, I knew I needed to take some with me to Vegas."

"Oh, wow. Well, thank you. I'm glad you liked it."

Andrew stepped closer to the table. "So I was hoping maybe we could meet up for a drink or coffee later when you're all done here. I'd love to catch up."

I felt six eyes burning holes in my back. "Oh, I would, but we're going to be here all night. By the time we've packed up and unloaded all over again, it's going to be super late. How about tomorrow morning?"

He shook his head. "I'm going to try to get back on the road around five."

"Oh, of course. Sorry, Andrew."

"That's okay. How about right now? Could I steal you away for five minutes?" he asked.

I looked over at Raul and he said, "Go on. Diego can help me fill the rest of the containers until you get back."

Diego didn't argue, but he also didn't smile.

"Sure. But only five minutes, okay?" I said.

Andrew nodded and then picked up his box of Sonrisa Secret Sauce bottles. We walked just a few feet away to the park's fountain.

"So what's up?" I said, using the opportunity to sit down for a few minutes.

He put down the box and sat next to me on the fountain's ledge. "Truth is, I didn't just come up here to check out the festival. I also wanted to try out your food before making my decision."

I squinted up at him. I wasn't following what he was saying. "What decision?"

"I want to offer you the head sous-chef position in my new restaurant."

The loud, animated voices of the people around us turned into a low rumble. I couldn't have heard what I thought I had heard. And because of the doubting, I almost didn't want to ask him to repeat it. He did anyway. "Did you hear what I said, Gabby? I want you to come to Vegas and help me open my restaurant."

"I . . . I don't know what to say."

"I know it's a big move," he said. "But you have an aunt who lives there, right? So it's not like you'd be all by yourself. I'm meeting with a few more chefs while I'm out there, and I'm hoping to have my team in place by the end of next month. The restaurant itself isn't going to open for a while, but I want to start doing some pop-ups and guest kitchens as soon as I move there."

"You're really full steam ahead with this," I said with a laugh.

He shrugged. "I've waited years for this kind of opportunity to land in my lap. Why should I wait any longer? What do you say?"

"I . . . uh . . ." I couldn't find the words because my mind was going a mile a minute. There was so much to think about. So much to consider.

Andrew spoke since I didn't. "How about you think about it and let me know?"

I could only nod before he gave me a light hug and told me to call him soon. I watched him walk away and couldn't help but wonder if maybe it had all been a joke. But deep down I knew it was 100 percent real. Andrew knew how important it had been to me to become a sous-chef. He had always been a friend to me, and there was no reason for him to play such a dirty trick. That meant Andrew was dead serious about offering me a job at his restaurant.

And now I had to figure out if I wanted to take it.

"Gabby!"

My name being screamed behind me distracted me from having to make that decision right then and there. I turned around and saw Carolina headed straight toward me.

Great. Just what I needed.

When she was only a few feet away from me, I stood up and began walking back to the booth. "I can't really talk right now, Carolina," I said over my shoulder. "I have to get back."

"But I have the best news!" she squealed and grabbed my arm. "Mr. Chambers wants to buy the house."

I blinked. I had heard the words, but it was like my brain had put up some sort of wall of denial because I wasn't understanding.

"Did you hear me, Gabby?" Carolina continued. "You officially have a buyer for the house."

Finally, I was comprehending what she was saying. "But he hasn't even seen it yet. I thought I was going to schedule a walk-through with him in a few weeks? We're not even done with all of the repairs."

"Apparently, he wants a fixer-upper. And the best, best part is that he's willing to pay market value . . . in cash."

My eyes widened in shock. "Wow. I mean, just wow."

"I know, right?" Carolina said. "He's ready to get the ball rolling. We can probably get all the papers signed next week."

A roar of laughter made me look over at the Carlita's Cocina booth. I watched Raul and Diego, and it was obvious they had just heard something funny. They looked just as happy as I had been just a few minutes ago.

Carolina's news was what I had hoped to hear for the past three months. It was the only reason I'd come to Sonrisa in the first place. And now Andrew was offering me an opportunity to get back on track for landing a head-chef position down the line. I had been questioning whether that was still my dream, but in my heart I knew it was. I had loved every minute of testing out the recipes from the journal and making them my own. I was thrilled by how excited everyone at the festival had seemed about trying my food. Suddenly, my life seemed to be turning around.

It looked like I was finally going to get everything I had ever wanted. So why wasn't I smiling anymore?

Chapter Twenty-Seven

I could tell something was wrong.

Auntie Martha had never been the best liar. It wasn't in her nature, and it was one of the many reasons why I loved her.

So the fact that she sounded upset but wouldn't admit it told me something was off. Something very, very bad.

It was the day after the festival, and I was exhausted. But I'd made myself get up early and start unpacking all the supplies from my car. Raul, Diego, and I had taken most of the stuff and the leftovers back to the restaurant the night before and hadn't left until almost midnight. And as much as I'd wanted to go back to Diego's, we'd both agreed to go to our own houses and get some sleep before meeting up today.

But just as I was about to head over to see him, Auntie Martha called.

Two minutes into the call, I knew something was wrong.

"All right, ma'am. Spill it," I said after I heard a sniffle in the middle of her telling me a very random story about how the store had been out of her favorite brand of ice cream for weeks. "I know you're not crying over butter pecan, Auntie Martha. What is going on with you?"

I heard her take a long, rattled breath. "I have to tell you something. And you're going to hate me, and I won't be able to bear it."

My chest tightened with dread. Yes, Auntie Martha was even more dramatic than Auntie Lily. But she would never make me worry unless it was something to worry about. I doubted there was anything she could ever do to make me hate her. It didn't mean I was going to like what she had to say, though.

It was my turn to take a breath. "Just tell me."

"I'm moving. I'm leaving Milagro Gardens . . . and LA."

My heart dropped. I couldn't believe it. If there was one thing I would've bet good money on, it was the fact that Auntie Martha would never ever move out of the projects. She was a third-generation resident. She knew everyone and everyone knew her. I knew her son and daughter-in-law had wanted her to move with them to the High Desert in California. But Auntie Martha had refused Bernard and his wife time and time again. She had told them and she had told me that she was going to die in that apartment just like her mother and grandmother before her.

"Are you going to live with Bernard?" I asked, careful not to let her hear the emotion in my heart.

"Yes," she squeaked. "I'm so sorry, Gabby. I promised you that you would always have a home here, and now I'm just a liar."

"You're not a liar, Auntie Martha. And if moving to Apple Valley is what's going to be best for you, then you need to do it."

She sniffled and then blew her nose. "I know. But it's not what I want. I was only supposed to stay for a week at Bernard's while they removed some mold from my unit and four others in the same section. But it's already been three weeks, and now there's talk that I might have to move to a studio on the other side of the complex. So Bernard said if I was going to move anyway, then I should move in with him. There's a lot of us that are going to have to leave if they can't save our units. I know it's affordable housing, but it doesn't seem right."

Anger replaced my sadness. "It isn't right. You and the neighbors should get together and fight back."

She scoffed. "Yeah right. We couldn't even get enough people to sign a petition for the city to add more speed bumps on the street after that little boy was hit on his bicycle. Plus, fighting sounds expensive. And no one around here has money for lawyers."

Auntie Martha was right. The people who lived in Milagro Gardens were a tight community. They didn't trust outsiders, including lawyers, since they'd probably try to get them to do something they had never done before.

Although I had wanted to tell Auntie Martha about the offer to buy the house, I didn't know now if it was the best idea. She was already worried about me not having a place to stay in LA; I didn't want to give her false hope. The deal could still fall through.

And, if I was being totally honest with myself, I was having second thoughts about the house and whether I should take Andrew up on his offer.

I knew, though, that I needed to talk to someone. And I knew who that someone had to be.

◆ ◆ ◆

In my defense, I had gone over to Diego's house determined to tell him about both offers.

But as soon as he opened the door, his mouth was on mine and the only thing I could think about was how much I loved kissing him. And how much I loved being in his arms.

So I didn't say anything and just let myself be with him.

A few hours later, a vibrating rattle on Diego's nightstand roused us both from a deep sleep. Slowly, I opened my eyes and thought we must have slept through the night and it was the next day. I watched as Diego reached for his cell phone and brought it close to his face. He swiped the red "Ignore" button.

"What time is it?" I murmured.

"A little bit after four," he said and rolled onto his side to face me. "Are you hungry? Should we go get dinner?"

"Why do I feel like I slept for twenty-four hours?"

"You had a long day yesterday. We both did."

Diego brushed his fingers along my bare back. Then he moved closer, entwined his legs around mine, and started kissing my shoulder. I giggled a little and scooted closer to his chest.

"I like this," he whispered in my ear.

"Of course you do," I murmured. I turned onto my back and smiled up at him. "All men like sex."

"Not just the sex. I like this . . . I like us."

His words warmed my heart, and part of me wanted to ask him what he meant. But I knew there was another conversation we had to have first. And as soon as I thought about telling Diego about the house and Andrew's job offer, my pulse quickened. I didn't want him to know just how anxious I was beginning to feel.

So I said, "Me too." Then I rolled away from him. "Get dressed. I'm starving."

I got off the bed, picked up my discarded clothes, and went into his bathroom. My heart was beating so fast. I knew if I didn't calm down I'd have an anxiety attack right there. And that's when I realized that I hadn't had an attack since I'd arrived in Sonrisa.

It wasn't like I hadn't been stressed about things here. Why had they disappeared?

Whatever the reason, I just needed to get ahold of myself now.

After a few minutes, my breathing normalized. I got dressed, splashed water on my face, rinsed out my mouth because it was so dry, and then walked back into the bedroom. Diego was already dressed and sitting on the bed, tying his shoes.

I took a few steps closer. "So, before we go anywhere, there's something I have to tell you."

"Shoot," he said, still fixing his shoes.

"Carolina told me last night that her buyer wants to make an offer on the house."

He stopped what he was doing and looked up at me. "Oh. Who?"

"The same guy that she had told you about. And she said he's willing to pay cash."

"How much?"

"Three hundred thousand. So, what I expected. She said we don't even have to finish the rest of the improvements since he'll be making his own."

"Wow. I don't know what to say. So are you going to take it?"

The air between us seemed to thicken. My heart was beating so fast I could hear the blood pumping in my ears.

His phone rang a second time.

"Just answer it or they'll just keep calling."

Diego made a face, turned away from me, and answered, "Hey, what's up? Of course I didn't forget," Diego lied. "I, um, I've just got to finish up some work before I can go. I'll call you when I'm able to get away and let you know what time to be there."

Diego hung up the phone and swore.

There was only one person in town who demanded Diego's time like that. Carolina.

Familiar annoyance prickled my nerves.

I let out a long sigh. "So should I assume you're finished now with—what did you call me? Oh yeah, work?" Diego almost jumped at the sound of my voice. He turned around, and I hated how guilty he looked. I hadn't meant to sound so sarcastic. Or bothered.

"Sorry about that. It was Carolina," he told me.

"I figured."

"I totally forgot we had made plans to meet up for coffee. I promised her."

"I get it. She's your friend. You don't need to explain." I turned on my toes and walked into the living room to get my purse. I hated that the idea of Diego leaving me to go see Carolina was bothering me so much. I didn't want it to turn into a thing, so I tried to push down my irritation.

He followed me, trying to explain. "I'm sorry I lied. I just didn't know if you wanted me to tell her about us yet. I'll call her back and cancel."

"You don't have to. It's fine. Go have coffee with your friend."

Diego raised his eyebrows and went from sheepish to amused. "Wait. Are you jealous?"

I couldn't believe he had the nerve to ask me that. Even worse, I hated that it might have been true. "Jealous? Are you kidding me right now?"

He held up his hands. "Okay, okay. But why does it seem like you don't like Carolina?"

"Because I don't! And I really don't understand why you do!" I hadn't meant to yell. At least not as loud as I did. Diego's eyes grew big, and then I knew he was as pissed off as I was.

"You don't know what she's done for me," he said slowly. "I'm sorry you don't like her, but I owe her. And if that means I have coffee with her once a week, then that's how I'm going to repay her. I didn't realize that I had to get your approval to spend time with my friends. Am I going to have to call you when you're in LA and ask if I can go have lunch at Carlita's?"

"Okay, now you're just being ridiculous."

"And you're being unreasonable."

"Maybe. Or maybe I'm allowed to get a little upset at you ditching me."

"I'm not ditching you, Gabby. I'm just postponing. We can have dinner after."

In other words, he would make time for me because I was the one he could have sex with later. Not her.

"I'm busy later," I said. "So you'll just have to go to bed alone tonight."

I turned to walk away, but he moved in front of me and put out his hands. "Whoa. What's happening here? Why are you so mad about this?"

"Because I need to tell you something very important, but it's obvious I'm not a priority to you like Carolina is."

He winced as if I'd slapped him. Based on the clenching of his jaw, I knew he was trying to control his anger. "That's not fair. And you know it."

I did know it, but I couldn't take back my words. And instead of being a grown-up and apologizing, I dug in just like I always did when my mom called me out for trying to make everything her fault. "I don't know anything because I don't know what we're doing anymore."

"I guess neither do I. The only thing I know for sure is that you can't wait to sell Teresa's house. And now you're finally getting your wish. So what do you want me to say about the fact that you're going back to LA?"

"Not LA," I said.

He stilled. "What do you mean?"

I crossed my arms against my chest and stuck out my chin, as if that would dampen the hurt I'd felt when he admitted that he didn't know what we were doing together. "I got offered a sous-chef job in Vegas. That was my news."

"With that guy who came to the festival?"

"His name is Andrew, and yes. He's opening his own restaurant, and he wants me to go work for him as his sous-chef. That's why he came to the festival, to ask me in person."

Diego dragged his hand through his hair. "And you didn't bother to tell me?"

"I'm telling you now."

He paced the room, just shaking his head. "So two big things happened to you, and it didn't occur to you that I might want to know right away? Thanks for letting me know that I'm not a priority to you."

"Don't do that," I told him, my heart breaking because of his words. And just like that, old defenses were back up. I felt as if I was losing control. "Don't you dare turn this around and make me feel bad about this. I told you from day one why I came to Sonrisa. As far as I'm concerned, nothing has changed."

"Wow," Diego said, stopping in front of me. "I thought . . . well, it doesn't matter anymore what I thought. So I guess this means you're going to say yes to both?"

I told him the truth. "I haven't decided. I have a lot to think about. But it's not like I have any other real options."

"You could stay here. You could live in Teresa's house and work at Carlita's."

"That's not going to help me pay my debts, Diego."

"And what does Raul say about everything?"

"I was going to talk to him after I told you."

"I see. Well, you may say you haven't decided, but to me it sounds like you have the excuse you need to leave."

"It's not an excuse. Do you think I want to live like this? I have no home, no job, no real family. I need something more. Don't you understand?"

Part of me knew that wasn't totally true. But I didn't care, because it was how I felt in that moment.

Alone.

He nodded slowly and looked at me like he didn't know who I was. "I do understand. In fact, maybe it's the first time I really do. Sounds like you have lots of thinking to do, so I'll give you some space to do just that." Diego walked over to his front door and grabbed his car keys from a nearby table. "Lock up when you leave."

And then I really was all alone.

Chapter Twenty-Eight

The day after my fight with Diego, I tried to distract myself with the one thing I'd been putting off for months—finishing what I had started in Teresa's room.

I still couldn't quite believe how things with Diego had taken such a terrible turn last night. It was still so raw. Especially since we'd left things up in the air. So instead of moping around the house all alone, I'd called Lola and told her I was ready to finally finish packing up the master bedroom. We'd spent the last hour throwing the majority of things in garbage bags.

In the end, I was a little sad that Teresa's life had come to this.

Even though I had never met the woman, she was still my great-grandmother.

"I feel like maybe I should keep something of hers," I told Lola as we went through the shoeboxes and suitcases that had once been stacked inside her closet.

"Like what?"

I shrugged. "I don't know. A keepsake? Or some type of memento? Maybe a piece of jewelry? I even asked Raul if he wanted me to put some stuff aside for him. He told me no."

Lola didn't respond to that, so I continued flipping through old utility bills and tossing fifteen-year-old receipts in a trash bag. When one box was done, I moved on to what looked like an old typewriter case. It wasn't very heavy, so I already knew it didn't have the typewriter in it. I unclasped the handle and pushed it open. I had expected more envelopes and receipts. I hadn't expected picture frames.

As soon as I saw the top photo, I knew what I had found.

"Lola. Look." I handed her an 8 × 10 wooden frame containing a photo of a little boy.

She took it and gasped. "It's Raul. It's Teresa's little boy."

We spent the next several minutes pulling the frames and loose photos out of the case. There were at least a dozen. There were more of Raul as a baby and when he was only a few years old. But there were others too. There were pictures of Teresa and the rest of her little family—birthday parties, Christmases, and even some at the restaurant.

"She kept them all," I said. I wanted to cry for the little boy who never became my great-uncle and for the little girl who became so lost that she never had the chance to become my grandma. "I think I should give this one to Raul." I showed Lola the photo that was contained in a silver metal frame of the family posing at the restaurant's counter. "Maybe he can hang it on his history wall."

Before Lola could answer, her phone began ringing. She pulled it out of her cleavage and glanced down at it. "Oh," she said. "It's Raul."

I pointed to the picture. "Ask him."

Lola nodded and answered the phone. But then she walked out of the room, and I thought it was a little strange that she didn't just talk to him here. I continued looking through the framed photos and decided to wrap each of them in newspaper before putting them back in the box. I didn't want to risk any of them getting broken once I figured out what to do with them all.

I had just finished wrapping a photo of Teresa and her husband on their wedding day when Lola walked back into the room.

"That was a quick call," I said, grabbing another frame to wrap. "What did Raul say?"

"I didn't ask him. I think you should be the one to give it to him. I don't think he even knows about his mom's brother. You should go over there today."

I looked up at her and nodded. "I can't today, but I'll go tomorrow. I need to see him anyway so we can talk about whether he wants to finish up some of the improvements we had already started or just leave them for the buyer to deal with."

When Lola didn't answer, I continued, "I was thinking we should take the rest of her shoes and handbags to Goodwill."

"Okay."

"Oh, and remind me to get more Bubble Wrap. I only have one roll left."

"Okay."

Lola's brief answers made me look up again. That's when I noticed. Her big eyes darting in every direction but mine. Her lips pinched so tight that she seemed to be hiding something behind them.

Anxiety stirred my insides. "What is it? Did something happen to Raul?"

Lola's brown eyes widened even more. "What?"

"You look like you have something bad to tell me. So is Raul okay?"

"Yes, yes. He's fine. I promise."

"Then what is it?"

"I don't know what you mean."

I sighed and threw up my hands. "I may not be as sensitive as you when it comes to other people's thoughts and feelings, but I'm not dumb either. I don't have time to play guessing games. I can tell you want to tell me something, but also *don't* want to tell me something. So let's save us both some time and get it off your chest."

Lola's shoulders sagged in agreement. "Okay. Pero, no te enojes."

Why did people say that? Like promising not to get mad over something that was definitely going to make you mad would ever work.

"Fine, I won't get mad," I said anyway.

When Lola hesitated again, my anxiety ramped up a notch and my cynical mind conjured up all sorts of scenarios. All of them ended with the one I feared the most.

"Oh my God. Did something happen to Diego?"

Lola walked over and placed her hand on my shoulder. "Diego is fine. You're right. I do want to tell you something, but I just promised Raul that I wouldn't because he wanted to be the one to do it."

I grabbed Lola's hands. "Just tell me. You know it messes up your inner whatever when you try to hold things in. Let it out."

She groaned. "Okay, fine. Me and Raul . . . well, Raul and I . . . we're dating!"

"Okay," I replied and went back to wrapping.

"Okay? That's it?" Lola said, obviously offended.

I laughed and put my hands on my hips. "Did you want me to challenge you to a duel to defend Raul's honor or something? You're both adults. You both seem to like the same things. If you guys like spending time together, then why would I have a problem with that?"

"Because I know your relationship with Raul is complicated, but I see it growing into something you both need. And I don't want you to worry that I'm going to get in the middle of that."

"Well, thank you for saying that. But I'm perfectly okay with you two being a couple, or whatever it is you want to call it. You have my blessing, okay?"

Lola grabbed me and pulled me into a strong hug. "Thank you."

When we broke apart, she added, "But we never had this conversation, right? So act surprised when Raul brings it up."

I laughed and then promised to pretend I didn't know anything.

"Maybe we can even double date," she said. "I like it when the four of us hang out."

My heart tightened with dread. "Sure. If Diego still wants to hang out with me, that is."

"Oh no. What happened?"

I knew Lola wouldn't leave it alone unless I told her the truth. But I wasn't ready to divulge all the painful details.

"We had a big fight, and he's not really talking to me right now," I said instead. "Anyway, I'm mad at him, too, so it's fine."

"Why are you mad at him?"

As usual, Lola wasn't going to let me off the hook that easily.

"I texted him this morning to let him know I'd told Carolina I was going to accept the offer, and he texted back, 'Fine, if that's what you want. I'm going to California for a few days. I'll see you when I get back.'"

"California?"

"His parents live there."

"So why is he mad?"

"I guess because I'm selling the house? I'm not really sure. We both knew it was going to happen eventually. I moved here to sell this house. Raul hired him to make all of these improvements because I was going to sell this house. He's acting like I just sprang it on him."

Lola put her hand on my shoulder. "Because maybe he thought you had changed your mind. Can you honestly tell me that you weren't considering staying?"

"Yes. No. I don't know," I said and plopped onto the bed. "I'm not going to pretend that I haven't started to become comfortable here. And, yes, maybe it didn't seem like the worst idea in the world to stay. But if I did, then what?"

"You live here in this house. You go work with Raul at the restaurant. You be with Diego."

"That's what he said. Well, the house and the restaurant parts, anyway."

"Gabby, can't you see this is the path you're supposed to be on? Do you know how many things in the universe had to collide in order to bring you here? Why are you still fighting against that?"

"Don't tell me it's fate," I scoffed. "I don't believe in fate. I believe in making things happen myself, and I'm not going to stay in Sonrisa in the hopes that one day Diego might want a real relationship with me. I'm not going to be Carolina and wait around for something that might never happen."

I was too old for crushes or unrequited affections. I wasn't some lovesick teenager pining away for the football player who didn't even know I existed. And I deserved more than a friendship with benefits or whatever it was that Diego seemed to want from me.

"What if you're wrong, though?" Lola said. "What if Diego does feel the same way?"

"And what if he doesn't?"

"Ay, Gabby. I thought I fixed you." Lola dropped her bombshell and then proceeded to continue packing as if she hadn't.

It caught me off guard. "What's that supposed to mean."

"You still don't think you're good enough, do you?"

Even after months of Lola's abrupt statements, I still wasn't used to them and I couldn't help but flinch. "Good enough for what?"

"For Diego. For Raul. For your mother."

I stared at Lola for what seemed to be an eternity. My mind tried to process, but my heart only deflected. "I don't understand what you're saying," I told her.

"You spent most of your life believing that you had to earn your mother's love because you thought she'd made all these sacrifices just for you to be born. It was the same with Raul, right? You were scared that if you let him into your life, he would be disappointed and change his mind. Yes, there are going to be times when you are going to love someone more than they love you. It doesn't mean you don't deserve to be loved ever again."

"No. But it does mean they have the power to hurt me."

"You can't think of it as who has more power and who has less power. You'll never be happy guarding yourself from hurt. It's not possible. People you love are going to hurt you. People you love are going to leave. People you love are going to die. That's life. Teresa tried so hard to hide herself away from being hurt again that she never got to experience love again. That's the real tragedy."

I looked around the room. It was so different now from that first day. Her presence had been so strong in here because of her things. And now that the things were getting taken away, she was disappearing. Besides Raul and me, who would remember that she had ever existed? I guess that's what happens when you're too afraid to let people in, or too afraid to love and be loved. Not because you don't want it, but because you're afraid of risking your heart getting broken.

I didn't want that. I didn't want my life to be reduced to boxes of things that would either be donated or thrown in the garbage. I wanted people to remember me long after I was gone. I wanted the people I left behind to hold me in their hearts and know that they were loved by me.

Teresa might be my family, but I refused to be like her.

I decided that love was worth the risk after all.

Chapter Twenty-Nine

Diego had been gone for two days, yet it had felt more like two years.

I knew we had to talk when he got back. I wanted to apologize for being such a brat about Carolina and for not telling him sooner about the house or the job offer. He had been right about me not making him a priority. I owed him an explanation. I owed it to him to be honest about my feelings.

I'd tried to keep busy by packing up the rest of Teresa's things. I'd been able to sell most of her clothes to the vintage store I'd found over in Santa Fe. The drive had also been a good distraction. But once I was back in Sonrisa, it was hard to keep Diego out of my mind.

So of course I did the worst thing I could do. I stopped at the bakery to grab a latte.

And then I regretted my decision even more when I saw Carolina sitting at one of the tables. I had been ignoring her calls and texts about getting Raul to sign the papers to finalize the sale of the house. I wasn't even sure why.

Perhaps running into her now was the sign I needed to just get it over with.

I grabbed my latte and headed over to her table.

"Gabby! Oh my gosh, I was just about to call you again. You are a very hard-to-get-ahold-of lady."

"Yeah, sorry about that. I've just been in packing and cleaning mode. In fact, I just got back from taking the last of Teresa's stuff to a vintage store over in Santa Fe. I guess you've been trying to get ahold of me because the papers are ready to sign?"

She gave me a huge grin. "They are! In fact, I had taken them over to Raul just a little while ago, but he said I needed to have you look them over first."

Carolina opened up her tote bag and pulled out a manila folder. I took it from her but didn't open it. I was going to need something stronger than a latte to go through them.

"Thanks. I'll take a look tonight."

I was about to leave, but then remembered something. "I wanted to give Mr. Chambers a complete list of all the improvements we made and also add in the things we never got to do. There are a few he will probably want to prioritize once he moves in."

"Oh, he's not moving in," Carolina said as she gathered her things from the table.

I froze in confusion. "What do you mean he's not moving in?"

Carolina's eyes grew wide. She looked as if she'd just said something she wasn't supposed to. I actually expected her to jump up and take off. But she didn't.

She took a long sip of her iced coffee. "I guess it's not a big deal, really. It's not like you care what's going to happen as long as you get your money and get out of Sonrisa, right?"

I didn't like her tone. Or any of her words, for that matter. But my gut told me I had to behave if I wanted to know the truth. "Right," I said through my teeth.

"Well, Mr. Chambers works for the finance company that works for Neighbors.com."

"The real estate website?" I asked. I still wasn't sure why that would be a big secret.

"Yes," she confirmed, with a roll of her eyes. "Anyway, Mr. Chambers finds properties for Neighbors.com to buy. So he's not going to be the owner, and that's why he's never moving in."

"And how did they even know it was for sale if I never even listed it with them?"

"Because of me, silly. I've helped Mr. Chambers find properties before here in Sonrisa. I get a nice fat finder's fee for every house Neighbors.com buys."

"I'm confused. Why on earth is a real estate company buying houses?"

"For money? Duh."

"I'm still not following. Explain it to me like I'm a five-year-old."

Carolina blew out a long breath that fanned her bangs. "It's not that complicated. The company picks a neighborhood, buys up a couple of houses in the neighborhood at asking price. Then they buy one last house, sell that one at over the asking price, and that drives up the comp average. Now they can go back and sell those other houses at the new higher comp price. Voilà! Instant profit."

I had worked with Auntie Lily long enough to know this wasn't a usual practice. "And then who buys those more expensive homes? I'm assuming not locals."

"How would I know?" Carolina shrugged. "And why would I even care?"

An uneasy thought came to me. "Carolina, did Neighbors.com buy the other three houses on the street."

She nodded with a proud smile. "They sure did. Made myself a pretty penny off those too. I was disappointed when Raul wouldn't put Teresa's house on the market earlier this year, but now it's all going to work out for the best since I'm going to make double my usual fee once your sale is closed."

"Why is that?"

"Because your house—well, Teresa's house—is the clincher house."

"What's the clincher house?"

"It's the final house—the one that's going to clinch their profits on the other homes later."

My stomach turned. Although I knew that what Carolina, Chambers, and Neighbors.com were doing wasn't against the law, it wasn't good. Especially for Sonrisa, which had successfully retained a large percentage of its homegrown population. After a hundred years, the townspeople had managed to keep out large corporations and developers who wanted to turn small towns into the next hot tourist destination, complete with chain stores and vacation rentals. It was basically slow-motion gentrification, since locals eventually got priced out of homes and had to move out of town.

If I sold the house to Neighbors.com, would I be just as bad as the city officials pushing Auntie Martha and everyone out of Milagro Gardens?

I looked at Carolina with as much disgust as I could muster. "You're actually proud of doing this, aren't you?"

She either didn't get it or she didn't care, based on her smile back at me. "I am. And I should really thank you. With all the money I'm making, I can finally get out of this god-awful town."

I froze. "I thought you loved Sonrisa?"

Carolina cackled. "Puh-lease. The only thing I loved about this place were all the old people I thought were going to kick it soon and leave me lots of houses to sell to Mr. Chambers. But these folks are hanging on way longer than I had planned. I've been ready to move on for months now."

"What about Diego? I thought . . . I thought you wanted . . . that he wanted . . ."

"Well, obviously I had hoped for him to finally come to his senses. I really thought that when he moved here it was because he wanted to be with me. It turned out he just wanted a place to hide. From what, I don't know, but he was a mess."

"He never told you why?"

"Never. Honestly, it didn't really matter. I was happy to be his shoulder to lean on. I was the one who started referring him to my clients who needed to get their houses ready for sale. That's how he started his little handyman business. Eventually he got better, and he got successful, and I was just waiting for Diego to finally realize that we should be more than friends. Well, I'm tired of waiting, and I'm ready to go someplace new. Turns out, he really does love this town. He once told me that this town saved him, and he's not interested in anyone who can't see themselves staying here with him forever."

That explained his reaction to my job offer and me agreeing to sell the house to this Mr. Chambers. Could it be that Diego wanted me to stay because he had feelings for me after all? There was a time when I could've convinced myself that I was reading into things and there was no way that a man like Diego could want to be with me. But now? Even my usual self-doubt couldn't deny the very strong feeling that there was something special between us.

And if that was the case, was it already too late?

But it wasn't too late for Teresa's house.

"I'm sorry, Carolina. But I've changed my mind. I'm not selling to Chambers after all."

Her perfectly tweezed eyebrows arched to the sky. "Excuse me?"

"I said I'm not selling."

She jumped out of her chair and got in my face. "You can't do this. It's not even your house."

"Technically, no. But Raul has given me the power to accept or deny an offer. You just said so yourself. Everything has to go through me."

Carolina looked as if her head were about to explode. "But why? Why do you care who buys the house or any of the other houses down the street? Didn't you come here just for the money?"

"I did. And someone once told me that pride wouldn't pay my bills. But sometimes it does help me see when I need to do the right thing, instead of the easy thing."

"You are ridiculous. It's just a fucking house."

I shook my finger at her. "See. That's where you're wrong. It's not just a house. It's a piece of history. It's part of a community. It would be a shame for Sonrisa to become just another city with overpriced homes and big chain stores. You and Neighbors.com don't seem to understand that small towns like Sonrisa are becoming endangered. If we allow corporations to buy up businesses and homes here, that will displace a community of people who have lived here for generations. I may have just moved here, but I can trace my roots back to one of the founding families. Why on earth would I help destroy a town my family helped build?"

Carolina rolled her eyes. "These small towns are dying anyway. Even without Neighbors.com buying up the houses, Sonrisa can't hide from progress and development. It's inevitable. Just like everything else, you grow or you die. Do you know how many ghost towns there are in the Southwest? I'm not destroying anything. I'm saving it."

The bitterness of my laugh was unmistakable. "Right. Of course. Keep telling yourself that. You're still not getting my house."

Chapter Thirty

It was hard to believe that it had been nearly three months since I first walked into Carlita's Cocina. I had been nervous then, just like I was now. And even though tonight was for an entirely different reason, it still had to do with facing Raul.

The restaurant was already closed, so he had to unlock the door and let me in. We walked to our usual two seats at the counter, and I was surprised to see a coffee cup waiting for me.

"Is this a latte?" I asked as I sat down.

"Yes. I figured the bakery would be closed by the time you got here, and I know how you like your nightly coffee."

Usually, he would've been right. But I didn't think caffeine would help my heart palpitations tonight. "Thank you," I told him anyway.

Raul took the seat next to me, and I swiveled in my chair to face him. "So you said you needed to talk to me about the house. Are the papers ready for me to sign?"

I cleared my throat. "No, they're not. And they won't be."

He raised his eyebrows. "Did the buyer back out?"

"I did."

"Can I ask why?" he said, his expression neutral.

I told him about Carolina's agreement with Neighbors.com and how they had already worked together to buy three houses on the same street. I told him how Teresa's house was going to be the house that drove up the prices for the neighborhood, and there was a very good chance it could open the door to gentrification.

"I just couldn't bear the thought of being responsible for that, just because of money. I'm not saying it still couldn't happen, because Neighbors.com could very well just buy the next house that goes on the market. All I can do is make sure it's not Teresa's."

Raul nodded in understanding. "Wow. I can't believe something like that would ever happen in Sonrisa. I agree with your decision. And I'm sure it wasn't an easy one to make because I know it means you have to stay a little bit longer to wait for another buyer. So thank you."

I knew that my not wanting to go through with the sale wasn't going to be too big of a deal. After all, he had made it clear from the very beginning that it was going to be my decision, and he would back whatever that was. But I wasn't sure how he would take what I had to tell him next.

"Well, actually," I began. "I think it will be more than a little bit longer. If it's okay with you, I'd like to stay in the house and not sell it. I want to stay in Sonrisa."

After finding out about the real buyer for Teresa's house, I knew there was no way I could let the sale go through. And if the house didn't sell and I still couldn't afford to get a place of my own, it seemed logical to just stay where I was.

But it was more than that too. Once I realized how easy of a choice it had been to give up the money, I knew that Sonrisa had gotten a grip on me. I belonged here. I belonged with Diego.

And although it was scary to admit it, I knew I loved him.

Once I figured that out, it hit me. I knew exactly where to spread Mom's ashes.

After telling him that I was staying, a smile spread across Raul's face and seemed to reach the top of his head. But before he could speak, I continued. "I want to be clear, though. The house still belongs to you—I plan to start paying you rent as soon as I can. And hopefully that will be in a few months, when I find a job."

I knew he would argue with me about the rent, and he did exactly that. "No. Your money is no good here at the restaurant, and it's not any better at the house. Besides, we both know you don't have any income right now."

I took a breath and began to share my third piece of news. "Remember my friend Andrew who came to the festival?"

Raul nodded. "He bought about two dozen bottles of your hot sauce."

"That's right," I said, amused that's how he remembered Andrew. "Well, I didn't tell you this, but that day he offered me a job to come work for him at the restaurant he was going to open in Vegas."

"I'm confused. I thought you just said you were staying here."

"I am. That's why I called him last night to turn down the job."

It wasn't like I could work in Vegas and still live in Sonrisa too. And when I really thought about it, there was only one place that felt like home to me. Andrew, as I'd expected, was disappointed. But then he said something I hadn't expected at all.

"Andrew wants to carry Sonrisa Secret Sauce in his restaurant and is offering me a distribution contract," I told Raul. "Auntie Lily's lawyer is going to take a look before I sign anything, but I trust Andrew, and fingers crossed, this means I will be able to pay off the credit card bills and my student loans."

Raul clapped. "That's amazing. Congratulations."

"And since the original recipe belongs to Carlita's Cocina, I want you to get some money from this deal too."

"I appreciate that, Gabby. But you are the creator of the sauce that Andrew is buying. This is your deal. Not mine."

"Well, let's revisit this after the lawyer gets a look at the contract."

"Okay. But I don't think I'll be changing my mind."

"We'll see," I said with a laugh. "Now, I have something to give you. It's for your history wall."

I pulled out the framed photo from my tote bag and handed it to him.

He studied it for a few seconds, and then his eyes grew wide. "Is that . . . ?"

"It's Teresa, your abuelo, your mom, and your mom's little brother," I explained. "His name was Raul, and he died when he was just a little boy."

"Raul?" he said softly. "I'm named after him?"

I nodded my head.

"I . . . I never knew," Raul continued. "Look at my mom too. I don't think I've ever seen any photos of her as a little girl. Where did you get this?"

"I found a case of photos in Teresa's closet. Lola told me that after Teresa's son died, she basically just fell apart. She didn't want to see any painful reminders of him, so she took down all of his photos. Unfortunately, Teresa's grief also pushed away the rest of the family, according to Lola. We think that's why your mom and her never reconciled."

"And why she treated me the way she did," he said.

My heart broke hearing Raul's admission. Up until that moment, I had never heard him say one bad thing about his abuela. I couldn't imagine the pain of knowing that your mother and your grandmother didn't love you the way they should've. I never wanted him to feel like that again.

"I'm sorry," I said softly. "You know it's not your fault. This was all set in motion way before you were born."

He looked at the photo again. "I know. But it explains a lot. Thank you for telling me."

"Can I ask you something?" I said.

"Of course."

"Where's your mom now? Does she even know that Teresa died?"

Raul sighed. "I'm not sure. Last time I talked to her, she told me she was moving to Ohio or Iowa, one of those states. That was when I had called to tell her that Teresa had passed away."

"But she didn't come for the funeral?"

"No. As soon as she found out that Teresa had left the house to me and not her, she told me she would never set foot in Sonrisa again. And I haven't heard from her since. The phone number I had for her doesn't even work anymore, so I have no way of contacting her. But she has my number, and she knows I'm always at the restaurant. If she wanted to, she could call. Honestly, I don't think she ever will, and I've learned to accept that she is never going to be a part of my life. Or your life."

"Me?"

"Yes. I mean you are a part of my life, Gabby. I would never ever think I could replace Juan as your dad. It's obvious you loved him very much, and I'm sure he loved you too. Anyone who steps up to raise another man's child as his own has to be pretty damn amazing. I know that you will never see me as your father, but I hope that we can figure out how to have some sort of relationship outside of the restaurant."

The usual defensiveness that would sprout up whenever Raul talked about my dad or wanting a relationship with me was gone. In its place was a feeling of warmth and tenderness for this man I had only known for a few months but in a way I had known my entire life.

My dad had always been the buffer between my mom and me— stepping in to make sure neither of us said or did things we would regret. But when he was gone, that was gone too. After one particularly nasty fight, she yelled, "You're just like him." Of course, I thought she had meant my dad. As soon as she'd said the words, I could see she had regretted them. So much so that she had immediately started crying and apologizing.

I knew now she had meant Raul.

From his love of cooking to his hazel eyes, there were parts of me that had always been a part of him. And maybe that was why my mom was always so hard on me. Just like Teresa, she couldn't handle the reminders of what might have been. But that wasn't going to be me. I wasn't going to look at Raul anymore as the father who had abandoned me, but as the man who gave me a second chance to chase my dreams.

Raul was right. He would never be my dad. But he could be my friend.

"I would like that," I said, tears welling up in my eyes.

He smiled and then he hesitated. I knew why. So I stood up first and gave him a hug. Strong arms pulled me even tighter, and he held on to me as he began to quake with quiet sobs.

We stayed there like that for a while. And when he finally let go, I could tell he was embarrassed.

"I'm sorry. I don't usually like to cry around other people."

I shrugged. "Well, I'm a big crier. I cry at commercials, TikTok videos, a lost-dog poster. Diego calls me a chillona? Did I say that right?"

"You did." He laughed and grabbed a napkin from a nearby dispenser to wipe his eyes. When he handed one to me, too, he seemed to consider something. "Can I ask you a question?"

I nodded and blew my nose into the paper.

"Is everything okay between you and Diego? I know it's not any of my business, but when he came to tell me he was going to California for a few days, I asked him why. All he said was that he needed time to figure things out. And although he never said your name, I got the idea that it had something to do with you."

Old Gabby would've been irritated by Raul's question. But I could see the concern in his eyes, and I knew he was only asking because he cared.

I plopped back onto my seat and let out a long sigh. "We had a big fight over me selling the house and possibly moving to Vegas."

"Okay. But now you're not doing either, so why isn't he back?"

"I haven't told him yet. I think I need to have that conversation in person because there's something else I need to tell him."

"That you love him?"

My eyes must have doubled in size, because he quickly added, "It's kind of obvious. And it's obvious that the feeling is mutual."

"It is?"

"Do you feel it?"

"I don't know what you mean?"

"Look, I'm the last guy to give advice when it comes to relationships. But I've always believed that love is more than just acts or words. Real love is like a presence. Someone can say 'I love you' all they want, but if you don't feel it, then they're just words."

I nodded. "That makes sense. When I'm with him, I feel like he would do anything for me. He makes me feel beautiful and wanted . . . and I can't believe I'm having this conversation with you right now." My face burned hot from embarrassment, and I fanned myself.

"Sorry. I didn't mean to . . ."

"It's okay. And it means a lot that you asked. So the answer to your question is that I don't know if me and Diego are okay. But I hope we will be."

"I'm glad," Raul said with a nod. "He's a good man, and you deserve someone who will treat you the way you deserve to be treated. And I can really see a change in him since you two got closer. He was always a friendly guy, always kind and caring. But you could tell he carried something dark and heavy on his shoulders. I don't see that anymore. Whatever it was, I think you've helped him unload it."

"I hope so. Thank you for saying that. I'm pretty impressed with how insightful you've become. Hanging out with Lola has rubbed off on you."

As soon as I said it, I regretted it.

"She told you already, didn't she?" Raul said. He didn't sound angry, though. Or even that surprised, actually.

I shrugged. "You know her. She can't keep things bottled up inside like the rest of us."

"And what did you say?"

"I told her that if you two were happy, then I was happy for you. Are you happy?"

Raul's face immediately brightened, and I knew the answer before he even said a word. "I am. This is the first relationship I've had in years. I wasn't even looking for this. But now that I'm in it, I'm happy it found me. Lola is unlike any woman I've ever met. And she has this way of helping you see things about yourself you never really understood. Not only that, but she's trying to get me to do yoga with her, and she makes me these green juices every morning to get rid of all the junk I've eaten over the past thirty or so years."

"Oh, she's tried to get me to drink those things too. I refused. I prefer her aguas frescas."

"They're so good, right?" he agreed.

"Well, it sounds like being with Lola has been good for you. I really like her. And I promised I wouldn't say anything, so you can't tell her that I told you. Okay?"

He laughed. "I think I understand what you just said. Don't worry, it will be our secret."

As Raul continued to talk about Lola's attempts to live a healthier lifestyle, I couldn't help but think about how secrets can come in different forms and sizes. Some are so big that you hide them in a closet and try to forget they're there. Others could be tiny, silly ones you keep with a friend just so you have something to bond over. But no matter how overwhelming or insignificant they are, secrets always find a way to come out.

So, sometimes, it's just better if you're the one who sets them free.

Chapter Thirty-One

Auntie Martha, Auntie Lily, and I arrived at Jemez Falls around ten in the morning on Saturday.

I wasn't quite sure what to do once we got to the spot I had in mind. I'd figured it would come to me once we were there.

I was wrong.

Instead, I held the box containing my mom's ashes and just stared at the roaring water in front of us.

"Should we say something?" Auntie Martha asked after several minutes. "Or I can play some music on my phone."

"That's a good idea," Auntie Lily said. "But let's use my phone. Your speakers are horrible."

Behind me, the instrumental beginnings of "Amazing Grace" began to play.

"Not that," I finally said. "Play something Mom liked."

After a few seconds, "Don't You (Forget about Me)" by Simple Minds filled the air around us. I couldn't help but smile. It was perfect.

"Do you know why she didn't want to be buried?" I asked, still watching the forceful streams falling off the edge of the rocks.

"Not really," Auntie Martha said.

"No, I never asked," Auntie Lily admitted.

"Because of my dad. She wasn't prepared when he died, obviously. They had never talked about his final wishes—there was no burial plot, nothing. She says she barely remembered meeting with someone from the mortuary to pick out the casket and the flowers, or even his headstone. Anyway, we visited his grave once, on Father's Day. She could barely bring herself to get out of the car. After that, she refused to go. She said she hated the fact she wasn't more thoughtful about it all. She felt guilty because she'd hated every minute of it and now my poor dad would be stuck with her choices for all of eternity."

"Oh, Sandra," Auntie Lily whispered.

"Yeah. So that's why she was so determined to plan out everything for herself. But she told me she never wanted me to feel pressured or feel guilty about not visiting her at a cemetery. That's why she chose this." I looked down at the wooden box in my hands.

"Well, I think this is a beautiful place," Auntie Lily said. "Sandra would have loved it here."

I turned to look at her. "Do you really think so? I mean, the first time I came here, I just felt so much peace and light. But you know, Mom was not much of a hiker. She probably would've complained the whole walk up here."

Auntie Lily wiped her eyes. "Probably. But once she saw this view, then she would've forgotten all about the journey to get here."

Satisfied I had made the right choice, I turned back to look at the falls. "Okay, Mom. I didn't really have anything prepared to say. I hope you like this place, and I plan to come visit you often, okay? I miss you. I love you."

"We love you, Sandra," Auntie Martha cried out.

Auntie Lily came up beside me and put her arm around my shoulders. I looked over at her through the blur of my unshed tears, and she nodded. Slowly, I opened the box and untied the small bag inside. I stepped out a little farther onto the rocks and then turned the bag upside down, releasing my mom's ashes into the water below.

She led me away and back to the large boulder she had been sitting on. I sat with Auntie Lily and Auntie Martha in silence. I closed my eyes and raised my face to the sun. The rays warmed my skin, and for a few seconds, I felt at peace.

And then the emotions came roaring back, and I jumped up from the rock as if the feelings had bitten me like a snake.

"What are you feeling, Gabby?" Auntie Martha asked.

"Guilt," I admitted. And then I burst into tears. "It's not fair that we get to move on with our lives and she doesn't. It's not fair that she can't be here to see me finally do something she can be proud of. She's never going to grow old or have grandchildren. I just feel so guilty and sad that she's going to miss out on so much. It's not fair."

Both of them were crying with me and nodding their heads. "She always wanted us to take a trip to Napa Valley, but we never did," Auntie Lily said between sniffles. "The other day I saw a commercial for this beautiful inn and started looking at my calendar to see when I could go. But then I felt awful for even thinking about it. How can I go there without her?"

Auntie Martha leaned her head against Auntie Lily's shoulder. "We were in the middle of reading the latest thriller from our favorite author when she passed. I still haven't finished reading it. I can't bring myself to even pick it up because I don't feel like I should get to know who the killer is if she can't."

"How are we supposed to go on like nothing happened?" I asked.

"I don't think that's really what we do," Auntie Lily said. "We can't. Losing Sandra has changed us forever. Of course something happened."

"Then how do we go on?"

"We just do," she said after a long sigh. "All right, all right. That's enough crying. We've cried enough this year, I think."

"Ain't that the truth," Auntie Martha said and stood up. "People are going to be arriving soon at the house. It wouldn't be right if their hostess was late to her own party. Are you ready, Gabby?"

I knew Auntie Martha was asking if I was ready to go back to the house. But she could've also been asking if I was ready to go on.

Yes.

Yes.

And even though I knew Mom wasn't going to be at my side for whatever came next, something told me that I would be okay. Because she would be here at Jemez Falls and she would be in my heart.

Chapter Thirty-Two

"Here's to you, Gabby."

Raul clinked his can of Coke against my beer bottle. We both smiled, and I wondered if he was thinking what I was—how so much had changed between us.

I scanned the backyard and looked upon the faces of those who had helped me survive one of the toughest times in my life. Auntie Lily, Auntie Martha, and Lola were all here to celebrate. I had also invited Antonio, Lupe from the library, and a handful of other neighbors I'd gotten to know from the restaurant. It was a combo housewarming and congratulations-on-my-partnership-with-Andrew party. I had wanted the party to be for both Raul and me, but he declined. He hated the spotlight and being fussed over. But nobody could stop him from basking in my accomplishment.

There was only one face missing.

I glanced down at my watch and tried not to worry that Diego still wasn't here. He'd returned yesterday and had sent a text only to let me know he was home. I had texted him back and asked if he could come to the house at 12:30 p.m. so I could show him something. In a way, this was also a surprise party for Diego to let him know that I was staying and to finally tell him how I felt. And if it went badly, then, hey, there was an ice chest full of beer to help me get through it, along with some of the most important people in my life.

I channeled Mom and went into hostess mode to distract myself from checking my watch every five seconds. I went inside to grab three large plastic bowls and then set them up side by side on the folding table next to the large container of chips that Antonio had brought from the restaurant. I had just finished filling up the last bowl when I happened to look up and see Diego walking through the back door onto the patio.

My stomach fluttered as I noticed how his jeans and charcoal-gray T-shirt fit his body perfectly. He looked so good that my knees and resolve to confess my feelings began shaking.

"Diego!" Raul and Antonio announced.

He waved at them but looked utterly confused. Then his eyes fell on me, and he raised his eyebrows in a question.

I took a deep breath, straightened my shoulders, and walked over to him.

"Hey," I said, barely able to get the one word out because of my nerves.

He nodded back. "Hey. What's going on?"

I tried to smile. "It's a party. We're celebrating."

His face instantly fell. "Raul signed the papers to sell the house?"

"No. We're celebrating something else." I grabbed his hand. "Come with me."

I led him through the house—the house he had worked on for the last three months. Gone were the stained Formica countertops, avocado-green linoleum kitchen floor, eighties wallpaper, shag carpeting, and decades' worth of clutter. Like me, the house had undergone a transformation. And I wanted to show him the biggest change of all.

For both of us.

We entered what used to be Teresa's bedroom. It was basically empty now.

"Raul and Lola helped me take apart the bed and huge dresser," I explained. "But I need a handyman to replace the rug with tile and paint the walls. Plus I'd like to take off the doors to the closet, and that whole master bathroom is going to need a lot of work."

"I don't understand. I thought you said the house wasn't sold yet."

"Oh it's not. But it is getting a new permanent resident."

He looked at me then. "Who?"

"Me. This is going to be my bedroom because I'm staying in Sonrisa."

I had thought—no, I had hoped—he would've been happy to hear my news. Instead, he looked so serious and concerned. My anxiety made my heart rate launch into the sky.

"What about Andrew and Vegas?" he asked.

I shrugged. "I turned down the job offer."

"So you're not leaving?"

"Nope. I guess you're stuck with me." My self-deprecating attempt at humor was my being desperate to change the tone of our conversation. I was starting to second-guess if this was the right time for this discussion.

He nodded and just continued to stare at me.

"Maybe this was a bad idea," I said with as much conviction as I could muster. "You don't have to help me with the room if you don't want to. Are you hungry? There's lots of food." I didn't want him to see that I was on the verge of crumbling.

Then he finally spoke. "I just want to ask you one question," he said roughly. "Just one question and then you can go back to your party."

"What if I don't want to answer it?" I replied, half-joking, half-serious.

"Please, Gabby . . ." The softness of Diego's voice made me hold my breath. I put my hand over my heart in a foolish attempt to stop the pounding. I had never seen him like this before. It scared me a little. What if I was wrong about his feelings for me? What if he was actually upset that I wasn't leaving? I began to rethink everything I had wanted to say to him. Maybe it would be better if I told him that even though I was staying, that didn't need to change things between us?

Pretending that I didn't care was a game I was used to playing. The old Gabby would've tried to laugh off the tension or escape the entire situation. It was easier to turn and run than face the hard feelings you knew were coming. The old Gabby had been just like Teresa.

I looked around the empty room, and it hit me that I hadn't just cleaned out the physical space; I had also wiped away the heaviness that had existed here for so many years. I'd laughed when Lola had insisted on saging the room twice. Maybe it had worked?

The old Gabby, like Teresa, didn't live here anymore.

So, I made myself stand there in front of Diego, and I told myself that I would answer whatever question he had. And then I would live with it.

"Okay, Diego. Ask me what you need to ask me."

He looked at the ground and shoved his hands into the pockets of his jeans. He took them out again and then folded them across his chest. He looked up finally, and I couldn't decipher his expression. Diego wasn't smiling, but he wasn't frowning either.

And just when I thought I would pass away from the suspense, he met my eyes and said, "Do you . . . do you love me?" He whispered the last four words, and I wasn't sure if I had heard what I thought I had. He must have seen the confusion in my eyes, because he grabbed my hands and held them tightly between his. "I asked if you love me," he said, this time a little bit louder and clearer.

My resolve came crashing down, and the tears started to come. Even though I was the one who was going to tell him how I felt, I couldn't get the words out. I dropped my head—shaking it from side to side—desperately hoping to fling the drops from my face before he saw them. He still held my hands. "Gabby, just tell me, just say the words."

I refused to look up, instead looking down at where my tears were now splashing onto my shoes. I thought I had been ready to tell him how I felt. Now I was panicking at how exposed and vulnerable I would be if I admitted how I felt about him.

So much for my pledge to risk it all for love.

"I can't," I whispered. "I can't."

He let go of my hands and pulled my face up to look at him. His anguished eyes searched mine. "Why can't you answer the question? Because you don't feel it, because you don't love me?"

"Because it scares me," I finally cried out. *Terrified* was more like it.

His eyes softened. "Then I'll say it."

I inhaled a sharp breath. His face was only inches from mine now. "I love you, Gabby. I love you. I love you," he whispered and then put his lips on mine. At first, I did nothing. The shock of his words left me frozen. But his kiss grew deeper, and when his tongue gently pressed at my lips, I finally began to melt. My mouth opened, and I allowed him to engulf me.

Seconds or minutes later—I couldn't tell—but when we both had our fill of each other for the moment, I broke from Diego's lips to rest my head against his shoulder. I inhaled his cologne and wrapped my arms around him. What I was feeling was nothing like I had ever felt before.

My chest tightened. But it wasn't from anxiety or fear or even doubt. It was tight because my heart was full of love for Diego and my new home in Sonrisa. So many secrets had been brought to light over the past few months. Some sad. Some surprising. But I believed they had all served a purpose to bring me here to this moment.

It was time to let go of everything that was holding me back from my future. It was time to be brave and be free.

"I love you," I told Diego. "I love you with all of my heart."

Diego's arms tightened around me, and he kissed the top of my head. I smiled and closed my eyes because I knew I was finally home.

Epilogue

One year later . . .

"I'm ready!"

"We're coming!" I heard Raul yell back. "We're coming."

I let go of the restaurant's back screen door, and it slammed closed as I ran over to my truck. I had parked it in the middle of the rear parking lot of Carlita's Cocina after picking it up from Fernando, Sonrisa's best and only sign vendor. He'd added decals of yellow Mexican sunflowers and white yucca shrubs (the official flower of New Mexico) to the bright-turquoise truck. Until my planned big reveal, large cardboard panels were taped over the areas where he had also added the food truck's name and logo. As I waited for everyone to join me, I took a second to bask in the fact that it was really mine.

Because up until this moment, I hadn't quite believed that I was about to launch my own food truck business.

As I had hoped, the money from the distribution deal with Andrew to carry Sonrisa Secret Sauce had been enough to pay off all my debts months ago. Then a second deal with a restaurant in Albuquerque had given me enough to buy the truck. While I was basically the chef, operator, and owner of the food truck, Raul was an investor in the business. The idea was to offer both my dishes and a few menu items from Carlita's in order to drive customers back to the restaurant.

It was amazing when I thought about how I'd come to Sonrisa to sell a house and had ended up buying my future instead.

"Okay, okay, we're here," Raul announced as he, Lola, and Antonio joined me in the parking lot.

Lola clapped in excitement. "I can't wait to see it," she said with a wink. Even though I had wanted to keep the name of the truck a secret until the signage was ready, Lola had already guessed it, of course. At least she had promised not to share it with anyone else—even her new fiancé, Raul.

"Pues, let's see it," Antonio said.

I glanced at my watch and was about to tell him we had to wait a few more minutes. Then Diego pulled into the parking lot and parked behind my truck. My heart did a little leap as if I hadn't just seen him at breakfast four hours ago. He'd moved in with me last month, and the plan was to sell his place after making a few improvements. Of course, we were still arguing over what projects should be done first. And I had already told him that I refused to do anything where gutters or scuppers were involved.

Sometimes, late at night when I couldn't sleep, my mind wandered to that dark place where I still couldn't quite believe that Diego loved me. But all I had to do was look over at him snoring away and my doubts were silenced once again. I'd learned to trust that he was exactly where he wanted to be—right by my side. It helped that he was always telling me that I was stuck with him forever.

And I actually believed him now.

My feelings for him had only grown stronger. Sometimes so strong that it actually took my breath away. I loved how much he loved this town and the people in it. Being such a good person, he knew exactly what I needed, when I needed it. He made me feel like I could do anything—like start my own business.

"Sorry I'm late," he said as he came up to me. He gave me a quick kiss on the mouth and then pulled out his tablet. Within two minutes, both Auntie Lily and Auntie Martha were on a video chat so they could be a part of the reveal too.

"Martha, we can only see your forehead again," Auntie Lily droned. "I told you not to answer the call on your phone. You were supposed to use the tablet I gave you for Christmas."

"I don't know how to work that thing. Anyway, you don't need to see me. As long as you can see Gabby's truck, that's all that matters. Wait. Where's the truck?"

I laughed and motioned for Diego to lift his tablet a little higher. "Now can you see it, Auntie Martha?"

"Oh yes. Thank you."

"All right, all right. Let's get this show on the road. I have been waiting for weeks to finally see this name, and I don't want to wait a second longer," Auntie Lily said.

Diego nodded and met my eyes. "Go ahead, Gabby. Show us."

A bundle of mixed feelings came over me. I was excited and nervous to finally reveal the name of my food truck. But at the same time, I couldn't help but feel sad that my mom or dad weren't here to see it. I had visited Jemez Falls over the weekend by myself to have a chat with my mom and to tell her the name. I tried to go there at least once a month now. Sometimes Diego would come with me. And this past May, Auntie Lily, Auntie Martha, and I all went together again for the one-year anniversary of her death.

I know some people say that grief gets better with time. But I would argue that it just takes on a different form. You don't get over losing a loved one; you just learn how to live with it. For me, that meant visiting Jemez Falls whenever everything seemed too much and not enough all at the same time. And even though I couldn't see her, I could feel her presence. She was there in the sound of the wind blowing through the trees and in the thunder of the water crashing onto boulders. A perfect final resting place for a true force of nature.

I blinked back tears as I walked to the side of the truck that had the largest cardboard panel. Then I cleared my throat of that choking emotion and said to my small band of supporters, "I wanted to give the food truck a name that would not just be memorable, but I also wanted it to be meaningful. When I came to Sonrisa over a year ago, I was lost in more ways than one. I thought that my future depended on selling another woman's house. Instead, I found it by allowing myself to accept my past and where I came from. And I couldn't be prouder of my roots and my heritage, especially the women in my life who have shown me what it means to fight for who you love and what you believe is right. So this truck is dedicated to them."

I nodded to Raul, and he walked up, and together we pulled the cardboard off the side of the truck to unveil the name: Adelita's.

Everyone cheered and clapped, and I could feel myself bursting with happiness and pride. Tears filled my eyes, and I didn't try to hide them anymore. Diego handed the tablet to Antonio and took me in his arms.

"I love you," he said against my temple.

"I love you too."

"All right, all right, my turn," I heard Lola say behind me.

We both laughed, and he let me go. After giving me a long hug, I noticed that Lola was crying too.

"Why are you crying?" I asked through new tears.

"I just wish that Teresa could've been here to see this," she said, pulling a tissue from her cleavage to dab her eyes.

"Really? Why?"

"She always knew she was to blame for breaking her family apart. I think in the end she did regret not ever trying to fix that. But, now, I can see that Teresa did have a hand in bringing us all together, didn't she? I hope that wherever she is, she knows that and can finally be at peace."

My voice caught in my throat. Since I couldn't say anything, I just hugged Lola again. When we separated, I noticed Raul standing off to the side, just staring at the truck. I walked over to him. "You're studying that decal pretty closely there. Did Fernando mess up something?"

He shook his head and continued staring. "The name is perfect," he finally said.

"Thanks. I thought so."

"I know you are going to be so successful."

"We are going to be successful. This is your business too."

"Maybe. But this is your dream. And you alone made that happen. I'm so proud of you. And I know your family would be, too, if they were here."

The tears were back. Not just because it was an emotional day, but because I finally believed that I wasn't alone. I would never be alone.

"Well, my family is here," I said. "And I think it's time I took them out to lunch to celebrate."

Raul smiled at me, and I could've sworn his eyes were glassy with emotion like mine. I motioned for Diego to come over to us, and he did.

"What's up?" he asked and put his arm around my shoulders.

"We're going to lunch to celebrate."

"Great! I am starving. Where should we go?" he asked.

I looked over at the restaurant in front of us and realized we were probably standing in the same spot where the photo of Miguel and Carlita had been taken all those years ago. I couldn't help but wonder what they would think of their great-great-granddaughter introducing their treasured recipes to a whole new generation.

I took a deep breath and then let it go. It was my turn to carry on their legacy. But I didn't see it as a burden. I didn't see it as an obligation either. Because I wanted to do it. And I knew exactly where to start.

"All right. Who wants tacos?"

AUTHOR'S NOTE

Would you believe me if I told you that this story was inspired by a hot sauce? Well, it's true. Kind of.

Before I even typed one word, I knew this story was going to be about a woman's journey to connect with her father, her past, and her Mexican roots. I also knew that it was going to be about grief and the different ways people deal with it. But it really didn't come together until I saw a TikTok video about the popular Mexican hot sauce Valentina. Legend has it that the hot sauce was named after Valentina Ramírez Avitia—a woman who fought in the Mexican Revolution. She was a real soldadera. A true Adelita.

I have always known that my great-grandfather Gregorio Ramirez fought in the Mexican Revolution and rode alongside the infamous Pancho Villa. But I had never heard of the Adelitas until that video, and I was instantly intrigued. I looked up articles, watched more videos, and even listened to the famous corrido. Then the idea of a woman discovering that one of her ancestors was an Adelita came to me. And it was the thread I needed to stitch this story all together.

While my first women's fiction release, *Big Chicas Don't Cry*, was dedicated to the strong women in my life, this book was my way of honoring the memory of two of the most important men I've ever known.

Unlike Gabby, I was blessed to have had my biological dad, Arturo Chavez, always in my life. He immigrated to the United States from

Mexico at the age of eighteen and went on to serve in the Vietnam War. When he met my mom, he didn't speak English and her Spanish wasn't the best. Still, they found a way to communicate and fall in love. They were married for almost forty-seven years. My dad was a quiet man—except when it came to his two greatest loves: family and soccer. When we lost him in 2018, it became more important than ever for me to celebrate my Mexican heritage and teach my children to be proud of our roots. It's how I keep my dad close to my heart.

My husband and I both lost our dads within eleven months of each other. My father-in-law was not my husband's biological dad. My husband was thirteen years old when he first met John Dominguez, who had come by to pick up his mom for a date. But the date was quickly forgotten when my husband experienced his first seizure. John was the one who drove everyone to the hospital, and he stayed until he knew my husband was going to be okay. From that moment on, my husband said he knew that John was a good man. And, later on, he became a good dad to my husband and his sisters, and a good grandpa and great-grandpa too.

Our family has had our share of losses in the past few years, and the ongoing grief can sometimes feel overwhelming. I read somewhere that grief is just "love with no place to go," and I think that's a perfect way of explaining it. This book, then, is my way of giving my love for my dad and John and all the other people I've lost a place to go.

Thank you for taking the time to go on this journey with me. I hope you enjoyed my book.

ACKNOWLEDGMENTS

Despite what it might look like, writing a book is never a solitary effort. I absolutely could not have finished this book without the support of some pretty amazing humans.

First, I want to thank my agent, Sarah Younger, for her continued faith in me and my writing. I am so blessed to have you in my corner.

I also want to recognize Maria Gomez, Charlotte Herscher, and the rest of the fabulous Montlake team. I am so proud of how this book turned out, and I know I have all of you to thank for that!

To Marie Loggia-Kee and Nichelle Scott-Williams, thank you for always being just a text message away. I will always treasure our friendship.

To my amigas queridas—my Latinx Romance hermanas—I can't even put into words just how much your friendship and support mean to me. From the bottom of my heart, thank you to Zoraida Córdova, Alexis Daria, Adriana Herrera, Priscilla Oliveras, Mia Sosa, and Diana Muñoz Stewart.

And, finally, thank you to my wonderful family, especially my husband, Patrick, and my kids, Samantha, Patrick, and Bella. I love you all. Always.

ABOUT THE AUTHOR

Photo © 2021 Sabrina Kay Vasquez

Annette Chavez Macias writes stories about love, family, and following your dreams. She is proud of her Mexican American heritage, culture, and traditions, all of which can be found within the pages of her books. For readers wanting even more love stories and guaranteed happily ever afters, Macias also writes romance novels under the pen name Sabrina Sol. A Southern California native, Macias lives just outside Los Angeles with her husband, three children, and four dogs.